SECRETS, LIES, AND FAMILY TIES

BALDWIN'S SHORE
BOOK 2

ELISE NOBLE

Published by Undercover Publishing Limited

v7b

ISBN: 978-1-912888-46-7

Edited by Nikki Mentges, NAM Editorial

Cover design by Abigail Sins

www.undercover-publishing.com

www.elise-noble.com

A smooth sea never made a skilled sailor.

1

GABRIELLE

Scheiße.
            For fanden.
Helvete.
Voi vittu.
Fuck.

I could curse proficiently in five different languages—none of them in public, of course—but somehow, *somehow*, I didn't have the words to convey just how screwed I was today.

Or rather, how *not* screwed.

A weird gurgle burst out of my throat, the sputter of hysterical laughter turning into a sob, and I kicked the tyre of Siri's Audi. Then winced because my stupid satin wedding shoes gave my toes no protection whatsoever. Dammit all to hell! German cars were famed for their reliability, but five minutes ago, a red light had illuminated on the dash, so I'd pulled over to check the glove compartment for an owner's manual—there wasn't one—and now the engine wouldn't start again. Was this karma?

Probably. Siri hadn't wanted me to take the car, but I'd squashed myself behind the wheel and sped off anyway, her words ringing in my ears.

"Gaby, do you even remember how to drive?"

"I'll figure it out," I'd called over my shoulder.

And now I was stuck.

Stuck at the side of a highway in... Well, I had no idea, but I was fairly sure I was still in Oregon.

I began to regret hurling my phone at Emmett. If it had hit him, I could have taken some small measure of satisfaction from that at least, but the asshole had ducked and the phone had smashed against a vase of flowers, which had teetered sideways onto the floor and shattered, and then Rosa, Emmett's maid, had materialised in an instant with a dustpan, and I'd tripped over her and nearly knocked my teeth out, and...

Don't think about it, Gabrielle.

But how could I not? Right now, I should have been feasting on smoked salmon and champagne with my closest friends, dancing my first dance and celebrating the fact that I was Mrs. Emmett Collins. The fireworks should have come *later*, when my family found out what I'd done. Would the fact that I hadn't actually gotten married mean they'd be happy now? Of course not. The circus had only just begun. The fact that I'd eloped instead of trotting down the aisle at the huge celebration my mother insisted upon would have made the gossip pages back in Europe, where the paparazzi fed off my blood like hungry jackals, but me eloping and then ditching my fiancé five minutes before we got hitched? Now, that was a good old-fashioned front-page *scandal*.

And I wasn't sure I'd survive another.

The ocean was to my left, out of sight but close enough

for me to smell the salt on the warm summer air. To hear the siren's call. Could I walk there? Not for the first time, I considered swan-diving into a watery grave, just vanishing under the waves and ending it all, but like so many things in my life, it wasn't to be. Three years ago, it had been my brother who found me on the cliff edge, but today it was a stranger who stopped to help.

"What seems to be the problem, ma'am?" he asked.

Everything. *Everything* was the problem.

The man was big. Big all over. Broad shoulders and strong arms, muscular legs stuffed into a pair of worn blue jeans. Handsome in a rugged, unpolished sort of way, an oak tree that needed pruning. Hair the colour of dark chocolate, a neatly trimmed beard, and an easy smile. Kind eyes, but still I stepped back on instinct and got my feet tangled in my stupid dress. Would have landed on my well-padded ass if he hadn't shot out an arm to catch me. The glint of a gold badge clipped to his belt drew my eye, along with something else. Yes, he was *definitely* big all over.

He followed my gaze and thankfully misinterpreted as I fought not to blush.

"I'm a sheriff's deputy right here in Baldwin's Shore." He set me back on my feet. "Having car trouble?"

Car trouble, man trouble, can't-put-a-foot-right trouble.

"The engine won't start."

He gave me a slow perusal, head to toe, but he was polite enough not to mention my attire. "Got enough gas? I always carry a spare can."

"I...think so?"

"Let's take a look."

A woman jumped down from the passenger side of his truck, a pretty brunette. The deputy's wife? He was clearly off duty. The back of the pickup was filled with furniture—a bed, something in bubble wrap, and a tiny pink dressing table. A girl scrambled out of the back seat, and the woman turned to wag a finger.

"Kiki, stay inside."

"But I want to see the princess."

I stiffened, but the little girl wasn't to be deterred as she ran in my direction.

"Sorry, she's fascinated by your dress."

"It's a princess dress! I love it!"

So had I once. The boutique owner had signed an NDA, and I'd snuck in under cover of darkness with Siri. Phil, my best friend, my sister from another mister, my partner in crime, had watched me try on dress after dress via Zoom, and I'd fallen in love with the jewelled bodice and sweeping chiffon skirt. Phil said the sweetheart neckline did magical things to my boobs, so she'd given me the thumbs-up too. The first time Emmett had seen me wear it was when I threw my engagement ring at him.

The little girl reached out to touch one of the pearls, but the brunette quickly lifted her away.

"Kiki, you shouldn't bother people."

"It's okay." I tried a smile, pulled it off through practice and sheer willpower. How old was the girl? Six? Seven? When I'd been her age, I'd dreamed of pretty gowns too, although the shine of dressing up wore off quickly when I was forced to do it all the damn time. "What's your name, little one?"

"Kinsley Hannah Haines. And I'm not little anymore—I'm nearly eight. Are those real diamonds?"

My earrings and necklace? Yes. The beads on the dress? No.

"I'm afraid not."

If they'd all been real, my bodyguards would have kept me on an even tighter leash. As it was, they were undoubtedly scouring the Oregon countryside in between squashing Emmett into a pulp and getting berated by my mother for losing me. Okay, so the first part was wishful thinking, but Phil had emptied a jug of Pimms over him, so I had to be thankful for that, at least.

"Your accent's weird."

Funny how children always said what adults wouldn't dare, wasn't it?

"I'm not from around here."

"Where are you from?"

"Uh, Denmark?"

It came out sounding like a question, probably because it was a lie. But it was close to the truth, and in my experience, most Americans couldn't find Denmark on a map anyway. Or many other European countries, which was why I'd chosen to come here in the first place. It was far easier to fly under the radar in the US. Or it had been until now. After today, I wasn't sure I'd ever be able to show my face in LA again.

"You sound kind of British," the brunette said, and dammit, why hadn't I just claimed to be from England? My accent was a product of all the places I'd lived, but the years I'd spent near London had been the most influential.

"I have a British grandma."

That part actually was true, although she'd moved to Finland at the grand old age of twenty-three. Luckily, the brunette seemed to accept it as an explanation.

The car coughed as the deputy tried to start it, and the vindication that I hadn't been a complete fool, that the car really was broken, was of little consolation. I was thousands of miles from a home I didn't want to live in, freshly single, with no phone and only the five hundred bucks in emergency money that Siri kept stashed under her car seat. Clean underwear was a pipe dream.

"Are you okay?" the brunette asked, the first one brave enough to broach what was clearly the bigger issue.

Claiming I was fine would have been an all-too-obvious lie, so rather than insult both of us, I simply shook my head.

"Do you have far to drive?"

"I don't even know where I'm going," I admitted.

"You need help with directions? I have a maps app on my phone."

"No, I mean I just got in the car and started driving without a destination in mind."

"In your...?" She gaped at my dress, and I honestly couldn't blame her for that.

"Yes."

"Oh. So, uh..."

Thankfully, the deputy's reappearance put an end to that non-conversation.

"It's not the gas. Did you know your alternator warning light is on?"

So that's what it was. "I was aware of a light. Is an alternator fundamental to the running of the engine?"

His eyes rolled halfway, then he seemed to catch himself. Hey, it wasn't my fault my first car had come with a chauffeur.

"It charges the battery and powers the electrics while the car's running. So if you want headlights, then yeah, it's key."

"I see."

"Is there somebody you could call?"

"My phone broke."

He fumbled in his pocket. "Here you go—borrow mine."

I just stared at it. Who on earth would I contact? Not my

mother—I already had a headache, and I didn't want to make it worse. My sister was too young, the baby of the family at fifteen. My brother? He'd help me, he always did, but I'd already burdened him with so many of my troubles. Not only that, he was working in India this week. So he'd be asleep, and when he travelled, he turned his phone off overnight because otherwise people kept bothering him.

That left Siri or Phil. Siri was on the family payroll, so technically she reported to my mother, and even if I swore her to secrecy, *Mor* would strong-arm my location out of her in one hot second. And Phil... Phil had only flown into the country two days ago. She didn't have a car, and practicality wasn't her strong suit. Plus there was a bigger problem—I didn't know her new number by heart. I'd merely programmed it into my phone, the phone that was now lying in pieces in a borrowed house in Gold Beach. The location had seemed so perfect when Emmett suggested it —his friend's parents' vacation home, secluded, pretty, and with a view of the sea. Available whenever we cared to visit. But I'd soon wished I was anyplace else.

Of course, now that my wish had come true, I found the reality wasn't much better.

"You don't have anyone to call?" the deputy asked.

"Is there a garage nearby? Maybe I could just buy a new alternator and carry on?"

How much did an alternator cost, anyway? At times like this, I missed my father more than ever. He'd have known the answer. I'd have called him in a heartbeat.

"Want me to arrange a tow?"

Did I have any other choice? I wasn't ready to face the people I'd left behind, not yet.

"Yes, please."

"What's your name?"

"My name? Uh... Uh..." I needed to remain incognito, and having people call me Gabrielle or even Gaby would hardly help with that. "I'm Brie."

My chest hitched as the word left my mouth. Nobody but my father had ever called me that, and I'd have given anything to hear his voice again.

"Brie." The deputy tested it out, then smiled. "I'm Deputy Haines—Colt—and this is Brooke. I see you've already met Kiki."

"You both have a beautiful daughter."

Why did Brooke look so horrified?

"Oh, no, no, no. We're not together." They weren't? I'd just assumed... Colt wore a wedding ring, and Brooke had a diamond on her finger. "Colt and my boyfriend—fiancé—are old friends, and they work together too. He just gave me a ride to the furniture store, seeing as I couldn't fit a bed into the trunk of my compact. But you're right about Kiki—she's super cute."

I liked Brooke. She was doing her best to make an awkward situation slightly more bearable.

"Thank you for stopping."

Colt tipped an imaginary hat. "It's not every day you see... Well..."

So much for things not being awkward.

But Brooke came to the rescue again. "Let's sit in Colt's truck while we wait for Ernie to get here."

"Ernie?"

"He owns the local auto repair shop."

"Do you think he'll take long?"

She scrunched her lips to one side. "Maybe an hour or two? Ernie runs the place with his wife, but she's gone to visit her sister. And Carl Tuttle often helps out too, but he broke his arm falling out of the Cave last week, so I guess Ernie's on his own today."

"He fell out of a cave? Didn't he use a safety rope?"

Brooke stared at me, puzzled. "A safety rope?"

"Spelunking can be such a dangerous pastime if one doesn't take the proper precautions."

What was so funny? Brooke's peal of laughter made Kiki giggle too, and Colt was smirking.

"The Cave is a bar. He got drunk and fell down the steps outside the door."

Perhaps I should have guessed? Rural Oregon was a whole different world from the one I was used to.

"A bar. Of course."

Brooke looped her arm through mine and led me to the truck. We both looked at the door, then at my dress, layers and layers of chiffon versus an opening designed for jeans and a plaid shirt. How had I ever fit into the driving seat of Siri's Audi? I had to conclude that it had been through grim determination mixed with sheer desperation to get the hell away from Emmett. And Vania, my now ex-friend. If I cared to think about it, her betrayal hurt even more than his.

"Maybe you could change your clothes?" Brooke suggested. "There's a stand of trees you could use for cover."

"I don't have any other clothes."

"This really was a spur-of-the-moment trip, huh?"

"Yes, it really was."

Colt joined us, and his expression said the news wasn't good. "Ernie's tied up fixing Bobby Graham's truck so he can tow his trailer to the cattle auction in Deschutes County tomorrow, but he'll come after that. Brooke, why don't you take Miss Brie to get coffee and something to eat while I wait here with her vehicle?"

Brooke looked to me, questioning.

Going to a café was the last thing I wanted to do, especially in this outfit, but I had to use a bathroom sometime. And I couldn't go without drinking for the rest of the day either. Better to get it over with, and at least out here in the middle of nowhere, there wouldn't be many witnesses to my humiliation.

"Thank you. I'd appreciate that."

2

GABRIELLE

"*I* don't suppose Deputy Haines carries a pair of scissors in his truck?"

"Scissors?"

"Or even a knife?"

Brooke braked at a stop sign and eyed me up doubtfully. "I'm not sure..."

I realised where her thoughts were going. Perhaps mine would have gone there too, given a few minutes, but I wasn't about to try anything stupid with a small child in the back seat.

"I just want to cut off the bottom of this dress."

Kiki gasped behind me. "Cut the dress? Noooooooo! You can't. You can't cut it!"

What choice did I have? "I doubt I'll fit into a bathroom stall otherwise."

And it was only a dress. Fabric and beads, forever tainted by the morning from hell.

"We could swing by my place if you want?" Brooke offered. "I'm sure I have clothes that'll fit you. Kiki's right—

you shouldn't ruin the dress. Even if you never want to wear it again, you could sell it."

Sell it? No way. If people found out who it had belonged to, it would become a macabre souvenir that popped up at auction every few years to remind me of my bad decisions. But the idea of borrowing clothes filled me with relief. Brooke was shorter than me, and thinner too, but if she had something stretchy... I hadn't cried since I left the house this morning, but now my eyes prickled, not with grief or longing or regret but due to her kindness. She had no idea who I was, and yet still she was willing to help me.

"That would be very generous of you."

Another sideways glance. "Okay, so I guess that's a plan."

Brooke pulled into the driveway of a two-storey house, a little dated but neat and tidy. A family home. She hadn't mentioned having children of her own, but since she was engaged, maybe she and her fiancé were planning ahead? I was about to pay a bland compliment out of habit when she carried on along the driveway and parked in front of a double garage at the back.

"We rent the garage apartment from my friend's parents. I should have moved out earlier in the year, but I had a few problems with a stalker, and to cut a long story short, we're having to rebuild part of the apartment I was meant to move into."

"A stalker?" I gave an involuntary shudder. Being watched gave me the creeps.

"Don't worry; he's in jail now." Brooke's smile looked as fake as my own felt. "It's over. But we'll be here for another month or two, and it's kind of the Crowes to let us stay. Do you mind dogs?"

"Not in principle, but I've never had one of my own."

"Vega's big, but he won't hurt you. It turned out that being a guard dog wasn't really his thing."

A flight of stairs ran up the side of the garage, and I scooped up armfuls of dress to follow Brooke to the door at the top. Kiki clambered on ahead, and when she reached the landing, she bent to pick up a small box.

"Cookies? Did we get cookies?"

"*Don't* shake them. Mrs. Crowe likes to bake," Brooke explained. "A perk of living here."

The apartment was smaller than my closet back home, but cosy. Colourful paintings decorated the walls, the couch looked squashy and comfortable, and the coffee table held a stack of well-thumbed magazines instead of a flower arrangement and a book of fancy photos that nobody ever opened. And it seemed Brooke enjoyed knitting, judging by the wool criss-crossing the floor.

"Vega! What have you done?"

The fireplug of a dog—one that looked like a German shepherd crossed with something much stockier—paused mid-leap and sat on his haunches, tail still wagging. He seemed quite pleased with his handiwork.

"This was meant to be a freaking sweater."

"Bad Vega," Kiki scolded, but then she flung her arms around his neck and giggled as he licked her. "He says he's sorry. Can he have a cookie?"

"No, he can't have a cookie. They probably have chocolate in them, and chocolate is..."

"Poisonous for dogs," Kiki finished. "Can *I* have a cookie?"

"How about you put the cookies on a plate while I clean up this mess, and then we can all have cookies?"

"Okay."

She ran to the kitchen, which meant she didn't run very far at all, and Brooke cursed under her breath.

"Sorry, I'm so sorry, it isn't usually this chaotic. Vega's going through a 'cat' phase. He's started playing with yarn and chasing birds, but at least he hasn't brought me any dead mice."

"Do you want me to unravel some of this?"

"I think..." Brooke surveyed the mess. "I think it'll be easier to just buy another ball. I work in a craft store, so I get a staff discount. Or Kiki might do the unravelling. She likes to keep busy."

"You spend a lot of time with her?"

"Sometimes I babysit to help out. Colt needs a break, and her regular sitter is on vacation."

"His wife works too?"

Brooke lowered her voice, and I had to lean closer to hear.

"Hannah died. Kiki was barely two years old, so—"

"They're double chocolate chip cookies! We get two each, and that leaves one for Daddy and one for Luca. Luca is Brooke's *boyfriend*."

My heart stuttered as Kiki giggled. Colt had lost his wife? Kiki had lost her mom? For so long, I'd been living in my own bubble with my own grief, but this was a reminder that I wasn't the only person who had to deal with tragedy. And Kiki did a better job of smiling than I'd ever managed.

"Thank you, *min skat*."

The endearment slipped out, the way it had from my father to me and from me to my sister before she went through her bratty phase, and Kiki tilted her head to one side.

"Why am I a mince cat?"

"*Min skat*. In Danish, it means 'my treasure.'"

Her smile turned into a full-on beaming grin. "Like gold?"

More like "honey," but she seemed to be fond of sparkly things.

"Yes, like gold."

"And diamonds?"

"Yes."

"And rubies?"

In some ways, she reminded me of my sister. At seven, Elin had been a magpie, always collecting shiny trinkets, which everyone thought was cute until she snaffled a pair of diamond earrings from our mother's dressing table and couldn't remember where she'd put them. The staff had searched for days, even used metal detectors, and eventually the earrings had turned up months later in Elin's dollhouse microwave. I made a mental note to keep my own earrings safe. They'd been a gift from my father for my eighteenth birthday, one of the few pieces of jewellery he'd given me.

"Yes, like rubies too."

"And emeralds?"

Brooke smothered a chuckle. "How about we go and find Brie something to wear?"

"Can you do my hair the same as Brie's? I want it all... all...all *fussy* like that."

"Well, I could try, but you'd have to sit still for a long while."

"I can do that."

"Why don't you practise while we eat our cookies?"

"If I eat mine really fast, does that mean I only have to sit still for a short while?"

Brooke herded Kiki into the bedroom, and I heard a closet door open. The sounds of rummaging. These people were so nice. So *normal*. And they treated me as if I were normal too. What would have happened if instead of moving to LA three years ago, I'd run to a small town on the Oregon coast? Back then, I'd figured that if I hid out amongst movie stars and music moguls, I'd be small fry for the paparazzi in comparison, but perhaps if I'd made my life so utterly uninteresting that they'd gotten bored with following me around, it would have been a better strategy? Maybe I'd have been able to make real friends? And as an added bonus, I'd never have met Emmett, or Vania, or any of the others who'd flocked around us like wasps on sugar.

I'd spent two hours driving this morning, and alone with time to think, I'd seen what I'd been blind to for so long. That I'd created a world in my head, the world I'd wanted, rather than living in the reality that existed. Grief had dulled my senses. Blunted my intuition. I'd assumed that because Emmett's family was wealthy, we were equals, but money wasn't everything. Phil, bless her, had tried to warn me the first time they met, but instead of listening, I'd brushed her concerns away.

More fool me.

"These might fit?" Brooke held out a pile of clothes. "You've got much bigger boobs, but I accidentally bought a sports bra that was too big and I never got around to returning it."

"I'm so very grateful."

"You can use the bedroom to change. Or the bathroom, whatever works. Do you want drinks here rather than going to the coffee house? I could make sandwiches as well if you'd like."

Anything was better than sitting in public. I couldn't take the anxiety, not today.

"Thank you."

"Cheese? Tuna? Ham?"

"Whatever you'd care to make would be wonderful."

The bathroom wasn't a bathroom at all—it had no bath, only a shower—but there was enough space for me to get out of the damn dress, which was the most important thing. I had to twist myself into a pretzel to get the fasteners undone, but finally I was free. I'd never been so grateful to see sportswear in my life. The yoga pants strained at the seams, and my breasts bulged out of the top of the bra, but the oversized T-shirt covered a multitude of sins and at least I could breathe again.

My hair stayed in place even when I removed the pins. It needed a wash, but I combed out as much hairspray as I could with my fingers and scraped the stiff strands back into a makeshift ponytail. Then I set about fixing my face. The black streaks around my eyes meant I looked more like a raccoon or a death-metal singer than a wannabe bride, but I managed to make myself presentable with the help of soap and tissue.

Then I took stock of the situation.

The logical choice, the sensible choice, would be to call for help, deal with the Emmett mess, and go back home. Hide away for a year or two and lick my wounds. But just the thought left me nauseated, physically nauseated, and I choked. Heaved into the toilet. Only bile came up because I hadn't eaten anything since last night, but my mouth tasted disgusting, and then the tears fell. I sank to the floor and sobbed, kneeling on a pile of wedding dress. I had so much I should be grateful for, I realised that, and yet...and yet...

"Are you okay in there?" Brooke called.

"F-f-f-fine."

Siri would have accepted my claim and left me alone. Phil would have told me there was no point in moping my life away, then dragged me outside to face my demons because that was how she handled everything. Head on, with no fear.

But Brooke just asked, "You sure?" and somehow that made everything worse.

"No, I'm not sure. I'm not sure about anything. Whatever I do, however I act, it's wrong in someone's eyes. I've spent my whole life trying to do what I think other people want, and at the end of it all, my fiancé still slept with my bridesmaid."

"Uh...wow. So, you want me to swap the coffee for wine?"

A laugh burst out of me, which was ridiculous because nothing about this situation was funny.

"I'd better stick with the coffee."

The last thing I needed was a DUI, and I really, really needed to get out of here. If I had a little bit of cash left after whatever repairs Siri's car needed, I could find a cheap motel and hole up with chocolate for a few days.

"Do you take milk? Sugar?"

"Milk and two sugars. Thank you."

Once I'd got my sobs under control, I wiped my eyes—again—and held my head high as I walked out into the living room. Every day, the mask got harder to wear.

"I'm so sorry about this," I started, but Brooke waved my apology away.

"Everyone has man trouble at some time or another. At least yours didn't end in a criminal trial."

"I hope. My best friend was threatening to chop off parts of my ex-fiancé's anatomy when I left."

"Relax—there's not a female juror in the world who'd convict her."

Kiki sidled up to me with the dog in tow. "Can I try on your dress?"

"Kiki!" Brooke scolded. "Leave Brie alone."

"But it's pretty, and she's not wearing it now."

I crouched down so I was at the little girl's eye level. "Sure you can wear the dress, *min skat*. You can keep it."

But Brooke shook her head. "You can't give her your wedding dress."

"Technically, it wasn't my wedding dress."

"It looks really expensive."

"I have no further use for it. If it makes her happy, then she can use it to play dress-up. I'll get your clothes laundered and send them back as soon as I'm able to."

"Oh, you can keep those. I never wear them anyway."

"I helped to make the sandwiches," Kiki called as she ran into the bathroom. "Vega licked a cheese one, but don't worry, 'cause I ate it."

Brooke put her head in her hands. "Sometimes, I don't know how Colt manages."

"She's very cute."

"Cute, but a handful. Colt messaged, by the way. Ernie's arrived with the tow truck, so once you've had something to eat, we can head on over to the auto shop."

And just like that, my bubble burst again.

"It's the alternator," Ernie said. "You need a new one."

Which wasn't a surprise, but what shocked me was how much it cost. Over five hundred dollars just for the part.

"That's all the money I have. You can't repair the old one?"

"Those things aren't designed to be fixed. Back in the days when quality came before profit, everything was repairable, but these modern cars, you're just meant to take the broken one out and bolt a new one in, and they don't even make that easy." His expression softened into what might have been a smile. "Colt told me you'd had some trouble today?"

"If by 'trouble' you mean running out of my own wedding, then yes."

"So I thought that if you were amenable, we could make a trade. To help you get back on your feet, like."

"But I don't have anything to trade."

"You have yourself."

Was he serious? That pig. My palm itched to slap him, but that would only have made a bad situation worse.

"I am *not* a prostitute."

Ernie's jaw dropped, and he looked as horrified as I felt. "No, oh no. Not that. I didn't mean that. I'm a happily married man. But my Judith is taking care of her sister this week—she's just had her hip replaced—and I could do with somebody to answer the phone. Every time it rings, I have to stop what I'm doing and wash my hands, and it's a pain in the patootie."

"You want me to...answer the phone? Just answer the phone?"

"Exactly. You do that until your car's ready to go, and I'll let you have the parts at cost and my labour for free."

"For how long are we talking? Hours? A day?"

"A week, most likely. Tomorrow through Saturday lunchtime. That alternator's a special order, and they'll have to ship it. Next time, you should buy American, young lady."

A week without the car? I couldn't... I'd have to go home and face the music instead. Siri could borrow my credit card to get her car fixed, and... A groan slipped out as I thought of an even bigger problem. The car had been a gift from Siri's boyfriend. Her *American* boyfriend. She'd be devastated about returning home to Scandinavia as well.

"But...but...I don't have anywhere to stay, and I can't afford a hotel."

Can't afford. Those two words had never factored into my vocabulary until today. Funny how quickly things could change, wasn't it?

"You can borrow our couch if you want," Brooke offered. "As long as you don't mind Vega snoring."

Kiki bounced up and down on her toes, fizzing with excitement. "Or you could stay at our house. We have a whole spare room."

Bless that child. "*Min skat*, that's kind of you, but you can't just offer your house to strangers." I caught sight of Colt's face, and it seemed that horror was contagious. "It's not fair on your father."

"He always says that if someone needs help, then we should help them. Isn't that right, Daddy?"

"Well, yeah, but—"

"So Brie can stay, and she can show me how to do my hair with the curls."

I couldn't, not without the stylist Siri had hired, and he'd driven all the way from LA. *Sven.* He hadn't stopped chattering for a second while he pulled and twisted and pinned, and he'd given me a lecture on split ends too. *These are so dryyyyy. You should use the sea kelp protein pack.* Would Kiki's hair even hold that style? She looked like a baby Beyoncé with the confident attitude to match. And did I really want to work in a garage? I'd never had a job before, not a proper one with set hours and a lunch break. But a part of me wanted to experience that rite of passage, to understand how people lived in small-town America.

"When I said—" Colt began.

"She gave me her dress, Daddy. Her beautiful dress. And I still have five whole weeks off school. You said that since we couldn't afford a vacation this year, I could do fun stuff at home, and I want to have princess hair."

He sighed, defeated, and then cleared his throat. "So we have a spare room..."

3

COLT

*W*hat the hell was Brooke playing at?

She had a ton of clothes—I knew this because I'd helped her to carry the boxes into her apartment when she moved back to Baldwin's Shore—and this was the best she could do? The idea had been that she'd take Brie to find a more appropriate outfit, something less distracting than a bejewelled wedding dress. So why did the woman look like an extra in a porn movie? Kiki might have been the only girl I had eyes for these days, but I wasn't fucking blind. Those breasts must've cost Brie a fortune.

And now my darling daughter, the light of my life, the apple of my eye, had offered an admittedly pretty blonde-haired stranger room and board, and I couldn't veto the idea without disappointing my little girl and looking like an asshole in the process. I got that Kiki was fascinated by a new face in town, but Deputy Dawkins was covering my patch from his base in Coos Bay this week so I could spend some quality time with her, and the last thing I wanted to do was escort a jilted bride around the place. Sure, it looked as if Brie had found herself a temporary job, but damn. What a way to screw up my vacation.

Ernie's motives weren't entirely altruistic either. True, he was happily married, but he kept an old Pirelli calendar stuffed down the back of his toolbox, and I hadn't missed the way his gaze lingered on Brie's ass.

Luca and Aaron—Brooke's brother—were gonna laugh their damn heads off.

For a moment, I considered trying to offload Brie onto Aaron, but she really wasn't his type. He preferred his women confident. Independent. A little wild. More like Luca's sister, which Luca either hadn't noticed or was in denial over.

Hopefully, Brie wouldn't cry. If she cried, Brooke could come over and deal with her.

"I start at eight o'clock sharp," Ernie said. "Got plenty of coffee, but you'll need to bring your own lunch."

"Okay."

"You ever worked in customer service before?"

"Not exactly, but I've had experience with public relations."

"Good, good, and you know how to use a computer?"

"I can handle the basics."

"Then I'll see you tomorrow morning. You need anything out of your car before I lock the gates?"

"Perhaps I'll just check."

Five minutes later, Brie came back with an armful of belongings. Random stuff like an umbrella, a waterproof jacket, and a flashlight. Did she want to bring the tyre iron while she was at it?

"We may be out in the sticks here, but my house has electricity."

"Uh, yes. Yes, I'm sure it does, but I just thought that if I need to get up in the middle of the night…"

"I have a night light," Kiki told her. "You can borrow it if you want."

"That's very kind."

It was more than kind—it was a real big deal. Kiki never slept without her night light. When she was three, bees had built a nest in the siding, and while I waited for an expert to come and relocate them, their buzzing and scratching combined with *creak*s of the house settling at night had convinced Kiki that monsters lived in the walls. She'd been scared of the dark ever since.

Why was Kiki so enamoured with this stranger? It had to be the dress. Had Brie really gifted it to Kiki? I hoped she hadn't because that would only cause problems when I told Kiki she couldn't keep it. Wedding dresses cost a fortune— we'd saved for months to buy Hannah's—and Brie obviously wasn't thinking straight today.

"We can sort the lighting situation out later."

"Uh, are we still coming over for the football?" Brooke asked.

Good question. Was Brie a football fan? Somehow, I couldn't see it. She seemed like the kind of girl who'd be more at home in a yoga class than cheering on the Seahawks with beer and tacos. Or what was that other thing Hannah used to do? Pilates?

"I'm not sure that's a good idea."

Even if it was the first preseason game and I'd been looking forward to it.

"Please, don't change your plans on my account," Brie said. "I can just stay out of the way."

Once again, Kiki chipped in. "We can *all* watch the football. Can we have ice cream?"

There was nothing to be gained by arguing, not today. The way things were going, I'd lose before I even opened my mouth.

"Sure, we can have ice cream."

"So... You have a house guest?"

Luca left it until half-time to mention the obvious, despite the fact that Brie had been sitting stiffly on the couch for the entire first half, squashed between Brooke and Kiki, looking alternately bored, puzzled, and miserable. Aaron had claimed the other couch, which left the armchairs for Luca and me. Deck had sprawled out on the floor, his head on a cushion. I'd gone to high school with Aaron and Luca, but even though I'd lived on the same street as Deck for the past two years, he'd only started hanging out with us in the aftermath of Brooke's stalker drama. Aaron had invited him tonight.

"Yeah, I have a house guest. Brooke and Kiki cooked up the scheme between them. It was either my spare room or your couch."

"Lucky escape."

"You couldn't have...I don't know, driven her to a hotel?" Aaron suggested. "She looks like the type of woman who belongs in the Peninsula."

By "Peninsula," Aaron meant the Peninsula Resort and Spa, the newest addition to the town's coastline. Like many of the locals, I'd viewed it as a monstrosity, a blot on the landscape, but I was gradually coming around to the idea that it might not be such a bad development. Luca and Brooke had joined the gym there, and I'd visited a couple of times with their guest passes. The place was fancy, real fancy, but it did offer much-needed employment, and better a hotel than the tanker terminal some oil company wanted to build in Coos Bay.

"Brie has five hundred bucks to her name, and she needs that much to fix her car." I kept my voice down because she was next door in the kitchen with Brooke and Kiki. "She was meant to get married today, but something went wrong."

Luca snorted. "Yeah, I got that. I can't fit into the bathroom at home thanks to three hundred layers of satin and chiffon. Brooke said her fiancé fucked her bridesmaid."

Aw, hell. I winced inwardly. If that was true, then no wonder Brie had been upset earlier, upset enough to climb into her car and drive off without any plan.

"How'd she find out?"

"Brie told her, I guess."

"No, I meant how did Brie find out about the bridesmaid?"

"Who knows? But hell, the guy must've been an idiot."

Aaron threw an empty beer can at him. "You're engaged to my sister."

"What am I supposed to do? Walk around with my eyes closed?"

"If that's what it takes."

"Chill—Colt's in pole position anyway."

What? No way. "Are you kidding me?"

"Hey, you think I missed the way you've been checking out her ass?"

"I wasn't—" I started, but what was the point in denying it? "I'm only human."

"Hey, I'm not criticising. And maybe you should move in for a little rebound action? How long has it been since you split with Jacqueline?"

Over a year, and I was in no hurry to get involved with a

woman again. Jacqueline had been a mistake. After Hannah died, it had taken over three years for me to consider dating again, and I'd tried so hard to do everything right for Kiki's sake. Taken things slowly, steadily. Waited until I was comfortable with Jacqueline before I'd introduced her to my daughter. Kiki might have been young when her mom left us, her memories hazy, but there was still no way that anyone could ever replace Hannah. Not for either of us. But I'd missed having female companionship, and I'd thought Kiki might appreciate another perspective too.

I'd been wrong.

Kiki had never warmed to Jacqueline, although Jacqueline had tried her best to develop their relationship. Or so I thought. We'd been dating for six months when Meli Snyder took me aside for a quiet word.

The Snyders had moved in next door when I was at my lowest. Hannah had been gone for almost a year, and I was struggling to cope with grieving and being a single father, hell, just with getting out of bed in the mornings. Everyone in town had rallied around right after Hannah's passing, but fast-forward several months, the help had tailed off, and I was lost. Brooke and Meli had been the people who stuck, the ones who refused to let me fall into the black hole I was edging toward.

And Meli didn't like Jacqueline either.

Because when I went out, Jac treated Kiki like shit. Meli had heard her from the other side of the fence one day, forcing Kiki to stand outside in the rain because she'd talked back. A *six-year-old*. Jac denied it, of course, but Kiki had confirmed the story, the tears she'd been storing up for months pouring in through the cracks in my heart as she sobbed out all the ways Jac had belittled her.

I'd broken it off with a phone call, which was more than

Jac deserved, and then I'd vowed no woman would ever treat my little girl that way again. And the safest way to ensure that was to stay single until Kiki hit her teens. The mere thought of dating again filled me with dread, and even the occasional hook-up took planning. Let's just say I had a well-developed right arm.

And now a temporary roommate with the face of an angel and the body of a Playboy centrefold.

"I'm not interested in any more complications," I told Aaron.

Aaron looked at Luca, and Luca looked at Aaron.

"It's true," I growled. "She's not even my type."

Did I have a type? Sure, Brie was very different to Hannah physically, but they both had a vulnerability about them that drew me in like a moth to a damn flame. Brought out my caveman instincts. Made me want to stand between them and the world.

Fuck, I'd drunk too much beer tonight.

"You sure about—" Luca started, but Aaron cut him a warning look as the girls reappeared with churros and ice cream.

Brie managed a half smile as she tucked herself into the corner of the couch, knees drawn up to her chin, and I smiled back without thinking. Then realised Aaron, Luca, and Deck were all watching me.

Shit.

Where was Ernie getting Brooke's alternator shipped from? Because at this moment, I was tempted to volunteer to go pick it up myself.

Kiki was barely awake, but she still struggled out of my arms when I tried to carry her upstairs that evening.

"No, no, not yet! We haven't put food out for Tigger."

"Who's Tigger?" Brie whispered.

"Our cat. She hasn't been home for a few days, and Kiki's worried about her."

So was I, if I had to be honest. Unlike some other places, folks in Baldwin's Shore tended to let their cats out in the day and shut them in at night. Our roads were quiet, coyotes were rarely seen in town, and cats kept the rodent population down. The system worked around here.

Tigger had always been the adventurous type, but she rarely missed a meal, let alone six in a row. And Kiki loved that kitty. We'd inherited her when Winnie Thoroughgood died, and neither of her kids wanted to take on a pet. I hadn't been keen either, but Kiki wanted a cat, so we got a cat. Three cats, as it turned out, because in between Winnie's passing and our house-warming party, Tigger had found herself a boyfriend. That problem was fixed now, and thankfully, Deck had taken one of the kittens—the little furball had kept following him around when he'd come to build Kiki a playhouse—and the Snyders had adopted the other. Everyone on our street was keeping an eye out for Tigger, but so far, there'd been no sign of her.

Brie crouched down in front of Kiki. "I'm so sorry she's missing. Do you need help with the food?"

Kiki nodded. "Do you have a cat?"

"Not now, but when I was your age, I did. Her name was Anka."

"What happened to her?"

"She crossed the rainbow bridge at the grand old age of eighteen, but my little sister still has one of her kittens."

"What's the rainbow bridge?"

"It's where animals wait for their humans so they can go to heaven together."

"Do you think Tigger's at the rainbow bridge?"

"I don't know, *min skat*. She might just be visiting with her friends right here on earth. Let's get that food for her, okay?"

"Okay."

Brie looked up at me, apologetic. "Uh, so I don't actually know where the food is."

"I'll show you."

By the time we'd put dishes of Kitty Krunchies and fresh water out on the deck, Kiki couldn't keep her eyes open, which I had to view as a good thing under the circumstances. I needed to talk with Brie before we went to bed. We hadn't had a moment alone together yet, and I barely knew this woman who was now living in my home.

"Give me ten minutes," I mouthed as I carried Kiki up the stairs. At least she'd put her pyjamas on before the football started. Trying to get her octopus arms into the sleeves when she was half-asleep was no joke.

When I got back to the living room, Brie was exactly where I'd left her. By the window, staring at her own reflection in the glass. What was she thinking? I was fairly certain I didn't want to know.

"Hey."

She jumped. Pressed one hand to her chest.

"Want a nightcap?" I asked.

"Uh... I shouldn't, but... Yes?"

"Wine? Something stronger?"

"My head says wine, but my heart says Jägermeister."

"I have whisky?"

"That's fine."

Brie kept her distance from me, wary, as I poured us

both drinks. I couldn't blame her for that, and I half wished she'd picked Brooke's couch instead of my spare room because she'd probably have been more comfortable having another woman around.

"How are you feeling?"

"Please don't ask me that."

Well, okay then. "Sorry."

She flapped a hand in front of her face. "No, I'm the one who should be apologising. I didn't mean to be rude, but when people are kind, it makes me cry, and I hate crying."

I passed her the tumbler, and she gulped down half of the whisky, then gasped.

"Shit, that burns. I mean, uh, shoot."

"Try sipping next time."

She did as advised but still wrinkled her nose, which shouldn't have been cute but was. I was a sick, sick man.

"Not much of a drinker?"

"I've tried to abstain in the past. But tonight...tonight, it seems like a good idea. I won't get any sleep otherwise."

"Ah, that delicate balance between needing to pass out and avoiding a hangover. I know it well."

She nodded, and from the understanding in her eyes, I knew somebody had told her about Hannah. Brooke, probably, or maybe Kiki had let it slip. She talked about her mom as if she were some kind of mythical creature, real but not real. Part of me wished they'd been able to spend more time together, but the other part was grateful that Kiki had been spared some of the pain of losing a parent.

"Do you need a wake-up call in the morning?"

"Please. I don't have an alarm clock. Or a toothbrush, or a comb, or proper shoes, or clean freaking underwear. *Sådan en røv fanden af en dag*," she muttered at the end.

"That last part—what does it mean?"

Now her cheeks turned scarlet. "It doesn't matter."

Never mind—I got the gist. "There's a spare toothbrush and a comb in the drawer under the bathroom sink. Use whatever you want. Can't help much with the shoes, but I can lend you a pair of sweatpants and a T-shirt, and if you don't mind boxers..."

"I'm actually desperate enough to take you up on that." Brie clapped a hand over her mouth. "Sorry, I didn't mean to insult your choice of underwear."

"I got what you meant. And can I make another suggestion?"

She hesitated for a moment, and then nodded. "Okay."

"I know everything's raw right now, and you're hurting. But people are gonna be worried about you. Tell me to get lost if you want, but I think you should consider calling somebody you trust to let them know you're okay."

"I can't face speaking to anyone."

"A text message is better than nothing. At work, I've had to deal with families whose loved ones have gone missing, and the uncertainty is difficult for them to deal with."

I'd seen it when I was a kid too. Luca's mom had disappeared when he was eight years old, left him and his younger sister at the mercy of their asshole of a father, and although Luca rarely spoke about it now, I could tell that her vanishing act still ate away at him.

"I..." Brie paused and pressed the heels of her hands against her eyes. "I could email a friend?"

"I'll go get my laptop."

4

GABRIELLE

För helvete, my head hurt.

One glass of whisky had turned into three as I'd sat in front of Colt's computer last night, trying to come up with the right words. And I'd caught sight of the background before Colt opened up the browser—a picture of him with his arm around a beautiful Black woman cradling a baby in her arms, sitting on the porch of this very house. His wife and Kiki? They'd been smiling, so happy, obviously in love. My heart ached for them.

In the end, I'd typed out a short message to Phil, letting her know I was staying with friends for a few days while I thought things through. Which sounded better than telling her I'd been taken in like a stray dog by a bunch of kind-hearted strangers. We used a secret email account to communicate with each other—we had done since we were twelve years old—and I knew she wouldn't show anyone else what I'd written. But she would get word to my family that I was safe and not to worry.

A soft knock came at the door, and I groaned out loud.

"Brie? You awake?"

"Unfortunately."

"It's seven a.m. If you want to shower before work, you'll need to get up."

I tried to say "okay," but it came out more like, "Urgh."

"I've left painkillers on the bathroom counter."

This man was my hero. "Thanks."

"You'll have to use my shower because Kiki's swimming in the tub right now. First door on the right at the top of the stairs—just walk through the bedroom. There's a spare towel on the rail too."

How could Colt sound so human at this time in the morning? Don't tell me he was one of those weirdos who liked to rise with the sun? I genuinely didn't understand such people. But the thought of a shower, of washing off the grime left over from Emmett's touch, was enough to get me out of bed and stumbling towards the door. Colt had made good on his promise last night, and I'd slept in a giant T-shirt and a pair of boxer briefs, which were surprisingly comfortable.

I heard splashing as I hurried across the landing. A giggle. A sigh. *A family.* Colt's bedroom wasn't messy, but it was lived in. Clothes flung over a chair, a stack of books on the bedside table, empty coffee cups on a chest of drawers. It felt cosy, comfortable. My bedroom at home had never felt much like my own because the maids constantly fussed and rearranged things, and Emmett was a neat freak. He'd have flipped at the sight of not only the multiple coffee cups, but also the lack of coasters on a polished surface. At the time, his OCD hadn't bothered me too much—I guess because I was used to living with everything in its place—but now that I'd taken a step back, I realised it was refreshing to be in a home where dust was acceptable.

Twenty minutes later, I both smelled and looked like

Colt. I'd used his shampoo, borrowed his deodorant, and now I was dressed in his sweatpants rolled over three times at the waist and cinched tight. His T-shirt came to mid-thigh, so I knotted it at my stomach. Was that acceptable attire for answering the phone at Ernie's Auto Repair? I truly had no idea, but nor did I have much choice in my outfit. It was my voice that mattered, right? And I'd had a lifetime's practice at being polite to strangers.

"Coffee's on the counter," Colt said when I got downstairs.

"I made it," Kiki told me proudly.

"You did?"

"Well, I pushed the button on the machine."

"Thank you, *min skat*."

Colt nodded towards the mug. "A good coffee machine is essential around here. I didn't know if you took milk."

"I do, and sugar too."

"Don't have sugar, I'm afraid, but I can pick some up at the store later."

"Honestly, it's fine. Sugar's bad for me anyway. Uh, do I look okay? For work, I mean."

"You look fine. Mighty fine," he added, then quickly turned away. "People around here are pretty easy-going."

Even so, I still tugged the T-shirt down to close the gap a bit. Mother would have lost her mind if she'd seen me with a bare midriff. She still hadn't forgiven me for wearing a bikini to the beach after I moved to the US, and to be fair, it had been a mistake. A *huge* mistake. The British tabloids had questioned whether I was pregnant, and when they found out I wasn't, headlines like *Gabrielle's Diet Despair* made me hide away for three whole years. Waking up to find I'd made number six on celebgossip.com's list of the ten worst beach bodies wasn't an experience I cared to repeat.

My weight never used to be a problem. With all the sports I'd once done, I'd been able to eat whatever I wanted and still stay thin. But after the accident, I'd turned to food for comfort and paid the price. For the last six months, I'd dieted and worked with a personal trainer so I could fit into my wedding dress, but now all I wanted to do was cry into a fondue fountain.

"What do you want for dinner tonight?" Colt asked.

"Not burned Eggos," Kiki said.

Colt pinched the bridge of his nose. "Two years ago, I accidentally overcooked one side of her waffles, and she's never let me forget it."

"I have standards."

"Brie, any requests?"

"Anything but fondue."

"I don't even know what that is, so I think we're good. Pizza?"

I looked at Kiki, and she shrugged.

"Pizza would be lovely."

Work wasn't as challenging as I'd feared it might be. Boring, yes, but not technically difficult. All I had to do was answer the phone, write notes, and if the caller said it was urgent, walk out to the workshop and relay the message to Ernie. He seemed to spend most of his time underneath cars, but I'd handed over my five hundred bucks earlier and he'd ordered my alternator, so that was something to be thankful for. The seller had promised to send it by next Monday. Yesterday, I'd been dreading the wait, but now... Now, I thought a week in Baldwin's Shore might not actually be that bad.

ELISE NOBLE

During the morning, only two people came to the garage in person—both men—and they spent more time staring at my boobs than my face, which under the circumstances was preferable. Worry over being recognised left me constantly anxious. But I'd found a reasonably clean baseball cap behind the counter and tucked my hair under it, and the folks in Baldwin's Shore didn't seem the type to read European gossip rags, so I figured I was safe, temporarily at least.

And at lunchtime, I had a visitor.

"Colt said you ran out of time to organise lunch this morning, so I swung by the coffee house while I walked Vega and picked up a sandwich. Hey, Ernie!" Brooke yelled. "I brought you a donut."

Tears prickled again. Simple kindness was a gift I was unaccustomed to receiving. Sure, I was given stuff all the time, but as Gabrielle, not Brie. There was always an expectation behind it.

"Thank you."

"And my boss is closer to your size than I am, so she's gonna look through her clothes tonight and see what she has spare. You might end up with a muumuu, but they're really comfortable." She glanced down. "Oh, damn, I forgot about shoes. What size are your feet?"

"In US sizes? An eight, but I can manage."

"My friend Addy takes an eight. I'll call her."

"There's no—"

"She's a shoe-a-holic. Every time there's a sale, she buys another pair, but she forgets to wear the ones she already has."

Addy would probably get on very well with my mother. "I appreciate this more than you can ever imagine."

Brooke lowered her voice to a conspiratorial whisper. "I have an ulterior motive."

My spine went rigid. "What motive?"

"I like having another girl to hang out with. Addy lives over in Coos Bay, and I keep getting outnumbered by the boys."

That was it? She didn't want to borrow a yacht or something? Wow.

"Uh, sure. We can hang out."

"Colt said you're having pizza with him and Kiki tonight, so how about tomorrow?"

"Tomorrow?"

"No pressure. If you just want to stay home—I mean at Colt's—that's okay too."

"We can meet tomorrow."

"Great—I'll call you on Colt's phone later to let you know when and where."

"Want some of mine?"

Kiki thrust a slice of pizza in my face, and I tried not to flinch. Until today, I'd always thought there was only one ingredient that didn't belong on pizza—pineapple—but now I realised there was a second: macaroni. Kiki had picked her own toppings, and her tastes ran to carbs, carbs, and more carbs. Plus she'd squirted mayonnaise over the top.

"That's very sweet of you, but I have plenty of my own."

"Then why aren't you eating it?"

Because I was still full from lunch. It turned out the local coffee house made sandwiches the size of trucks.

"I am, just slowly."

"You should eat faster. Otherwise the ice cream'll melt."

There was ice cream as well? My first instinct was to decline, but I hadn't eaten dessert in half a year, and what did it matter? Soon I'd be back in Scandinavia, hiding again. A few extra pounds wouldn't hurt.

"Wine or whisky?" Colt asked after he'd put Kiki to bed. If there was one good thing about all the carbs, it was that they made her really, really sleepy.

"Perhaps a small glass of wine? I've only just got rid of the headache from yesterday. But do you think I could borrow your laptop again? I should check for a message from Phil."

"Phil?" Colt raised an eyebrow.

"My best friend. That's who I emailed last night."

"Yeah, sure."

Miraculously, there was a message. Phil rarely bothered to carry her phone, especially when she was on a horse, despite lectures from her parents on the dangers of riding alone.

Bloody hell, woman! That was some disappearing act.

Your mother's doing her nut—she was ready to send the cavalry out to look for you until your brother convinced her to back down. I told them you're okay, but now they keep asking where you are. Want me to throw them off the scent? Emmett's been phoning around all of your friends, but he can't work it out either. He had a massive row with Vania, and she ran off with her tail between her legs. Any idea who sent the video? He thinks it was her.

Siri rented a storage unit for your stuff, and she's staying with her boyfriend until you come back. Any idea how long you'll be gone? I'm not sure whether to stick

around in Bumfuck, Nowhere, or head back to Blighty,
and Blaze already threw Pammie off. You know how he's
a one-woman horse.

   Luv Ya,
   P

Colt slid a glass of wine onto the table beside me as I
typed out a reply.

I'm still in Oregon, but if you could tell them I went back
to LA, that would let me breathe easier. Maybe hint that
I'm staying with an acquaintance from the university?
Emmett never paid attention to my school friends, and
Mor won't be able to get hold of the enrolment list that
quickly. Data protection, blah, blah. I should be back next
week, mechanical issues permitting. Siri's car broke down,
and I'm getting it fixed, but the part won't be here until
Monday.

   I don't know who sent the video, but I'm certain it
was someone at the wedding.

   Give Blaze a carrot from me,
   G xxx

With hindsight, I should have accepted the offer of
whisky. In bed, I tossed and turned for an hour, replaying
the video of Emmett and Vania over and over in my head.
And when I finally did manage to sleep, the real nightmare
came.

The accident.

I'd relived it a thousand times over. The crash. The fall.
Screaming for help. Giving my father CPR as I prayed for
him to open his eyes.

But while I woke up in a cold sweat, he never did.

And a wave of grief washed over me once again.

5

GABRIELLE

"There's good news and there's bad news," Brooke informed me.

"Is the bad news that you're calling me at a quarter to seven?"

"Did I wake you? I'm so sorry. I just wanted to catch you before you went to work."

"Oh, it's fine."

It wasn't. Mornings sucked. And I wasn't sure what was worse—croaking my way through a conversation in my sleep or the fact that when Colt had knocked on my bedroom door to hand me the phone, I'd staggered over and opened it without thinking. While wearing his underwear and T-shirt, sans bra and with my hair all over the place.

"Still, I'm sorry."

"You said there was news?"

"Okay, so the good news is that Addy has plenty of shoes. The bad news is that she's insisting on bringing them over personally."

"That's a problem?"

"It is when she's booked a table for dinner at Applejack's. I tried to get us excused, but Addy can be a little strong-willed."

"You don't want to go either?"

"Let's just say the place brings back bad memories." Brooke let out a heavy sigh. "But I can't avoid going there forever, I suppose. Luca says he'll pick us up at the end of the night."

How did I feel about that? Uneasy, but not out-and-out horrified. I'd prefer to avoid going out in public, but who would be looking for me with two locals in small-town Oregon? And if Addy was willing to gift me footwear, then the least I could do was offer my company in exchange if that was what she wanted.

"What time do I need to be there?"

We'd driven past Applejack's on the way to the garage this morning, so at least I knew where it was. I could walk there if necessary, and the prospect filled me with an odd sense of trepidation and excitement. When had I last walked *anywhere* alone? I honestly couldn't remember.

"Seven o'clock. Want to get ready at my place first? Addy's coming over at six."

A real girls' night? "I think I'd like that."

———

And that was how I ended up in a cowboy's arms at...at... Well, I didn't know what the time was because I wasn't wearing a watch, but it was late.

"Where's your hat?"

He smiled at me, bemused. Or was I the bemused one? Amused? Confused? Yes, definitely.

"My hat?"

"Yes, your hat." He had the cowboy jeans, and the cowboy shirt, and the cowboy boots. Even the cowboy stubble. Did cowboys have stubble? I ran my fingers over it. This one sure did. "Cowboys have hats."

"I'm not a cowboy. I'm a veterinarian."

"Aw, so *close*. You still do stuff with animals, right?"

"If by 'stuff,' you mean medical procedures, then yes." Boy, did he have a nice smile. "I'm Isaac."

"Ga— Brie."

"Gabrie?"

"Just Brie."

Even introducing myself was an occupational hazard right now. Luckily, Addy came to the rescue, and the nice cow-vet's arms disappeared. Hmm. *Was* that lucky? I couldn't be sure.

"No men! Have you forgotten why we're here?" She squinted at Isaac. "Sorry about this. You're very handsome, but tonight we hate anyone with a dick. Hows...However, if you'd like to leave your number at the bar, one of us will pick it up tomorrow."

He just chuckled, and Addy was right about the handsome part. "Brooke knows where to find me."

Addy half dragged me back to our table in the corner. Brooke had brought her colleagues for moral support, and Paulo was definitely drunker than me. Darla? She was stone-cold sober, and she watched the rest of us with an expression not so dissimilar from the cow-vet's. But she was nice. She'd brought me leggings with an appropriate amount of ass coverage, a bra that fit, and three dress things that swirled and floated in rainbows of colour. I'd worn the blue one tonight, and it matched Paulo's hair.

"This is a man-free zone. Apart from Paulo, obviously.

We have cocktails and chips, and that's all we need. Did I tell you what Jonas did?"

At least twice. Maybe even three or four times. But that didn't stop her from telling us again.

"He got his dates confused, like, literally, and me and his other girlfriend both showed up at the same restaurant on the same freaking night. Same table, everything. Except we got there earlier than him, so at least we were able to coordinate our yelling."

Brooke laid her head on the table. "That makes Steve's strip-club visits look saintly."

"He even told her it was his birthday so she'd buy him a gift, but he told me his birthday was next month. Does that mean there are ten more girls out there? Does he rotate them on a schedule?"

Paulo had to go one better. "I dated a guy who gave me a key to his apartment, and on his birthday, I figured I'd go over there and, you know, surprise him. But it turned out his two other boyfriends had the same idea, and…boy, that was some night."

"Did you do the yelling too?"

"No, I hooked up with both of them. I have no idea what happened to the other guy—I just blocked his number."

If this was a contest, then I had to have the winner. "At least your fiancé didn't make a sex tape with one of your bridesmaids."

Four jaws dropped. Yes, I definitely took first place.

"Are you serious?" Addy asked. "I mean, how did you find out?"

"Someone Airdropped me a clip as Vania was helping me with my garter."

"Holy shit."

"She tried to tell me it happened before I got together

with Emmett, but she was wearing the necklace I'd gifted her for her birthday. Her birthday was *last month*. So I whacked her with my bouquet, and then Emmett came in, and I threw my phone at him, and my ring, and then everyone started shouting, but there was no sycro...syncras..."

"Synchronisation," Darla put in.

"Thank you. Yes, that. None whatsoever."

"Look on the bright shide," Addy slurred. "At least it wasn't *your* shex tape that got leaked."

Even drunk, I still had the capacity to be horrified. "I'd never make a sex tape."

"You're sure he didn't record you?" Brooke asked. "Who filmed the clip you saw?"

"I... I..." I struggled to force out even a whisper. "I don't have a clue."

"If it was Vania, she obviously wouldn't have filmed you too, but if it was Emmett..."

For fanden. What if it *had* been Emmett? A week ago, I'd have said no way, but I never dreamed he'd sleep with Vania either. There was definitely a tape of him with one woman floating around in cyberspace, but what if there was another?

And more to the point, what the heck was I meant to do about it?

Should I file a police report? Call my brother to warn him? Beg Emmett to tell me the truth? None of those were good options. I couldn't file a report on something that might not have happened. And if nothing had happened, I could hurt my family for no reason. As for calling Emmett, he'd already proven he was a liar.

"Can somebody pass that jug of... Uh, the blue stuff."

Magically, my glass got topped off, although I would

have drunk from the jug if necessary. I raised my hand in a toast.

"To erasing the past."

Everyone drank, although Darla was basically cheating with orange juice. But soon I didn't care. I didn't care about anything.

COLT

*W*hat the...? Hadn't Luca heard of a doorbell? Why was he kicking the damn door down?

I swung it open and started to ask exactly that, but the curses died in my throat when he deposited Brie into my arms.

"I guess this one belongs to you. Good luck, buddy."

"What the hell happened?"

"The dream team of Addy and Paulo."

"Hi, Colt!" Brooke hung out the car window, waving. "Men are assholes."

Fuck my life.

"If Addy ever suggests going out again, handcuff her to something solid," I advised Luca. "Just a tip."

"Sure, if you take Paulo."

"How did *he* get home?"

"Darla drew the short straw. I could hear him and Addy duetting 'Survivor' in the back seat as the three of them headed out of the parking lot."

Brie's dress had come courtesy of Darla too, I could tell that from a glance. Darla's sense of style was—in a word—

unique. But miles and miles of fabric was better than yoga pants that weren't wide enough or long enough, especially if Brie was drunk in a bar.

"Better her than me. Well, thanks for returning Brie."

Luca saluted and strode back to the car to deal with his own problem. Why did Addy always do this? Yeah, I got that she wanted to have fun, and she did have good intentions, but she took it too far. I swore under my breath. Damn, I sounded like such a *dad*, and I still had all this to come with Kiki.

Brie's eyes flickered open. "Hi, Colt."

Then she bit her bottom lip, and my cock stirred in my pants. Fuck.

I must have spoken out loud because the sleepy smile slipped off her face.

"I'm sorry I was bad."

Somebody kill me now.

"Your crown is slipping."

"I don't wear a crown. Ish...ish...more of a tiara." She let out a giggle. "I might've starred in a sex tape."

What on earth was she talking about? Forget relying on Luca—next time Addy had one of her bright ideas, I'd handcuff her myself. Encase her dainty little feet in concrete, whatever.

"Let's get you to bed."

"Bed? Okay."

At least Brie was a compliant drunk. No fighting, no belligerence, just glassy blue eyes rolling in different directions and a few hiccups. She began humming softly to herself as I carried her up the stairs, a tune I didn't recognise, and by the time I laid her on the bed, she was back to smiling. I wasn't about to wrestle with the quilt, so I grabbed a spare blanket from the closet and draped it over her. She'd have to sleep in the dress. I might have thought about her wearing my underwear more times than was healthy, but no way was I going to check if the reality matched up with my expectations.

"I should... I shhh..." she started, but I pressed a finger against her lips.

"Not tonight, Sleeping Beauty. Just get some rest."

She'd need it if she planned on working at the auto shop tomorrow. And I wasn't going to let her sleep in. Whether tonight had been Addy's fault or not, Brie needed to learn that actions had consequences. And what was all that about a sex tape? Drunken rambling? Or was there some truth in it?

In the murky depths of my dark, twisted mind, I had the thought that I wouldn't mind seeing Brie naked, her face flushed and those luscious breasts—breasts I now suspected were real—bouncing free. But not with another man. *Hell*, not with another man.

I shut that thought down pretty damn fast.

Brie wouldn't make a sex tape, anyway. She was far too prim and proper to do anything that risky. Uptight in a prissy sort of way. Although she *had* let her hair down tonight...

In the kitchen, I headed straight for the whisky. I never usually indulged—that one bottle had been sitting at the back of the cupboard for the past year—but there was something about this situation that drove me to drink. I felt as if...as if the women in my life had dragged me onto a roller coaster, jammed the safety bar across my lap, and set the ride going on a constant loop. Safety bar...what a fuckin' joke. My head was screaming "danger, danger, danger," but my cock and my heart had teamed up to do their own thing.

The last time I'd felt this way was in those early days

with Hannah. Back when I was fifteen and barely even knew what love was, just that there was a connection between us I couldn't sever. That connection had led to a whole world of trouble, but if I'd had the opportunity for a do-over, would I have changed anything? That was a question I'd asked myself many times over the years, but I always came to the same answer. No. No, I wouldn't have made a different decision. The good times had outweighed the bad, and even though our happiness had been cut short, Hannah had left me the greatest gift of all. Our daughter.

Kinsley Hannah was my world.

But was there room in it for another complicated entanglement?

"Brie, time to get up."

Nothing.

"I have coffee."

Silence.

A flicker of fear zapped through me—had she run off in the middle of the night? Then rationality kicked in. She'd been in no state to walk anywhere yesterday evening, let alone run. I opened the door an inch and found she hadn't moved. Opened it another inch to check she was still breathing.

"Brie?"

"Go away," she mumbled.

"No can do. Today's a workday. You can't call in sick with a hangover."

For ten long seconds, she didn't stir, but then she suddenly knifed up with her nest of hair tumbling all over the place.

"*For fanden.*"

"You're gonna have to translate."

"No, it's best that I don't." She groaned and buried her head in her hands. "I can't believe I got drunk. I was running my mouth in a freaking bar! Oh hell, oh hell, *oh hell.*"

"Is this something to do with the sex tape you mentioned?"

She stared at me in abject horror. "I told you about that?"

"Not the details, just that there might be one."

She screwed her eyes shut and sucked in a breath. "How many other people did I tell?"

"At a guess? Brooke, Addy, Paulo, and Darla. Maybe Luca."

"And they'll tell their friends, and those people will tell *their* friends, and then everyone will know." Brie scrambled out from under the blanket. "I should go. How can I ever show my face around here again?"

"Shh, shh. Don't panic. Brooke and Luca won't say anything, and Darla's never struck me as a gossip. I'll call Brooke, see if she can keep the other two quiet." I put the coffee on the nightstand and perched on the edge of the bed. "So, there really is a tape?"

"I don't know. I don't *know.* There's a tape of my ex-fiancé with another woman, and Brooke suggested that if he'd recorded her, he might have recorded me too."

"But you don't know for sure that he did?"

"No, and I certainly did nothing to encourage it."

"So maybe it was the other woman who made the video?"

"Why would she do that?"

"Blackmail? A sick souvenir? Why would *he* do it?"

Because the woman was the one with the motive. What

would the guy have gained? An addition to his spank bank? The risks outweighed the benefits, and he'd lost the biggest prize of all: Brie.

"Because he wanted to admire his performance? I have no idea. Why do men like to record themselves having sex?"

Oh, we were *not* going there. I raised both hands in surrender.

"Hell if I know. How did you find out about the tape?"

"Someone Airdropped it to me right before the wedding."

"Who? I thought Airdrop showed the person's name?"

"It shows the phone's name, but that's easy enough to change. We do it all the time."

"We?"

"Me and my friends. Ex-friends, I guess, since they came as a package deal with Emmett. One of them had her email hacked a while ago, and it caused a great deal of embarrassment, so we got into the habit of Airdropping pictures because then there's no trail. Can I borrow your laptop again? I need to contact Phil."

This Phil guy again. Brie said he was a friend, but she sure didn't hesitate to turn to him when she had a problem. Maybe *he* was involved in Tapegate? I'd watched enough chick flicks with Hannah to know that the shy best friend often had designs on the girl.

But I had no right to get involved in their relationship. Brie needed help this week, not a jerk like me causing more problems.

"Emailing Phil doesn't worry you? From a hacking point of view?"

"Oh, we don't email in the conventional sense. There's an email account we both have access to, and we leave messages for each other in the drafts folder."

Smart. Or paranoid.

"Sure, you can borrow my laptop. You want French toast for breakfast? I'm making some for Kiki."

"That would be very kind of you."

And stop thinking about Brie's underwear, asshole.

7

GABRIELLE

*H*onestly, I was my own worst enemy. Everything I touched turned to *scheiße*.

What had I been thinking last night? Yes, I'd had fun, but I'd blurted out my secrets to Brooke's friends—virtual strangers to me—and what if another of the patrons in the bar had overheard? Our table had been in the corner and the jukebox made it difficult to hear conversations, but even so... Nightmares or no nightmares, I was never touching alcohol again.

Ernie had noticed me getting bored and brought over a stack of dog-eared paperbacks, bless him, but I couldn't concentrate on spy thrillers right now. All I could think of was my own unravelling horror story. Would Phil be able to help? I needed her now more than ever. She'd left me a note yesterday, and at least my family had backed off.

Your brother's called me seventeen times (literally, I counted), so I told him you're staying in LA like you wanted. I'm still in the US—Siri's freaking about the movers packing up your stuff properly, so I said I'd stick around for moral support and also to stop Emmett from badgering her. He's bought you a florist shop's worth of roses, but he doesn't know where to send them. Ha!

Pammie's been bribing Blaze with apples, so all seems calm for the moment at least.

Chin up,

P

Phil was still in the US? Thank goodness.

Freaking out here! What if Emmett recorded that clip of him and Vania and he has a video with me too? How the hell do I find out? And do you know what happened to the remains of my phone? Who has my SIM card?

Emmett can stick the roses up his ass. I hope they've still got the thorns on them.

G xxx

Now I was fidgeting on the high stool behind Ernie's counter as I willed Phil to check the message folder. Sometimes a whole week could go by without her looking—technology wasn't her strong point—but I liked to think she'd show a touch more urgency given the current situation. My head pounded with the ferocity of a pneumatic drill every time I moved, so I swallowed a couple more painkillers and washed them down with cold coffee. I could just see the headlines: *Oh, how the mighty have fallen.*

By lunchtime, I could take it no longer.

"Ernie, could I borrow the computer to check my emails?"

I was assuming the thing was hooked up to the internet —it was one of those old tower systems, and every so often, it whirred alarmingly.

"As long as you don't get none of those viruses. My Judith, she clicked on an ad for sewing machines, and every day after that, it kept popping up pictures of naked ladies. I'd've left the darn thing as it was, but Judith got some kid from Coos Bay to drive over and fix it. Cost me a hunnerd and fifty bucks."

"I promise I won't click on any advertisements."

"Maybe you could type my invoices too? Since you'll have the screen switched on, like."

"Sure, I can type whatever you want."

And perhaps the extra work would keep my mind off more concerning matters?

Ernie beamed at me through crooked teeth, and five minutes later, I had a stack of handwritten notes to decipher, car parts and prices and details of the work he'd done. What the heck was a manual transmission shift boot ring? This was like a whole other language.

Phil still hadn't replied when Colt called at ten to four. I was trying to work on the "no news is good news" premise, but damn, it was difficult.

"Hey, it's me."

I hadn't been prepared for the flood of warmth that washed through me at the sound of Colt's voice. It was nice. But also scary.

"Is everything okay?"

"More or less." But it wasn't. I could tell from the tightness in his voice. "I'll tell you about it when I see you, but I'm gonna be a little late picking you up."

"How late?"

"Twenty minutes? We're just leaving Coos Bay."

"Why don't I walk? It's less than a mile, and it'll save you from detouring."

"If you're certain you don't mind, I'd appreciate it."

"I'll see you at home." Too late, I realised my slip of the tongue. "Your home, I mean. Obviously."

"Obviously."

"Well, uh, bye."

I hung up before I made things any more awkward. This whole "friends" thing was harder when a girl didn't have money and status to do the heavy lifting. But also nicer. Every interaction was so much more satisfying because it was real.

Even with Ernie, who could be a tiny bit grumpy at times but was actually quite sweet underneath. He waved as I set off along the road, my first taste of freedom in years. Baldwin's Shore wasn't the prettiest town, but it had a tired charm about it and a spaciousness that made it seem like another world. In my country, land was scarce, and people tended to build up instead of out. Even in England, my second home, everything was closer together. And LA was a jumble of traffic and smog and fancy houses set behind high walls. Here, even the main street had an unfamiliar openness, with a park halfway along and gaps between the buildings. People greeted me as I passed, even though they didn't know me, and I found myself smiling back.

"Brie!"

I stiffened on instinct, but when I spun around, I saw Brooke waving at me from a shop doorway. The Craft Cabin. This was where she worked? I hurried over.

"Hi."

"I'm so sorry about last night. Is your head okay? Mine's throbbing, and Paulo's been lying in a darkened room all day. He had to swap shifts with Darla."

"Painkillers helped."

"Colt called me this morning. Don't worry about Paulo talking—he can't remember a thing that happened after the third pitcher of margaritas. And Addy won't say a word either. She's a huge gossip, but if you ask her to keep a secret, she absolutely will."

"And Darla?"

"She promised to stay quiet too." Oh, thank goodness. A fraction of the weight pressing on my shoulders lifted. Even if a sex tape never materialised, rumours were as good as facts for the media. The lack of actual evidence wouldn't matter. "Do you want a coffee? Or are you on your way somewhere?"

"I'd love a coffee, but Colt's expecting me back."

"I'll text him and let him know you're here. Milk and two sugars, right?"

She'd remembered? That was so sweet. Even after two years, Emmett had always forgotten one or the other, although his maid managed to get it right every time. Rosa was a real sweetheart. I'd miss her.

A cat sidled up and rubbed along my legs, purring. Tigger? No, this cat was black, and Tigger was ginger. Colt had shown me a picture, and I'd also seen her on posters as I walked. *Beloved family pet missing, reward offered.* And she wasn't the only cat who'd disappeared recently. The owners of Mojo, Padmé, and Gizmo were desperately looking for their pets too. Colt said the number of missing cats was becoming a concern, but nobody could find any evidence of accidents or foul play—they'd just simply vanished.

"This is Pickle," Brooke said, beckoning me inside. "She lives here."

Lucky kitty. The Craft Cabin was a riot of colour, shelves of paints and wool and pencils and beads and glitter—a real treasure trove. Finished craft projects were arranged on display shelves, and although I didn't know a knitting needle from a crochet hook, I could quite happily have spent a day poking around in there.

Baldwin's Shore was full of surprises.

But good ones.

And as I took a seat across from Brooke at an old wooden table splodged with paint, and Darla brought out a tin of cookies, I began to wonder what it might be like to live permanently in a town like this. To fit in. To know my neighbours and pop over for a chat on a whim.

I thought that maybe…maybe I'd like to do that.

Baldwin's Shore was also full of sadness.

When I got back to Colt's place, I knew straight away that something was still very wrong. He had a tightness in his jaw that hadn't been there earlier, a tension in his shoulders.

"What happened?"

He opened the door wide enough for me to step inside, and the first thing that hit me was the silence. Usually, there was some sort of noise—Kiki's giggles, or the TV, or the washing machine.

"Where's Kiki?"

"In her room."

"You sent her there?"

It had happened to me as a child on the occasions I misbehaved around my mother. My father would talk things over, take the time to understand what I was going through. Mother said he spoiled me. It wasn't that she'd been a bad parent, more that she didn't have the same empathy. The same connection. Having spent a little time with my grandparents on that side of the family, I understood why.

"No, she took herself there and slammed the door." Colt scrubbed a hand through his hair. "Shit, it's days like this that I start to question everything."

"Want to talk about it?"

I followed him into the living room, and he sank onto the couch, defeated. How had a father-daughter fun day gone so wrong? When I left for work this morning, Kiki had been brimming with excitement about going to the safari park a short distance along the coast, and my heart ached to hear that she was upset.

"When we got back from Bandon, Kiki wanted to go swimming, so I took her over to the public pool, which I don't usually do on my own because they don't have family changing, just male and female. I can't go into the ladies' section, and I'm sure as hell not taking her into the men's, so usually Brooke or Addy comes with us, or Meli takes her with Sophie. But none of them were around, and I figured *someone* would give Kiki a hand to get changed. But they didn't. A bunch of kids made fun of her instead."

I took a seat beside Colt, tucking my legs underneath me so I could sit sideways.

"Kids can be cruel."

"Don't I know it." His heavy sigh told me how much he was hurting. "I never thought this would be easy, but sometimes..."

"Do you have any family who could help? A female relative, perhaps?"

"I'm an only child, and so was Hannah."

"No grandparents? Feel free to tell me to butt out if you want to."

"Hannah's father was never on the scene, and her mom lives in Canada. We talk on the phone every week, but

Dorothea's afraid of flying, so we don't see her much in person."

Telling that he'd mentioned Hannah's parents before his own. Come to think of it, he'd never said a single word about his family, which was strange considering Baldwin's Shore seemed to be such a close-knit community. Unless they'd passed away? That had to be the reason, didn't it?

I laid a hand on Colt's arm. "I'm so sorry about your parents."

"They're not dead. Might as well be, but they moved to Florida a year after Kiki was born. The last time I spoke to them was to tell them Hannah was gone, and they asked what I planned to do about 'the child.' The fuckin' *child*. They wouldn't even use her name." Colt choked up, and I realised I was completely out of my league here. Offering comfort wasn't something I was accustomed to. Meaningless platitudes were my specialty. "The only time they ever saw her was when we crossed paths in the grocery store."

"Do you know why? Were they overwhelmed at the thought of becoming grandparents?"

"No, they were racist as fuck. They hated Hannah because of the colour of her skin. For years, they hoped I'd 'come to my senses,' but when I told them I was gonna marry her, they said it was her or them. I've never regretted my decision, but times like today... It's just hard, that's all."

Hard? It was...unfathomable. How could parents cut off their child in that manner? My own mother had very specific ideas of who I should marry—Emmett had been acceptable because his family had money and moved in the right circles —but even she wouldn't be so pig-headed. My father, he'd always told me that I should marry for love, but after the Emmett debacle, I wasn't so sure I knew what love was. Surely if I'd been in love, I'd be more upset about being betrayed? Yes, there was embarrassment and anger, but did I truly miss Emmett? I honestly couldn't say that I did. Not with the same all-consuming grief with which I missed my father.

"I wish I could fly to Florida and shake some sense into your parents."

"You'd be wasting your time."

"Then if you want, maybe I could come to the pool with you and Kiki this weekend?"

"You swim?"

"Not in a public pool, but I'd be happy to help Kiki in the changing room."

"Why don't you swim in public?"

"Because adults can be cruel too."

"I don't get it."

And I could see he genuinely didn't.

"Me and bathing suits, we don't get along too well."

"Huh?" Then he snorted. "Are you kidding me? I'd pay good money to see you in a bathing suit." His eyes widened. "Ah, shit, not in a pay-per-view way. I... Fuck. I'm gonna shut my damn mouth now."

I tried not to smile. Yes, Colt's comment was totally inappropriate, but I took it as a compliment.

"So, the pool at the weekend?"

"Uh, yeah. I mean, thanks."

"Do you want me to try talking to Kiki this evening? I know I'm not a parent, but my little sister's ten years younger than me, and I often had to deal with her moods when my parents were out of town."

"Your parents left you to look after your sister?"

Oh. Crap. "Uh, no? We, uh, we had a nanny." Which sounded so freaking pretentious given the present company, and that was without mentioning the butler, the chef, the maids, the gardeners... "But Elin was a real handful. One time, she locked herself in her bathroom, and I talked to her for an hour through the door before she agreed to come out, but then the lock jammed, and I had to climb through the window to rescue her."

I left out the part where I'd convinced a crew from the fire department to hoist me up three floors in a cherry picker while the head of my security detail lost his cool and called my parents. Kasper had been my favourite bodyguard, but honestly, he did have a tendency to overreact on occasion. Wasn't it far better for me to show a little initiative than lose a valuable antique door to an axe? Mother had been horrified—no surprises there—but my father just said, "That's my girl," and checked I was wearing a safety harness.

"Sounds as if you have an adventurous streak."

"I did, once."

"But not anymore?"

"Things change."

"Yeah, they do. Could you try talking to Kiki? I just..." Another sigh. "I'd appreciate it."

I'd do anything to see the two of them smiling again.

8

COLT

*A*fter the loss of Hannah and then the trouble with Jacqueline, I thought I'd never fall in love for a second time.

That evening, I began to think again.

I'd paced the living room for half an hour. Gotten the whisky bottle out of the cupboard. Put it back again. Paced some more, and then eventually climbed the stairs to see how Brie was getting on with Kiki. I hadn't heard any doors slam, and I had to take that as a good sign.

I'd found them both sitting cross-legged on Kiki's bed, Kiki in front of Brie as Brie gently combed through her mountain of curls. She was doing it properly too—Kiki's hair was wet, and I could see the bottle of conditioner on the quilt next to them. The sight brought a lump to my throat, and I had to step back for a moment.

Brie had walked into our lives less than a week ago, but she fit into place so easily.

"Hey," I began, but my voice came out thick and croaky. I swallowed and tried again. "Hey."

"Can we have mac and cheese tonight? *Pleeeeeeease*?"

That was it? Mac and cheese? No more "Daddy, I hate you, I hate swimming, I hate everything"? Hannah rarely used to get upset, but when she did, she'd stay in a funk for days, and Kiki had inherited that stubbornness. But now she wanted dinner?

"Sure we can. You want the box stuff or made-from-scratch?"

"The box stuff. I don't like lumps."

Fair enough. "Everything's okay here?" I asked, just to check.

"Brie's doing my hair, and *I* told her what stuff to spray on it. Did I get it right?"

"You did."

"And she said she'd come swimming with us, and if anyone's mean to me, she's gonna throw them into the deep end."

I raised an eyebrow, but Brie just shrugged.

"I'm stronger than I look."

Yes, I was beginning to understand that.

Brie was like a Russian doll—a woman of many faces, and every time another layer got revealed, I liked her more. But I still didn't know much about her. Part of me wanted to push for more details, but I also didn't want to scare her off, and secretly, I was enjoying the game. Putting together the puzzle that was Brie... Hell, I didn't even know her full name.

"What's your last name, Brie?"

"Uh, why do you want to know?"

"Just curious."

For a long moment, I thought she wasn't going to tell me, but then she shrugged.

"My last name's Westerburg. Brie Westerburg."

Brie Westerburg... It suited her. A pretty name for a pretty woman.

"I'll start dinner. Half an hour?"

Both girls nodded in perfect unison.

Fuck, I was in so much trouble.

"Did you get a reply?" I asked.

Brie had borrowed my laptop to check in with Phil again, and she nodded.

"Yes, thank goodness. Phil has my phone, although it's smashed to bits, completely beyond repair. I actually feel quite sorry for Emmett because Phil promised to discuss the matter with him."

"You feel sorry for Emmett? Phil's a tough guy, then?"

A peal of laughter wasn't what I'd expected. "A guy? Phil's not a guy." He wasn't? "Oh, she's a complete tomboy, but she definitely has boobs."

Clank, clank, clank... The irrational jealousy released its pincers. In my defence, how many women were called Phil?

"So... Philippa?"

"Philomena. I've known her forever. Well, thirteen years. We met when I was at school in England."

"Your family moved around? I thought you were Danish?"

"I went to England alone. It's kind of a family tradition to get educated there—my brother attended Eton College, and my sister's at Wycombe Abbey."

"You didn't miss your family?"

"Every day, but my parents worked so much that it made sense to board. I always went home for the holidays, and my father cleared his schedule those weeks so we spent plenty of time together."

"Your father? Not your mother?"

"What can I say? I was a real daddy's girl." Brie's words were upbeat, her tone light, but there was an underlying sadness lurking. Why? What had happened to her father? It was no surprise when she changed the subject. "Phil and I, we shared a room from the start, and we clicked straight away. We can tell each other anything. When I first started dating Emmett, she asked me if I was sure about him, and I thought I was, but it turned out that she was absolutely right and he was a bit of a dick. If I ever get involved with another man, I'm going to have her pick him out and then I'll just go along with it."

Ah, shit. So now I needed to get Phil's seal of approval too?

Or did that just give me an easy way out?

"And Phil's going to speak to Emmett?"

"You were right about the 'tough' part. If she can handle her horses, she can handle an American idiot."

"She rides horses?"

"When Phil's mother told her to settle down and find a nice man, I don't think she envisioned one with hooves and a tail. Rather her than me, though. The idea of bouncing around on an autonomous lump of meat makes me shudder."

"I'm disappointed. Maybe someday you'll reconsider." *Did I just say that? Shit, I just said that.* Slowly, deliberately, I pushed my glass away. "I apologise, that was inappropriate."

Brie took the opposite tack and drained hers. "Uh... Uh... For the record, I was talking about horses there. Not, uh, non-horses." She pointed to my drink, flustered. "Are you planning to finish that?"

"Have at it."

She did, and then smacked her head. "I'm not even meant to be drinking. My liver hates me right now."

"This week, it'll forgive you."

"I should go to bed."

And she did. Alone.

Tonight, it would just be me with my hand for company.

Friday afternoon, and I'd managed to survive a trip to the ice cream parlour in Coos Bay, plus stayed awake the whole way through a movie about a cartoon anteater. I was proud of my achievements but also counting down the minutes until I could pick up Brie.

And then my phone rang.

Deputy Dawkins.

I weighed up the pros and cons of answering. I wouldn't have described Dawkins as a friend, so he wasn't calling to shoot the breeze, and if I let it go to voicemail, I'd only have to deal with whatever shit he wanted to discuss later. And I had better things to do with my evenings.

"Haines speaking."

"How's your vacation?"

"Fine until thirty seconds ago. What's up?"

Dawkins's first name was Pete, but we all called him Deputy Dawg behind his back, partly because he had a jowly face but mostly because he was like a dog with a bone whenever he got his teeth into something. And that something usually created work and ultimately turned out to be inconsequential. But he'd volunteered to cover my time off, so I couldn't complain.

"Think I might've solved your cat mystery."

"Oh?"

Now I was more interested. Kiki was still putting food out for Tigger every night, and we had half the cats in the neighbourhood roaming our yard, hunting for scraps.

"Of course he denies everything, but I caught him red-handed with a cat in his vehicle."

"So who was it?"

"Name's Deon Jackson."

Deon? My first reaction was, *Are you fucking kidding me?* Like many of us, Deon had done some dumb shit in high school and been careless enough to get caught, but he wasn't a hardened criminal. He'd drawn a moustache on the principal's portrait and run underwear up the flagpole, and once or twice, he'd stolen candy from the grocery store and gotten a smack on the wrist. But I thought he'd outgrown all that. His grandfather had driven a cab in town for as long as I'd been alive, his father had a stable job at the port in Coos Bay, and Deon made deliveries for the grocery store on Main Street as well as transporting anything else that needed to be picked up or dropped off. Worked hard at it by all accounts.

"You're sure it wasn't his cat in the vehicle? Or a friend's?"

"According to the collar tag, it belonged to one Lillian Baldwin."

Suddenly, my day just got a whole lot worse.

Yeah, Lillian Baldwin was one of *those* Baldwins. The town had been named after her great-great-grandfather, a man who'd been into both property development and philanthropy, traits that had continued on down through the family until the current crop. The last of the old-school Baldwins, Easton the First, had died a few years back—a nice old guy—and now we were left with Easton Junior and his second wife, plus the kids from his first marriage. Easton the Third, the twins Lillian and Kayleigh, and Parker, in order of toxicity. Then there was Sara, their cousin. Her parents had had the sense to get the hell away from the nastiness, but after they passed in a car accident, Sara had ended up back in the family fold. She seemed okay. I didn't know her well enough to make much of a judgment. But Lillian? Lillian was pure poison.

"Do *not* call Lillian Baldwin."

"Already did that. She said it's definitely her cat."

As Brie would say, *for fanden*. I wasn't entirely certain what it meant, but I could take a guess. And if Dawg had called Lillian, that meant I'd be getting a call in three... two...one...

Call waiting.

That one could definitely go to voicemail.

"Did Deon say how the cat got into his vehicle? He was driving his cargo van?"

"That's the one. Pulled him over for a broken tail light and heard the thing miaowing inside. He claims the cat must've jumped in there while he was delivering groceries to Ms. Baldwin."

Which sounded plausible. But something niggled at me, and I focused until I remembered what it was. Tigger had gone missing on a Tuesday. And Deon delivered groceries to Mrs. Hardcastle next door every Tuesday, come rain or shine.

Could Deon have stolen the cats?

Whether he had or he hadn't, I needed to figure out the truth. Kiki was missing Tigger, and I hated to consider what might have happened to her.

"Where's Deon now?"

"I transported him to the sheriff's office. You wanna speak with him?"

"Yeah, I do want to speak with him."

———

"Why can't I stay at home?" Kiki asked as we drove back to our place. Brie had a well-thumbed paperback in her lap with a flattened spark-plug box wedged halfway through it, so I figured she'd had a quiet day at the office.

"Because I have to go into work for a while. You can sit at my desk, okay? And we can pick up dinner on the way back. Anything you want."

"But I hate going to your work. It's so booooooring. Can I go see Brooke instead?"

"Brooke isn't free this evening."

She had date night with Luca, the lucky asshole. They were just so damn happy together. And I was happy for them, so fucking happy, but that happiness was always tinged with an edge of melancholy because watching them together reminded me of what I'd lost.

"If it would help, I could watch Kiki this evening," Brie offered. "Although I'll understand completely if you don't want that. We don't know each other very well, after all."

We didn't, but did I know her well enough? I'd seen how Brie acted around my daughter, and Kiki sure seemed to like her. There was none of that hesitancy I'd seen around Jacqueline. Yes, it was soon, but I'd known within a week of meeting Hannah that I'd marry her someday, and heaven help me, I was beginning to get that same feeling about Brie.

She was a good person, instinct told me that much. And it was time to listen to my instincts again instead of trying to use my head. But the final decision was up to Kiki. If she wasn't comfortable with the idea, I wasn't going to push her.

"What do you think, kiddo? Do you want to come to the office or stay with Brie?"

"Stay with Brie! And don't call me kiddo."

Guess I'd been told.

"If you're sure you don't mind," I said to Brie.

"I don't mind one bit."

9

GABRIELLE

För helvete.

Colt had trusted me with his home and his child, and I'd messed everything up. Kiki giggled hysterically as I wafted the smoke with a tea towel.

"It smells so *bad*."

"Yes, yes, I know that."

"You're not very good at cooking."

"No, I'm really not."

The back door was open, the windows were open, and still the house smelled like burned plastic. Kiki coughed again. The pizza was ruined, the fries were still frozen, and not so long ago, Colt had called me on the landline when he left work. If my estimate was correct, he'd be back at any moment.

Ah, there was his truck now.

Every time things seemed to be going a little better, life fell apart. In the great scheme of things, ruining dinner wasn't a disaster, but on top of all the other things that had happened this week... I sniffed back my tears and wiped my eyes with a sleeve.

"Don't cry." Kiki wrapped her arms around me. "Daddy used to burn stuff every day."

The front door opened, and I heard the sound of running feet, heavy boots on the wooden floor.

"What happened?"

"I didn't realise you weren't meant to cook the pizza on that little tray thing it came with. The instructions said nothing about removing it, and now it's..." I pointed at the metal grill I'd pulled out of the oven, complete with ribbons of melted plastic. "I'm so sorry. What should I do? How should I clean it?"

"Forget it—I'll chip off the melted parts tomorrow. Haven't you ever cooked a pizza before?"

"No."

"How have you survived for the past decade?"

"By going to restaurants. Or sometimes other people cooked. I just thought that I could make an attempt, and it all went so horribly wrong."

Was Colt angry? He looked so stern, but then his lips twitched, and I realised he was trying not to laugh.

"Hey! It's not funny."

"Princess, it's hilarious."

"P-p-princess?"

What the hell had he been doing at work? Background checks?

"Aw, c'mon—you went to boarding school, and you've never cooked a pizza before. What would the Brits call that? Posh?"

Ah, crisis averted. "Yes, posh. Absolutely."

"I've never cooked a pizza," Kiki said. "Can I be a princess too?"

Colt swung her up into the air, and she squealed. "Sure you can. How's about we all go out for pizza?"

"Can I have ice cream?"

"You've already had ice cream today."

"But if Brie's with us, then it's a special dinner, so I can have more ice cream."

"That's not how ice cream privileges work, kiddo."

"Don't call me kiddo."

But Kiki got her ice cream, on the house courtesy of the restaurant manager who said that any young lady who dressed up for dinner deserved dessert. And Kiki had certainly made an effort. She'd picked out her pink satin gown herself, and her gold plastic crown, and I'd lent her my necklace because nobody would be likely to steal it. Who would believe a seven-year-old was wearing real diamonds? She looked so cute with all the sparkles.

Colt had dressed up too, sort of. Outside of his uniform, I'd never seen him in a shirt with buttons before, and he'd switched his jeans for flannel slacks and his boots for brown leather shoes. He didn't have the crispness of Emmett, but now that I'd had time to reflect, I realised I could have had a shop mannequin on my arm in Malibu and nobody would've been able to tell the difference. Colt was *rugged*, and every single woman checked out his ass. I wanted to poke their eyes out.

I was the underdressed one tonight, which was somewhat novel. I'd worn Darla's flowing red dress, which could best be described as cute-casual, but it was oh-so practical. Not only did it let me eat as much as I wanted without getting cut in half by a waistband, but it also had pockets. Six of them. Brooke said Darla made most of her dresses herself, and if that was true, then she should definitely start selling them. She'd rake in a fortune.

The whole evening was one of the nicest I'd ever had. No pressure, no expectations, just good food and better company. I wanted to repeat the experience a hundred times over, a thousand, but that was out of the question. Siri's car would be fixed next week, and then I'd have to go... somewhere. What was it called when you went into exile in your own country? Inxile?

"Ready to go, princess?" Colt asked softly, and I realised I'd been staring into space for goodness knew how long. Kiki was slumped over the table in a food coma, but it was also past her bedtime so that wasn't helping either.

I nodded, and Colt hoisted Kiki up onto one hip. Her head flopped onto his shoulder, and I wasn't sure she was even awake. Guess she wouldn't be needing a bedtime story tonight.

Ever the gentleman, Colt held the door open for me, and I stumbled through it. Tonight had been an eye-opener, proof that the simple things in life were worth more than—

"Wrong way." Colt took my hand and steered me in the other direction. *He took my hand.* And he didn't let go either.

"Directions aren't my strong point."

"What do you normally do? Get lost?"

"No, I ask Siri."

Voi vittu. I bit my tongue, but it was too late. Thank the deities that someone at Apple had had the foresight to name their assistant after mine.

"Technology's a wonderful thing."

"Yes, yes it is."

If I ever had to hire another assistant, they would be called Bixby.

This hand-holding thing—what did it mean? Did Colt like me? In *that* way? I might have been twenty-five, but having never had a normal, healthy relationship in my life, I found myself at sea, metaphorically speaking. Life with Emmett had been so much more straightforward. By our third date, Emmett's assistant had been coordinating schedules with Siri, and the information magically appeared in my calendar. I'd known in advance when we'd sleep together for the first time because somebody booked a hotel room and Siri packed my fancy underwear. I couldn't recall feeling any particular anticipation or excitement—it had just been something I accepted would happen, and it did.

With Colt, I was sailing into uncharted waters in a rough sea, and every time we crested a wave, my stomach did that flippy thing before we dropped back down again. This was fun. The little touches, the way he looked at me, his sweet chivalry... I loved it.

How was I meant to drive away from all that on Monday?

My last morning at work, and I'd actually kind of miss the place. Ernie said I could keep the book that I was three-quarters of the way through, and I'd gotten to know a bunch of people around town, by voice if not by face. Most of them were lovely salt-of-the-earth types, but as in every sphere, there was an asshole. His name was Easton Baldwin the Third. That was how he introduced himself when he called. Easton Baldwin *the Third*. Goodness, and people thought *I* was pretentious.

He'd phoned on Wednesday, Thursday, and Friday to complain about how long Ernie was taking to repair his car, which was pointless because Easton *the Third* also drove an Audi and Ernie couldn't magic up parts from nowhere. Plus several of the bolts had been rusted, and he'd had to brush off all the rust, apply a thread loosener, and let the liquid soak in overnight, so he'd told me over coffee yesterday.

But now the car was fixed, which meant E-Three could come and be rude in person instead of yelling down the phone.

And now here he was.

"Where's my car?"

I recognised the voice from his many, many calls, but I refused to give him the satisfaction of knowing that.

"Could I take your name please, sir?"

When I was younger, my mother had taught me an important lesson—the more obnoxious somebody was, the sweeter you became. It took the wind out of their sails and also confused them.

"Easton Baldwin. The *Third*."

"Thank you, sir. I have your paperwork right here, and if you'd care to take a seat, I'll just fetch your keys."

He grumbled, but he sat, and I sauntered out the door and around the side of the building. It was a lovely day. I stood for a while, breathing in the fresh air and watching as a flock of birds dipped and swooped across the blue sky. Then I fished E-Three's keys out of my pocket and ambled back inside.

"Here you go. And how would you like to pay?"

He thrust a credit card at me, and I slid it into the machine. Ernie had shown me how to use it because there was no point in him stopping whatever he was doing to take payment when I was perfectly capable of pressing a few buttons myself.

"You new in town?" E-Three asked.

"Just arrived last week."

"What are you doing tonight?"

"Tonight?"

"Yeah, later."

Was he...was he asking me on a date? A freaking date? He'd spent four days bitching at me and he thought I'd want to spend another minute in his company? As Phil would say, what an utter cockwomble.

"Tonight? I'm cleaning my oven."

"Fine. Tomorrow?"

"Aw, tomorrow is Netflix night."

For the first time, he looked slightly uncertain. "Monday?"

"Monday, I'm attending a lecture on misogyny through the ages at the Coos Bay Historical Society, but you're welcome to join me if you'd like. I think you'd get a lot out of it."

Ah, now he understood.

"Bitch," he muttered under his breath.

"Don't forget to take your invoice, sir. And please accept this sour-grape-and-raspberry air freshener with our compliments."

He slammed the door so hard it rattled.

Five minutes later, Ernie slunk in. "Easton's gone?"

"Didn't you hear the tyres squealing?"

"He happy?"

"I don't think he knows the meaning of the word."

"'Bout right. That boy's rubbed everyone in town the wrong way over the years." Ernie scanned the invoice. "What's this line at the bottom? This A55 tax?"

"The ass tax? Every time Easton shouted at me on the phone, I added ten bucks to the bill. When he came to pay, he was too busy staring at my chest to notice."

Ernie began to guffaw, bent over double, and then went into a coughing fit. "Ass tax. *Ass* tax? Now that, that I'll have to remember." He reached into his pocket and extracted a crumpled ten-dollar bill. "Why don't you run on down to the coffee house before you finish, get us a box of donuts?"

"Of course."

He shook his head, still chuckling. "Ass tax."

Yes, I could quite happily stay in Baldwin's Shore for a little longer. My father had always told me that everything happened for a reason, but after the accident, I'd lost my faith in that assertion. How could I not? But maybe he'd been right? Maybe I was meant to be in this place, at this time? I was happier now than I'd been in years.

"Get me one of them bear claws?" Ernie said. "And a Boston cream."

"Sure."

But how long could the happiness last?

10

COLT

*S*o *much for taking a whole week off.* Rather than making Deon spend a night in a cell, I'd let him out on the condition that he came in for an interview today. It wasn't much of a risk. For the most part, Deon was a good kid. Plus he had nowhere to go but home, and his pop would've kicked his ass if he didn't show. This morning, I'd talked to him for near on two hours, and he'd stuck to his story—that he'd left the van's side door open while he carried groceries to the Baldwins' kitchen, four trips so the door stayed open for a good ten minutes, and the cat must've climbed inside while he was busy. He hadn't checked the interior before he closed the door—why would he?—and the first time he'd heard the cat was when Dawg was issuing a ticket for a broken tail-light cover.

Damn by-the-book asshole. Who issued a ticket for a broken tail light? All that did was piss people off. Sure, if the guy had been warned before, that was a different story, but a first-time offence? I carried red tape in my patrol car to cover over the gaps—a helping hand and a friendly warning to get the glass fixed went a lot further than the heavy-handed approach in this town.

Deon didn't have an alibi for any of the cat disappearances, including Tigger's, but since the time windows were so wide, I wouldn't have expected him to unless he'd been out of town for a few days. He had no proof of his innocence, but I had no real evidence of his guilt either. All I could do was keep an eye on him.

However, the Baldwins didn't see things that way. Lillian had called me at nine, eleven, and one o'clock, and in-between times, I'd had Kayleigh and Easton on the phone. Easton the Third, that was. Easton Junior—EJ—could be an imperious prick, but he didn't have much of a spine, so he tended to leave the confrontations to his kids. Now that Deon was back making grocery deliveries, I gave it another thirty minutes before someone told Lillian and she screeched at me again.

Luca had bet on an hour.

Right now, we were sitting in the sheriff's office in Coquille, filling out paperwork. Mine related to Deon, and Luca's related to bureaucracy. From Monday, he'd be riding with me until he'd completed the next stage of his training, which we both bitched about, but in the way that two buddies who were in reality looking forward to working together did.

The phone rang, and Luca glanced at his watch. "Thirty-seven minutes. You win."

The victory gave me no pleasure. Was there any way I could transfer the call to Deputy Dawg? Probably, but he'd no doubt manage to make the situation worse.

"Afternoon, Lillian."

"How could you? How could you let that thief go?"

I covered the phone with my hand and let out a long

sigh. "Because there were no grounds to hold Deon, and we have procedures to follow."

"You didn't care about procedures when you barged into my home earlier this year."

"A woman's life was in danger, Lillian."

"And Burty was in danger today. Are you saying his life isn't important?"

"No, I'm not saying that at all, but—"

"Well, arrest that awful man again."

"I'm afraid I can't do that."

"Then I'm going to put in a complaint. Parker and Easton should have complained before, and then you'd have been fired already."

In truth, I was surprised they hadn't. I wasn't sure whether Parker had dug deep and found a grain of pragmatism or the Baldwin brothers had been concerned about retribution. Not from me or even Luca, but from the person we'd christened "the Bad Samaritan."

"Go right ahead. If you want me to transfer you over to our administration department, they can mail you a form."

She hung up.

"And you can stop laughing," I told Luca. "From next week, this is your problem too."

"Maybe I should rethink the career change?"

I flicked his shiny new badge. "And give up the jewellery?"

"Hey, I could get my ears pierced to celebrate graduating. What do you think? Diamonds or rubies?"

"What do I think? I think you should take Brooke out for dinner instead."

"The weather's meant to be good tomorrow, so why don't we all go to the Peninsula? Me and Brooke still have spare guest passes, and we can chill by the pool. Make the most of my last day of freedom."

Kiki didn't love the Peninsula. She called it the "old-people pool," but after her experience at the public pool this week, perhaps she'd be willing to give it another try? Plus Brie might be happier there. Her body hang-ups baffled me, but they worried her and that was what mattered.

"Reckon we'll take you up on that."

"Brie too?"

"If you have enough passes."

"We do, but I don't suppose Nico even cares. He said to come over whenever."

"That guy's weird. He's a billionaire, but he shoots the shit with us when he's in town?"

In a stand-offish sort of way, but he was thawing gradually.

"Brooke thinks he's lonely, and I guess that makes sense. When you have that much cash, how do you know who your friends are? He probably sees talking to us as a safe option."

"Money can't buy happiness, huh?"

"Something like that. And speaking of happiness... You and Brie? That going places?"

"Hell, I don't know."

"But you want it to?"

"She's only in town for a week."

"Avoiding the question?"

Fuck, that was the problem with having friends who'd just been trained in investigative techniques. They felt the need to practise.

"Yeah, I'd like it to go somewhere, okay? But last week, she was ready to marry another man, and I don't want to scare her off by making any heavy moves."

"So tiptoe. Have you given her any clues about how you feel?"

Had I? I'd held her hand when we left the restaurant last night, and she hadn't objected. Did that count? Or had she just assumed I didn't want her to meander off in the wrong direction again?

"Not what you'd call *solid* clues."

"So tell her."

"I have to think of Kiki as well. I don't want her to get hurt if things go wrong."

"But what if things go right? I'm not saying that Kiki's short of love, but she's not gonna complain if there's another woman who likes sparkly shit around. Brooke likes Brie too. Says she's a ditz sometimes, but sweet."

That was accurate. All of it.

But there were still so many unknowns. What if we did take things further and it turned out to be a rebound relationship? Did Brie have commitments elsewhere? She'd mentioned a PR job. And would she be happy with the life I could provide for her? Emmett might have been a douche, but I got the impression he was a rich douche, and some months, I had to make the decision between filling my truck with gas and eating breakfast. Kiki wanted for nothing—I made sure of that—but I wasn't rich. Last night's pizza trip had blown two months' entertainment budget. I was just damn lucky I had generous friends. Even today, Brooke was entertaining Kiki at the Craft Cabin so I could work. Technically, the Saturday morning craft sessions were meant to be for nine-year-olds and over, but as long as Kiki behaved, Brooke made an exception.

"I'll see how things go this weekend."

"Just don't fuck it up. I wasted a decade pussyfooting around Brooke, and that's a decade I can't get back."

"That's your advice? Don't fuck it up?"

"It's sound logic, buddy. Consider it. And what're we gonna do about these cats?"

The cats? We were going to put them on the back burner for the rest of the weekend. Burty Baldwin was back home with Lillian, and I was at a loss about the next step, other than to keep a watch on Deon. If there'd been even a hint of a clue as to where Tigger had gone, I'd have been on it in a hot minute, but I'd spoken to every neighbour, not only on my street but around the homes of the other missing cats too.

There was nothing. No sightings, no carcasses, no suspects seen skulking around. No cougar sightings. No coyotes.

The cats had just...gone. Good thing Beer Me Up had morphed into Applejack's because if Skip was still running the bar, he'd be muttering about alien abduction. Although I kind of missed the old guy and his craziness. Getting your picture taken on top of the giant flying saucer in the parking lot had been a teenage rite of passage. Too bad Skip had gone to jail for robbing an armoured truck.

So apart from our now-nightly routine of putting food out—which I'd carry on with for as long as Kiki wanted— we focused on other things. On Saturday afternoon, we went to the beach, and Kiki ran around the tide pools, hunting for fish and crabs and sea stars and anything else left trapped by the receding ocean. Brie wasn't far behind her, clambering over the rocks like a kid. I lagged behind because I liked watching the girls together, and definitely not because it gave me a great view of Brie's luscious ass.

"What's that?" Kiki asked. "The yellow-and-purple thing?"

I was ready to step forward and take a look, but it turned out I didn't need to.

"It's a nudibranch," Brie told her. "Don't touch, though—they're often poisonous."

"I never touch because Daddy told me not to. Will it kill me?"

"Probably not, but it might sting. They're clever little creatures—most don't produce toxins themselves, but they eat other animals that sting and store the stingers on their a — Uh, on their rear ends to protect themselves."

Impressive. And unexpected.

"What did you say you studied at college?" I asked.

Brie never had said, but I was curious.

"Political science."

"And you just read up on marine biology in your spare time?"

"When I was Kiki's age, my papa used to take me to see the rock pools at home."

"So you grew up near the ocean?"

"The Baltic Sea. Yes." Her voice turned wistful and, if I wasn't mistaken, held a touch of sadness. "This brings back so many memories."

And I wanted to make new ones with her. With every day that passed, Brie embedded herself deeper into my life, and if she left... I didn't want to think about it. *Couldn't* think about it. I might have tried for her hand again as we walked back, but Kiki beat me to it and insisted on walking between us.

My girls.

That evening, we grilled out in the backyard, all of us barefoot and happy, then settled in for movie night. Kiki made it halfway through *Finding Nemo*, and after I'd helped her to brush her teeth and settled her into bed, I headed back downstairs for some alone time with Brie.

"Did you pick another movie?"

"Yup."

What was it? *The Notebook? Titanic? Pride & Prejudice?*

No.

"*Godzilla?* You like action movies?"

"Yes, apart from *The Meg*. That one gave me nightmares. But we can watch a romcom if you want?"

Damn, this woman was perfect.

"Don't ever change."

I started off with my arm on the back of the couch, and when Brie leaned into me, I dropped it down to her shoulders. Neither of us said a word. Halfway through the movie, her eyes began to close, and when she keeled over into my lap, I didn't move a muscle for five straight minutes. Then I rested a hand on her shoulder, and her hand crept up in sleep to twine fingers through mine.

This wasn't just some rebound fling, was it?

This was more. So much more.

11

GABRIELLE

Way to go, Gabrielle.

The memory of yesterday evening made me smile and groan at the same time. Colt had acted unbelievably sweet, sort of cuddly, and I'd been wondering how risky it would be to try a kiss when tiredness overcame me and I'd fallen asleep on him. Like, *on* him. With my head in his lap. At completely the wrong angle for what I'd dreamed about doing, but still... He hadn't objected, but was it normal to do things like that? My experience with men was painfully limited. I'd lost my virginity to an absolute playboy who viewed me as nothing more than a notch on his bedpost—which was fine, it had been by mutual agreement—but that didn't provide me with any point of reference for future relationships. Other than Emmett, my only serious boyfriend had been a shipping heir who on paper had seemed like a good match but in reality had been so boring that I'd grown sleepy at the mere mention of his name, like Pavlov's dog if the dog had yawned rather than drooling. That dalliance had lasted for six months before we'd parted reasonably amicably.

För helvete, I was so bad at this.

"Ready to go?" Colt called up the stairs.

"Five minutes."

Today, we were heading to the beach again, but a different beach. A beach at an upscale resort, which sounded quite dull, but Brooke, Luca, Addy, and Aaron were going too, so perhaps it wouldn't be so bad? And at least Kiki could swim without fear of mean girls.

Was it a date?

It kind of felt like a date, but when we arrived, Addy made it very clear that she and Aaron definitely weren't dating. No way. Nuh-uh.

"Aaron's like a brother to me. And totally not my type. Did you know he's a lawyer? Soooo uptight. You're not swimming?"

"I'm happy just sitting here in the sun."

Since I didn't have any shorts, I'd worn Darla's red dress again. I'd send her some money once I got home because those dresses really had been the loveliest gift. Mother would roll her eyes when she saw them, and Elin too, but did I care? No, I did not.

The Peninsula Resort had two pools, and we'd set up by the smaller—and quieter—of the two. There was no bar, but waiters would bring drinks and snacks if you asked. I didn't ask. Apart from Kiki, I was the only person not paying my way, and I would have been blind not to notice how careful Colt was with his money. That his daughter had new shoes, but his were well-worn. That his house was homey and clean, but dated. That he studied the prices on the menu and avoided the expensive items. How much did a sheriff's deputy make? Not a fortune, I didn't suppose, and after he'd paid for childcare... I'd send him money too, although that seemed so...so...trite.

"Brie! Brie!" Kiki tugged on my skirt. "Come watch me."

She cannonballed into the deep end, squealing, and splashed me, a passing waiter, and an older couple sipping cocktails. They didn't say anything, but the woman looked pained.

"I'm so sorry," I told them. "She's just excited to be here today."

"Perhaps you could encourage her to be a little quieter?" the woman suggested.

"We'll try." The voice came from behind me, a man. A man with an accent. Russian? "I'll have fresh drinks sent over for you."

The woman beamed at him, the man not so much.

I turned to see who'd been speaking, expecting a member of the service staff but finding a dark-haired man in board shorts and a T-shirt rather than the tan slacks and polo shirt the employees wore. He held out a hand.

"Nico."

Ah. The resort's owner. Colt had mentioned he showed his face sometimes. I sized him up in the way I'd become so used to doing after years spent attending tedious functions, and recognised him doing the same to me.

Early thirties, kept in shape, the shirt was faded but looked as if it had been made that way rather than weathered by the sun. Designer sunglasses pushed up on top of his head. Good nails. The nails were always a giveaway with men, and Nico's said he got manicures on a regular basis. He was rich, but not frat-boy rich or Emmett rich. There was a hard edge to him I couldn't quite put my finger on. Wasn't sure I wanted to.

But I held out my own hand, and he shook it rather than kissed it. So, charming but not a sleaze.

"Brie."

"You're Colt's friend?"

"Something like that."

Water cascaded over us, accompanied by a "Yee-ha!" and I bit out a curse. Quietly and in German, but loud enough for Nico to hear, and I could tell by his raised eyebrow that he also understood.

"Sorry," I muttered. "Kiki, please!" The grey-haired couple were wet again. Dammit. "*Min skat*, you can't keep splashing people."

"But at the other pool—"

"We're not at the other pool today. And we need to apologise to those people."

She walked over, head down and hair dripping.

"But—"

"It's okay to swim, and it's okay to be excited, but not everybody likes water or quite so much noise." I took her hand in mine. "Let's go and say we're sorry."

Kiki managed to be reasonably gracious, and by the time I'd finished grovelling, Colt was talking with Nico. Two men, both devastatingly handsome if I looked at them objectively, but I knew which I preferred. My whole life, I'd been conditioned to seek out the Nicos of this world, and yet I wanted Colt, a devoted father whose T-shirt really had been faded by the sun.

"Hear you got into some trouble, kiddo."

"Don't call me kiddo. And I was just swimming."

"Well, Nico said that we can go swim in his private pool, and if you want to jump into the water there, you can. How about that?"

I glanced at Nico, and he shrugged. "I was a child too, once."

Same. And my father was the one who'd taught me how

to cannonball into the pool, much to my mother's exasperation.

Their marriage had been…not exactly arranged, but very strongly encouraged by both of their families. They'd grown to love each other, but my father had once confessed that when they walked down the aisle, they'd been virtual strangers. Chalk and cheese. Night and day that had eventually merged into dusky twilight. He'd rubbed away some of her sharp corners, and she'd curbed some of his wilder ways. Then the accident had happened, and those corners had come right back, sharper than ever. I knew it was only Mor's defence mechanism, but they still hurt whenever I walked into one.

The waitstaff helped us to pack up our stuff and carry it to Nico's garden. He seemed friendly with Colt, with Luca and Aaron too. A regular boys' club. And Kiki's frown turned into a smile when she saw the ball of fluff stretched out on a sunlounger by the pool cabana.

"You have a cat? What's its name?"

"She's called Snezhinka."

"Sne-what?"

"Snezhinka. It's Russian for 'snowflake.'"

"Can I pet her?"

"If she'll let you."

"Didn't know you had a cat," Colt said.

"Yes, well, I started out with a girlfriend. And she wanted a cat, so I bought her a cat. And then the cat brought her a dead mouse, and then a dead bird, so she decided the cat had to go. Which didn't seem very fair, since the cat was only doing what cats do, but Maraya gave me an ultimatum: her or the cat. So now I have a cat."

A pure-white long-haired diva of a cat who allowed Kiki

to pet her for thirty seconds before she stalked off, tail held high in the air. And then Kiki was back to splashing again, but my attention was elsewhere.

The private garden had the best view in the resort, out across the beach to the sea with Turtle Rock in the distance. Turtle Rock was exactly as it sounded—a rock shaped like a turtle—and apparently also a local landmark. But that wasn't what had caught my eye.

"You sail?" I asked Nico.

He had a sheltered dock beyond the pool, and tied up at the dock was a sailing yacht, a rather nice one. Fifty feet long at a guess, with what looked like a dual-headed Solent rig. A million-dollar boat. Her name was *Checkmate*, written across the hull in elegant script.

But Nico just laughed and shook his head. "No, I don't sail."

"Not your yacht, then?"

"Oh, she's mine."

"You bought a sailing yacht, and yet you don't sail?"

"There was a man who owed me some money, and it turned out he didn't have the money, but he did have a boat. So now I have a boat."

"And she just sits there at the dock?"

What a waste.

"No, she also has an engine, so I take her up and down the coast on occasion."

Heathen.

I was saved from further incredulity when something hit me on the side of the head. I stooped to pick up the scraps of turquoise fabric, then made a "What the...?" gesture at Addy.

"Colt said you didn't have a bathing suit, so I brought you one."

"This isn't a bathing suit. It's a...a..." A series of tiny triangles connected by string. I couldn't wear that, not in front of people. Never in a million years. "No."

"You'd look hot."

"Just no."

"Perhaps a different style?" Nico suggested. "We have a small boutique here."

"I'm afraid I can't afford to visit a boutique. Honestly, I'm fine in the dress."

"Money isn't a problem. Let me help." He waved a hand, and a waitress practically sprinted over. "Mandy, would you mind taking Brie to the boutique and helping her to find whatever she wants?"

"You don't have to—"

"Please, I insist." His phone rang, and he turned away. "Excuse me."

Great. If I turned down Nico's offer, I'd look ungrateful, but if I accepted, then I'd have to parade around the pool with my cellulite on display. Perhaps if I wore the suit under the dress, stripped off at the edge of the pool, got straight into the water, wrapped myself in a towel immediately afterwards...

"You don't want to wear the bathing suit?" Colt asked quietly. "I can tell Nico 'thanks but no thanks.'"

"I'm a few pounds heavier than I used to be."

"Without wanting to sound like a horny asshole, if you were in front of me in a bikini, the last thing I'd be thinking about is your calorie intake."

It was just the two of us in that moment, standing close, too close, and I heard the thickness in his voice. The lust. A wave of heat rolled through me, slow and powerful. A little scary too.

"You want to see me in a bathing suit?"

"Can't say I'd mind that."

"Then maybe..." I swallowed the cactus lodged in my throat. "Maybe I could take a look and see if there's something suitable."

"Need a hand?"

"Uh, okay."

Colt's Adam's apple bobbed as he swallowed too. "Brooke, can you watch Kiki for a while?"

"Sure," she called.

The boutique didn't only sell swimwear and summer clothing, it sold gourmet snacks and a whole range of local handicrafts. I recognised Deck's name on several of the sculptures, spotted Brooke's signature on a cluster of paintings, and it turned out that Darla did sell her dresses. Were they available by mail order?

Mandy hovered at a respectful distance while I looked through the swimwear. It was all high-end designer labels, cut to lift and shape and flatter. I knew from experience that there was only so much tailoring could do, but it might offer a modicum of assistance.

I picked out a plain one-piece at the same time as Colt held up a floral bikini with a tie at the front.

"Too ambitious?" he asked, sounding a tiny bit sheepish.

"Yes. Sorry." I grabbed a couple of other options from the rack and headed for the changing room in one corner. "I'll try these."

My first choice was too tight, but the second did magical things to my cleavage and also smoothed out most of the bulges. My pulse spiked as I opened the door, and I realised just how much Colt's opinion mattered. I cared what he thought. I cared about him.

"What do you think?"

He whirled his finger, and I turned slowly, my skin prickling under his gaze.

"If I told you what I thought, you'd slap me."

"That's unlikely." I wasn't a violent person, and I doubted he'd say something deliberately hurtful. "Tell me. Be honest."

"Okay, so... I like you in the bathing suit, but I'd like you better out of it."

Oh.

Wow.

That was *blunt*.

Was it normal for men to be so blunt?

Whether it was or it wasn't, I preferred it to Emmett's non-committal shrugs. At least I knew where I stood. Kind of.

"When you say out of it...are we talking on my back?"

"I'm saying I'm interested, and now that you know I'm interested, it's up to you whether you want to take things further. You've had a rough time lately, and I'm not going to add complications you don't want."

If only he knew how complicated things really were.

But I was interested, all right. My ovaries were beating my brain with a stick. But there was also so much that Colt didn't know about me, and I didn't want to hurt him.

"I think... I think that maybe I'll keep this bathing suit."

I couldn't commit, not yet. I needed to think things through. Perhaps I could go for a walk on the beach? Water had once been my happy place, and I missed it. I missed everything about it. The ever-changing sea breeze, the perpetual motion of the tides, the way the sun sparkled off the rippling ocean at sunset. Waves had been crashing against the shores of Valetia when I squalled my way into this world, and they'd be crashing still when I faded my way out of it.

I just needed a little time to myself. To consider my future.

But I wasn't going to get it.

12

GABRIELLE

"We're gonna look for dolphins! I love dolphins!"

So much for a quiet walk alone. But I couldn't stomp on Kiki's enthusiasm, and if she wanted to go dolphin-spotting, then that should be encouraged.

"You want to go sit on the beach?"

"No, no, in the boat. Nico said we can go in the boat."

He what?

"The boat?" Colt asked, perplexed. Were his thoughts as jumbled as mine right now?

Nico was sitting on a steamer chair beside the cabana, a glass of what looked like orange juice in his hand, except it had a tiny umbrella sticking out of the top and a cherry hooked over the rim.

"I said we could take the boat out *if* you agreed."

"Please, Daddy. Pleeeeeeease."

"Is it safe?"

"Well, nothing's one hundred percent safe, but I have life jackets and there's a coastguard station in Coos Bay."

He was right. No matter how experienced a sailor you

were, the water was never a hundred percent safe. But I kept my mouth shut because I didn't want my freak accident to colour everyone else's view of the ocean.

"I'm a good swimmer," Kiki insisted. "You said I was a good swimmer."

"It's not as if it's a dinghy," Addy put in. "Let's take a picnic. Have lunch out on the water. Nico gave us a tour of the boat, and it has two bedrooms and a salon."

"Saloon," I said automatically.

"A picnic is certainly possible," Nico agreed. "I can have the staff prepare something."

Kiki's pleading and the fact that everyone else clearly wanted to go play on the yacht swayed Colt.

"I guess we could go on a short trip, as long as you're sure it's no trouble."

"I have to justify the boat's existence somehow. Any lunch requests?"

"Have you got any of those pastries with the cheese?"

"I *need* wine."

"Cookies and candy and cakes with pink frosting."

"Does somebody have a good camera?"

"I need sunblock. Can I borrow some sunblock?"

"What if we get seasick?"

The excited chatter was non-stop, but Nico turned to me. "Brie? You've been very quiet."

"I hope you all have a wonderful time, but I think maybe I'll just stay here."

Colt touched my arm, barely a brush, but I still broke out in goosebumps.

"You don't like boats?"

"I actually do, but...but..." What was I meant to say? I didn't want to bare my secrets to an audience. "I also like sunloungers."

"We don't have to go."

"Kiki's looking forward to it. I'll be perfectly fine here on my own."

"I can stay with Brie," Brooke offered. "There's no need for everyone to miss out."

And Brooke shouldn't miss out either. I'd been avoiding boats for three years—could I really do so for the rest of my life? Sailing had once been part of my soul. Ingrained into my DNA courtesy of my father.

With friends, perhaps a trip on the water wouldn't be so bad? *Checkmate* was a big, stable yacht, undoubtedly well-maintained, and we'd just be puttering along the coastline on engine power. If we were all wearing buoyancy aids and Kiki stayed in the cockpit, the risks were low.

"Don't worry; I'll come."

"Are you sure?" Colt asked softly.

"Yes, I'm sure."

"There's another one!" Kiki squealed. "That's six."

"Did someone get a photo?" Addy asked.

Aaron held up the fancy camera he'd borrowed from Nico. "At least a hundred."

We'd found the dolphins, a pod of them swimming four miles offshore, and now they were following us, leaping in the boat's wake and looking for all the world as if they were playing.

"You okay?" Colt asked, settling beside me on one of the cockpit seats. Being out at sea hadn't been as traumatic as I'd feared. My heart rate wasn't exactly normal, but I didn't feel as if I was on the verge of a coronary, which was a vast improvement on my last excursion. The one other time I'd been in a boat since the accident, I'd had a panic attack and ended up being rescued again.

"I'm fine."

"You didn't eat much."

"I'm not really hungry. Do you know when we're heading home?"

"When the girls finish ooh-ing and aah-ing at dolphins, I guess."

"I think we should turn sooner rather than later. It'll take us two hours to get back, and the weather's deteriorating."

"It is?"

"There's a storm coming. Not imminently, but sometime tonight."

"How do you know?" His tone was curious rather than dismissive.

"I can feel it. There's a heaviness in the air, and look at the waves. See the whitecaps?" Nico seemed pleasant enough, but he wasn't a sailor. He didn't understand the ocean. And I didn't want Kiki's first experience at sea to involve puking over the side. "Perhaps you could mention it to Nico? It's probably better coming from you."

Colt didn't question me, which was a miracle in itself. Whenever I'd told Emmett a storm was coming, he'd immediately opened his weather app to check, so I figured that if he didn't believe me anyway, what was the point in mentioning it? Then he got soaked on the golf course and his electric golf caddy short-circuited, and somehow, it was all my fault.

Whatever Colt said to Nico, we were soon turning to starboard, and I began to relax. We were more than halfway, and nobody had fallen overboard. We had plenty of fuel—

I'd checked twice—and the only kraken we'd seen was on the bottle of rum in the galley.

With everyone else occupied by mammals that probably had a higher IQ than all of my exes combined, I ventured into the saloon. There was something special about boats in general and yachts in particular. They were just so beautifully made. A house, you could throw together and keep adding parts to until it turned into a labyrinth of confusion—my ancestors had been fond of that—but boats weren't so forgiving. You had to utilise every tiny bit of space. A place for everything and everything in its place, as my father had been fond of saying.

If Nico's business acquaintance had run out of money, it was because he'd spent it fitting out *Checkmate*, even if Nico didn't seem to know how to use most of the bits and pieces. Such as the barometer, for example. Since I wasn't feeling quite so queasy now, I tried a leftover pastry, and it practically melted in my mouth. Whoever Nico had working in the kitchen, they sure knew how to cook.

I ran my hand over the smooth wood of the cabinetry and carried on to the double stateroom in the bow. An interesting layout. They could have crammed a couple of bunks in as well, but they'd chosen to leave the room open and spacious. The "spacious" part was of course relative, but—

"There you are."

Colt stood in the doorway, resting one arm against the side. If he were an inch taller, he'd have had to duck to get through.

"Just being nosy."

"I never realised boats could be this complicated."

"They're marvels of engineering. Think about it—a yacht half this size can sail all the way around the world, across vast oceans, and provide everything the crew needs along the way."

"You know about boats, huh?"

"My father used to have a yacht."

"Used to?"

"Well, I suppose technically it still belongs to him; he's just not around to sail it anymore."

"I'm so sorry, princess."

Colt's face morphed into oh-so-familiar sympathy and he reached out a hand, but then the yacht lurched, and he stumbled forward into me. A second later, I was underneath him on the bed.

"Guess this isn't quite the rose petals and candlelight I'd imagined," he murmured. "Hey, your heart's racing."

I pushed at his shoulders, then levered with my legs, and he scrambled backward as an alarm began beeping in the engine room.

"Shit, Brie. I'm sorry. I didn't mean—"

I made it to my feet, grabbed his shirt and pressed a hurried kiss to his lips because it was the fastest way to convey that the problem wasn't with him.

"There's something wrong with the engine."

After the initial judder, its pitch had changed from a smooth rumble to a higher, lumpier whine. Dammit, I'd brought my bad luck out to sea again, and this time there were even more people I cared about on board. I ran through the saloon and up the stairs to the cockpit, where Nico was staring at the dashboard, brow creased.

"What happened?"

"The engine's overheated. I'm not entirely sure why. It was only serviced a month ago."

If the boat had been well-maintained, that ruled out a bunch of potential issues.

"Did you turn the engine off, or did it stop automatically?"

"I turned it off."

"Can you try starting it again? No throttle, just let it idle."

"I'm not sure that's a good idea."

"Only for a moment. I want to check something." I cursed the fact that I was wearing a dress as I scrambled up onto the rear deck and leaned over the stern. "Okay, now."

Nico did as I asked, the engine coughed into life, and... nothing. No water coming out of the exhaust.

"It's a problem with the cooling system. Either a belt's broken or debris has been sucked into the raw water intake."

"Dare I ask how you know this?"

"She doesn't want to talk about it at the moment," Colt said, and I could have kissed him again. "But I bet you twenty bucks she's right."

Nico looked to me, then back to Colt.

"I'll pass on that wager, but I do have another question. How do we fix it?"

"Out here, we don't. If it's a broken belt, you'll need a mechanic, and if it's a blocked intake, you might be able to dive under the hull and pull out whatever's in there—a plastic bag, maybe, or a fish—depending on where the strainer is. But not in this sea. Otherwise, you'll have to get into the engine room and start disconnecting hoses, but that isn't a five-minute job, so I'd suggest calling for a tow."

Just then, a particularly strong gust of wind hit, and with no engine power, *Checkmate* turned beam to the seas and began rocking. Kiki burst into tears.

Voi vittu.

Perhaps I could heave-to while we waited?

"Do you know if this yacht has a full keel or a fin keel? And is there a sea anchor?"

"You might as well be speaking Swahili, but I have marine breakdown insurance, a life raft, a working radio, and a satellite phone."

Kiki clutched at Colt's hand. "I d-d-don't like this anymore."

"Take Kiki into the saloon. If she stays in the centre of the yacht, it'll be smoother." Hell, the tears were streaming down her face, and we couldn't even see land. "Don't worry, *min skat*. We'll be fine."

I hated that we'd gone farther out to sea than we'd planned. I hated that we were stuck. But more than anything, I hated that a little girl would grow up scared of the sea rather than learning the joy it was able to bring.

Could I get us home? Four years ago, we'd have been on our way already, but all I could think about was the crippling fear I'd experienced last time I'd stepped up to the helm. The sweat that had poured down my back. The pounding headache. The scream that had brought my bodyguards racing alongside in their chase boat.

"Brie, it's okay." Colt wrapped an arm around my shoulders as Kiki clung to his other hand. "It's not your fault. None of this is your fault."

"I just feel so helpless."

"Try to breathe steady. Focus on my face. What colour are my eyes?"

"What? Why?"

"Look at me. What colour are my eyes?"

"Brown."

Brown with flecks of cream and gold. Kind eyes.

"And what colour are my shorts?"

"Blue."

"How many bottles of beer on Luca's shirt?"

I quickly counted as I realised what Colt was doing. Distracting me.

"Six."

"One for everyone except him." Colt smoothed my flyaway hair and tucked it behind my ears. "Feel the deck under your feet?"

"Yes."

"Solid ground. We're on solid ground." He gave me a squeeze, and I leaned into him. My wall of strength. "Why don't you go inside and sit with Kiki?"

Because if I did that, I'd feel like even more of a failure. I'd been a sailor. I'd won an Olympic freaking medal on the water. And now I was scared of boats.

I'd been a sailor.

Helvete, I was *still* a sailor.

And if I didn't conquer my fear, I might as well bury myself at sea because that spark I'd only ever felt behind the helm would always be missing.

"I think... I think I can take us home."

"How?"

"Because this is a sailboat. And I sail boats."

"I'm worried about you, princess."

"I have to do this."

Mind made up, I grabbed the hem of the dress and dragged the garment over my head, relishing the feel of the chill air on my skin. Should I reef the mainsail? Better to reef too soon than too late, that's what Papa always said. Unless of course you were a lunatic who liked hanging off the edge of a boat in a storm to stop it from capsizing, which was both of us.

"Is this a wise idea?" Nico asked.

"It's a perfectly wise idea. All the sail controls are

cockpit-led. This yacht was literally designed to be sailed short-handed. She's beautiful. Beautiful."

Great, now I was babbling.

"Go into the saloon and drink rum or whatever it is non-sailors do. Oh, and work out where we're heading. I presume you'll want to take her to a port with an engineering service. You'll need to call ahead on your radio or your satellite phone and arrange a tow from the port entrance because I'm not even going to try to berth her in this wind." When Nico didn't move, I flicked a finger at him. "Go on, shoo. This is a *sail*boat now."

"I'll be back." Colt leaned in close, close enough to brush my ear with his lips. "Reckon I kinda like bossy Brie."

13

COLT

*W*asn't Princess Brie full of surprises?

And confusing as fuck.

The more I learned about her, the more I came to think she was out of my league. But she'd kissed me. Not a real romantic kiss, but lips-to-lips had to count for something, right?

"That was one hell of an adventure," Luca said. "Where'd Brie learn to sail like that?"

We'd made it safely to Coos Bay, and once Brie had gotten over whatever that freak-out was at the beginning, she'd handled the trip like a pro. Even looked happy while she did it. I'd dug a pair of shorts and a T-shirt out of Nico's closet for her, then had nothing more to do while she just handled that shit. Yeah, she might have been a ditz sometimes, but not while she was driving a boat. Even Kiki had managed a smile once we were underway, although she'd spent the last half hour desperate to go potty. There were two bathrooms on board, but she refused to use either of them because she didn't want to pee while the boat was rocking. Once we reached the marina, Brooke and Addy had taken her to answer the call of nature while Brie explained things I didn't understand to a boat engineer.

"Her father taught her," I told Luca.

"He must be proud."

"I think he's dead, but it hurts her to talk about it."

"Probably always will if they were close," Aaron said. He and Brooke had lost both parents when they were young, and even now, he didn't like to discuss them. Brooke found it easier, said she hated the thought of forgetting, but Aaron preferred the "bury it deep" approach. "Don't push her."

"I don't intend to."

"Did you talk to her yet?" Luca asked. "Tell her how you feel?"

"I did, but I fucked it up."

"Fucked it up how?"

"Phrased it all wrong."

"In what way?"

"Let my cock do the talking and told her I'd like to see her out of the bathing suit." They both winced. "Yeah, I know, I'm an asshole."

"It might be salvageable with grovelling," Aaron suggested. "Flowers, dinner, jewellery."

"I don't have the budget for jewellery. I'm not sure I have the budget for Brie either. Her father owned a fuckin' yacht."

"She seemed happy enough eating nachos at Applejack's the other night," Luca pointed out. "And if she was after money, she'd have been shoving Addy out of the way to shake her maracas at Nico earlier, not telling him to shoo." Luca's mouth creased into a grin. "Don't suppose he's accustomed to that."

"They're coming this way," Aaron warned us.

Brie looked more relaxed than I'd ever seen her walking along the jetty. With the setting sun behind her, she was almost ethereal. Did I sound like a sentimental fool? Probably, but I was beyond caring.

"I've arranged cars for everybody." Nico appeared as well, tucking his phone back into his pocket. "They'll be here within half an hour. How's Kiki?"

"Better now that we're back on dry land."

"Aren't we all? Brie's quite a woman. Colt, you're a lucky man."

"Yes, I know."

Because even if this was all I ever got of Brie, I'd been lucky to have her in my life. She'd pushed me out of a rut, shown me that it was possible to find a woman who Kiki and I could both love. Love? Hell, yes. When you knew, you knew.

But was there a chance Brie might forgive my foot-in-mouth tendencies and feel the same way?

I was beginning to think the answer to that question was "no."

Brie seemed to be avoiding me when we got home—not giving me the cold shoulder, exactly, more keeping herself busy with other things. Taking a shower, reading a story to Kiki, staring out of the kitchen window with her back to me. The door squeaked loud enough to wake the dead when I walked in, and I cursed under my breath because I'd forgotten to oil it again, but still Brie didn't turn. She wanted space, that much was clear, but all I could hear was the clock ticking in the background. Counting down the minutes until she went home.

"Any requests for dinner?"

"Not really."

"Pasta?"

"Pasta's fine."

Fine. No, nothing was fine.

"Do you want to talk about it?"

"About pasta?"

"No, about what happened today."

"I..." Brie finally turned to face me. "I... I don't *want* to talk about it, but I realise I have to. There's so much I want to tell you, and I don't know where to start, and...and... It's hard for me."

"Just tell me a small piece at a time, okay? Nothing's going to change the way I feel about you. Well, unless you killed someone."

I was trying to make a joke, but Brie burst into tears. Oh, fuck. I took a step toward her, but she backed away until her ass hit the counter. This was bad. Really bad. And also concerning.

"You didn't... You didn't actually kill someone, did you?"

"I might as well have."

"Are we talking self-defence here?"

"An accident. A *freak* accident, but it was my fault. *I* was the one who wanted to go sailing that day. *I* was steering the boat."

Ah, shit.

"That's why you were upset earlier?"

She nodded.

"Princess, I'm sorry you got pushed into sailing today. Sorry you felt pressured to go out on the boat at all."

"I was so scared at first, but Kiki was scared too. And then...then I started to enjoy myself, but as soon as I realised, the guilt hit. Guilt that I was out at sea having fun but my father wasn't."

"Your father? That's who was with you when you had the accident?"

Another nod, and I wrapped my arms around her. Not making any sort of a move because I wasn't *that* much of an asshole, but because she looked as if she desperately needed a hug.

"What happened?"

"We...we had a new boat." Brie choked out a laugh. "The *Penguin*. We named our watercraft after birds, and we'd gone through all the cool names by then..." How many boats did they have? "So I jokingly said, 'How about *Penguin*?' and it stuck. She was a C-Cat—a Class C racing catamaran—quite small and very fast."

"You used to race?"

"Sometimes. I was always happiest on the water. And that day, the weather was beautiful—not too hot, not too cold, plenty of wind—so I convinced Papa to go for a quick sail. Mor was so annoyed. We were meant to be entertaining dinner guests, you see, and she took those duties very seriously. *För helvete*, I hated the fancy dinners. Always having to dress up and be nice to people I didn't even know. Papa had this theory that each person has within them a sort of...reservoir of social energy. And some people have huge reservoirs, while other people's are much smaller."

"And yours is small?"

"Tiny. More of a puddle, really. And in order to replenish the reservoir, you basically have to be antisocial until the waters rise, or else your soul ends up dried out and unproductive. Mor didn't understand, but her reservoir is enormous, and so is my little sister's. My brother, he's somewhere in the middle, but he still wasn't amused when

Papa and I snuck off. I wish with all my heart that we hadn't."

"You can't turn back the clock."

"I know. Believe me, I know. We left the bay, and we were zipping along at thirty-five knots or so when we hit a whale."

"You hit a *whale*?"

"A humpback. It breached right underneath us, and I doubt it even noticed our tiny little boat, but we flipped right over. One second, we were bitching about three courses and wine, and the next, we were in the water. I went under, and when I surfaced again, Papa was just floating there, face down, so I dragged him over to the hull and started rescue breaths, but...but..."

I hugged her tighter. The pain in her voice was still so raw, the grief a gaping wound that had never been allowed to heal. With Hannah, we'd known what was coming. Had months to prepare for it. Hannah wrote letters and made videos for Kiki, wrapped enough birthday gifts to last her a lifetime. We said our goodbyes slowly, and at the end, we'd made our peace with what was to come. But for Brie to have the person who, by the sound of it, meant the most to her torn away in a heartbeat... That was a whole other kind of agony.

"He didn't make it?"

"He's still alive. The doctors said he hit his head, probably on the boom or the gunwale, and now he just sleeps. He's had so many scans and examinations, and the specialists say that he still has brain activity, that maybe he'll wake up someday, but it's been three years..."

The shoulder of my shirt was soaked through with Brie's tears, and all I could do was hold on while heartache poured out of her like a waterfall. Three years, and she was still torturing herself for something that wasn't her fault.

"Have you talked to anyone about this before? A therapist?"

"In my family, that's not really the done thing. I just try to block it out, but every time I have to smile, my face feels as if it's going to shatter. I thought that things would get easier—doesn't everyone say time heals?—but this...this wretchedness, it won't go away."

"Time does heal, but only if you let the pain out."

"People will judge me. Everyone *already* judges me. Mor, she says she doesn't blame me for the accident, but words and actions are two different things. And then when I said I wanted to finish my schooling in the US, she was so angry. I overheard her talking to my brother, complaining that I'd made all this mess and now I was running away from it. *For fanden*, I miss Papa so much."

How could a parent be so cruel to a child? Even if Brie wasn't meant to hear her mother's words, to even think them was wrong. I kissed Brie's hair, and she stiffened, but only for a second. Then she went limp in my arms.

"Do you get along with your brother?"

"For the most part. Sometimes he can be a little cold, but he's fair. He was the only person who supported my decision to come here. Grudgingly, but he said he understood. Can we sit down for a moment? I think I've lost my appetite now."

I kept an arm around her as we headed to the couch in the living room. She didn't seem too steady on her feet. But uncomfortable though it was to see Brie hurting so much, I was glad she was talking to me, opening up about her problems. If I knew how she was feeling, then I could help. And I was all too well acquainted with family pressure to conform.

"Would a glass of wine help?"

"Perhaps just a small one to take the edge off?"

I kissed her forehead, and she let out a small whimper and pressed closer. This was the real Brie I was seeing now. The cool walls she'd built around herself were gradually crumbling away.

Damn, I was gone for this woman.

14

GABRIELLE

Colt was the best listener. If he ever wanted to change career, he could make good money as a therapist. Despite her misgivings, Mor had sent me to a therapist once, after the accident, but he'd been patronising and obsequious rather than helpful. Plus I knew very well that he'd reported every word I said back to her, patient confidentiality be damned. So I'd stopped going. And when I realised I could no longer rely on the water to heal me either, I'd just felt...lost.

Until now.

"From what you've told me, a fresh start wasn't a bad idea," Colt said. "What could you have done if you'd stayed?"

"Helped out with family stuff. PR work, that sort of thing."

"And would that have made you feel better or worse?"

"Worse. So much of the time, I felt as if I was just a prop in other people's lives."

"Then taking a break was probably sensible."

"I go back to visit my father. For a few days every month,

I sit with him and tell him about everything that's been happening." The doctors said it would help, that he needed external stimulus, although as the days passed, the months, the years, they struggled to muster up any optimism. Sure, there were new drugs and therapies, and they tried them all, but still...nothing. "I guess this month's update is going to be quite dramatic."

Papa heard me, I was certain he did. Occasionally he'd twitch or groan, and when I'd told him about my move to the US, he'd squeezed my hand. Even though the doctors had viewed me with scepticism when I told them, I knew what I'd felt. And when I wasn't there, I made sure he didn't get bored. I'd recorded stories for him, everything from his favourite novels to me reminiscing about our sailing adventures, and skiing, and rock climbing, and that time we'd gone sandboarding in Egypt... I'd set up a playlist of his favourite songs and placed a fan in his room to remind him of the breeze, and a sunrise lamp, and I'd even tried misting water on his face. And because I didn't want to neglect his sense of smell, he had a bottle of his favourite aftershave, plus I'd arranged for pizza to be delivered to the hospital each week for the nurses to eat in his room. Pizza was his guilty pleasure. Studies showed that patients whose families involved them in their lives and also reminded them of the past made the best recoveries, and that waking up was a gradual process over time as reactions slowly improved, yet still he slept. Quietly, peacefully, sometimes with a smile on his face.

He slept.

But I refused to give up. I'd never give up.

And while I waited, I knew he wouldn't want me to waste my life.

"What will you do after your visit?" Colt's voice had

changed. Become flatter. More guarded, and I understood why. "Will you stay in Europe?"

Translation: would we ever see each other again?

"Papa's in Scandinavia. And I want to return here, I really do."

"But..."

"But it's not as easy as just jumping on a plane. I'm afraid that if I go home and come back again, everything will change."

He took my hand in his. Caressed my knuckles with a feather-soft touch that made me shiver inside.

"Nothing needs to change. Not if you don't want it to."

But it would. The chances of me slipping away alone for a second time? Zero. No way would my bodyguards make the same mistake twice. If I set foot in Baldwin's Shore again, I'd bring the whole damn circus to town. I couldn't—wouldn't—cut my family off, so simply staying in Oregon wasn't an option either. I was stuck between Turtle Rock and a hard place.

"Some things are out of our control."

I drew my legs up onto the cushion and twisted to face Colt. My knees rested against his thigh. We were close, so close that I could smell the citrusy aroma of his shampoo. Or maybe that was me, since I'd been borrowing it all week? Another reminder of how tight we'd become in such a short space of time. I hadn't even shared a bathroom with Emmett, and the shipping heir had lived in a whole other house.

"That's a lesson we've both learned all too well, don't you think?" Colt said. "Why don't we take things one day at a time? I can't make you stay, but I sure would like you to."

"I'm meant to be picking up my car tomorrow."

"Do you have anywhere you need to be?"

If you asked my mother that question, she'd list a hundred places, none of which were important and all of which would be unpleasant. A ball, a party, a ribbon-cutting ceremony... They'd go just fine without me.

"Not until I fly home to visit my father at the end of the month."

"Will you give me a couple of weeks and see where fate takes us?"

Maybe if I had Phil run interference and didn't venture out in public too often, I'd be able to pull it off? I'd owe Phil a pony by the end of it, but the debt would be worth it to spend more time with the only man who'd made me feel alive in three years.

I cupped Colt's cheek with one hand. He'd trimmed his beard this morning, and the wiry hair scratched at my palm.

"I'd like that."

How would he react if I kissed him? I wanted to. He watched me with those big brown eyes, and I saw my uncertainty reflected back at me.

"Is it normal to be so nervous?" I asked.

"Don't know about that, but if you're asking whether *I'm* nervous, then the answer is yes. Because you matter, princess. *This* matters."

För helvete, if I didn't kiss him, I was going to cry.

I hooked a hand around his neck and tunnelled my fingers through his thick hair. In the near-silence, all I could hear was the rasp of our breathing.

"Let me taste you," he whispered.

My pulse took off like a racehorse from the starting gate.

But it seemed natural to tip onto my knees, to lean in and press my lips to his. And then his arms were around my waist, lifting me, pulling me onto his lap. I felt a hint of what was to come between my legs and gasped into his mouth.

"You okay?" he asked.

"Uh, yes?"

"You sure?"

"Just the tiniest bit daunted."

"Daunted?"

"As you said, this matters. And I don't know what your expectations are."

Colt chuckled, and the vibrations reached my core.

"My expectations are that we'll fool around a little, maybe lose some clothing and a few inhibitions. Get to know each other. If you feel ready, we can move things upstairs, but if you don't, we can cuddle on the couch, eat dinner, and watch a movie." He brushed hair away from my face. "And we'll do all of that quietly because Kiki's a light sleeper."

"I'll definitely keep the noise down. Perhaps I should gag myself?"

"You like that kind of thing?"

Huh? Being gagged?

Oh!

Oh my goodness.

My cheeks burned. "No! I mean, I don't know! I've never tried it or ever really considered trying it." Curiosity got the better of me. "Do *you* like that kind of thing?"

"I've never tried it either. But unless you've got a particular ambition to experiment, I'll have to pass because taking your mouth out of play seems like a real waste. Speaking of which..."

He pulled me close again, and this time, he let his tongue join in the action. Colt tasted of Cabernet Sauvignon and magic, and for once in my life, I had to congratulate myself on making a good decision. Colt was the whole package. Until now, I'd always figured that relationships were based on an either/or premise—if the guy knew what he was doing in bed, he was disappointing out of it, and vice versa. So far, that had been borne out by my experience. But Colt... If he screwed like he kissed, he might just turn out to be the holy grail of men.

When he slid his hands under my dress and ran them slowly up my thighs, I forgot to be nervous. How could I be when he gazed at me with such fire in his eyes? I pressed against him, relishing the hardness of his muscles and the softness of his soul. This man could ruin me. Probably *would* ruin me, but at this moment, I couldn't bring myself to care.

I was, however, unprepared for his laughter.

"What?"

"I thought Brooke got you underwear?"

"She did."

"Then why are you still wearing mine?"

"Because it's comfortable and also practical."

No VPL, no ass-flossing... What more could a girl want? Okay, better colours, but I'd willingly sacrifice style for comfort. For the most part, I wore pretty lingerie, but this time in Baldwin's Shore had been a revelation in so many ways.

"What's mine is yours, princess," Colt said as he ran a finger under the waistband. Just one finger, and I pressed my thighs together to suppress the need coursing through me.

The dress had to go.

I stood to wriggle out of it, then quickly had second thoughts. The overhead light was on. He could see almost all of me. I should have shrivelled under his gaze—that's what I usually did when a man studied me—but instead, I felt every nerve ending come alive. Colt was looking at me with such desire that I forgot about stretch marks and fat folds and all the other hang-ups that had become so important over the years and leaned in for another heavenly kiss. When I pressed against him, I discovered his abs weren't the only part of him that was hard.

This man... He was perfect, and he was also wearing too many clothes. He didn't say a word when I unbuttoned his shirt and flung it across the room, at least not until it landed on a floor lamp and cast us into shadow.

"Probably a fire hazard," he muttered.

Oops. "You know how you mentioned moving this upstairs...?"

"You want to?"

"Where you're concerned, I want *everything*."

He took me by the hand as he retrieved the shirt, and then I was treated to the sight of rippling muscles in his back as I followed him up to his bedroom. Colt truly was a Leonardo-da-Vinci-life-study of a man. I'd seen a set of weights in the garage out back, and it was clear that they and he were well-acquainted.

The window was open, and as Colt lowered me onto his bed, a cool breeze washed over my skin, bringing with it the smell of the ocean and laughter as someone ambled past on the sidewalk outside. Another reminder to keep the noise down.

"How the hell do you get this bra off?" he muttered.

"Over my head. One second... Better?"

"Princess, I've been dreaming about those tits since the day I first laid eyes on them. On you. Laid eyes on you. Shit."

My turn to laugh. "It's okay."

Sort of flattering, actually. Better to be wanted for my boobs than for my money or my title. My breasts felt swollen and heavy as Colt palmed them. I'd spent most of my life wishing my cleavage wasn't quite so generous, but now...now those regrets disappeared along with my last shred of self-consciousness. When his mouth closed over one hardened nipple and sucked, I arched off the bed and groaned his name. But quietly.

Scheiße, his tongue was magic, soft and sweet in contrast to the delicious roughness of his beard against my skin. Then he nipped gently, and a jolt shot straight between my legs. This time, I cursed out loud, and he laughed.

"Give me more of that dirty mouth."

"Only if I get more of yours in return."

"Deal."

I'd meant he should be liberal with his language, but he took my words literally, and I gasped as he peeled off my underwear and then buried his face between my legs. Phil had told me stories of this, of men so skilful they could bring a woman to her knees with their tongue alone, but I always assumed she was exaggerating. In truth, I'd thought it sounded a bit icky and swore I would never—

"Ohmigosh!" I cried when Colt flicked the tip of his tongue in exactly the right spot and then grinned up at me, totally unrepentant. "Don't you dare stop."

He chuckled against my core, and that alone sent another ripple of pleasure rolling through my body.

Emmett was a man who always read the manual and followed the instructions to the letter. Sex with him had been no different. One, remove clothing. Two, find an appropriate horizontal surface. Three, insert penis into vagina. Four, thrust until the desired result was achieved. His result, not mine, obviously. I'd kept a vibrator in my bathroom drawer for that purpose. Phil had acquired it for me—clearly I couldn't make such a purchase myself.

But Colt? Colt was a man who tossed the manual over

his shoulder and dove right in on a voyage of discovery. Every new revelation was a wonder, and he was definitely results-driven.

The first orgasm ripped through me like wildfire, and I smothered myself with a pillow to muffle what would definitely have been a scream.

"*For fanden*," I gasped.

"Does that mean 'holy fuck'?"

"Just 'fuck.'"

Colt grinned like a kid on Christmas morning. "Your wish is my command."

"Do you have a condom? Tell me you have a condom."

"I might've picked up a box at the store on Friday."

"Because you knew this was going to happen?"

"Because I *hoped* this was going to happen."

Before I managed to get my breath back, he tore open a foil packet, sheathed himself, and slid into me on a groan. Stilled. Took a moment to study me as I lay there, drenched in sweat.

"Just give me a minute," he murmured, and I froze as old memories rushed back.

"A minute to do what?" I asked suspiciously.

"To get my dick under control so I don't shoot my load like a horny teenager."

"Oh. Oh, okay then." Phew. I mean, that sounded reasonable. "Super."

"What did you think I was going to say?"

"Uh, nothing?"

"You asked a question and thought I'd say nothing?" When I didn't explain further, he raised an eyebrow. "Brie?"

"Okay, fine." My cheeks heated. "The last time a man said that, he needed to send an email."

Now both of Colt's brows winged up. "Let me get this

straight... A guy was buried inside you balls deep, and he put things on pause because he needed to send a fuckin' *email*?"

"Apparently, it was urgent."

I'd lain there awkwardly, pinned down by his weight as he typed out the message on his phone. My snarky suggestion that he might want to check in with his PA while he was at it had been met with a roll of the eyes.

"Was that the same douche who cheated on you?" Colt asked.

"No, his predecessor."

"I realise that given the position I'm in, I probably shouldn't say this, but you've dated some real assholes."

"Yes, I know." But Colt wasn't one of them, and I pulled him closer so I could whisper in his ear. "Help me to forget them all. Please?"

He kissed me hard and deep, his hands tangled in my hair as he filled my head with better memories and my body with his exquisite cock.

"They're gone," he murmured when our lips parted. "It's just you and me now." He raised himself up on his elbows and looked down at where he disappeared inside me. "You're a perfect fit."

"*We're* a perfect fit," I said, and I meant it. In the moment, I meant it, although in the cold light of day, it would become all too obvious where the gaps were. "Give me everything."

He moved slowly at first. Smoothly, gently as we grew used to each other. It was more than a joining of bodies. Our hearts were connected too, although the thread that held them together was worryingly fragile right now. As he got closer, he rolled me, let me ride him, and I blocked out the past as I took everything he gave, everything I wanted and more. He skimmed his hands over my hips and dug his fingers in as I clenched around him. Heat poured into me, pulsing, and I collapsed forward to meet his lips with mine.

"I think I got my appetite back."

"Princess, I'll feed you anything you want."

15

GABRIELLE

"*A*re you coming out for lunch? We're going to the coffee house—it's a Brooke and Kiki tradition."

With Colt back at work, Brooke had come over to spend the day with Kiki. They were meant to be doing crafts, but so far, the only thing they'd made was a mess.

"If I clean up, I get a donut," Kiki told me.

"But you haven't cleaned up."

She had paint on her clothes, glitter in her hair, and I wasn't sure what she'd used to decorate her eyebrows, but it didn't look as if it was coming off in a hurry.

"We work on the honour system," Brooke explained. "If she doesn't clean up today, she doesn't get a donut next time."

"I already earned today's donut, but you can share it if you want."

Kiki really was the sweetest girl.

"Thank you, but I need to stay here today."

Not only was walking difficult, but I also wanted to check my messages. Phil had been playing detective, in between getting co-opted into representing her family at various events she had no desire to attend and shopping for a new equine friend she absolutely didn't need and wasn't meant to be purchasing. Basically, she was a hoarder. Of horses.

But she'd grown cunning with her acquisitions. Last time she'd snuck a horse home, she'd bought a new horse jacket first—what were they called? Rugs? Blankets?—a garish hot-pink thing covered in purple and yellow stars, and put it on one of the horses she already owned. The first thing her parents did was ask her if she'd bought a new horse, and oh-so innocently, she'd told them no, merely a new horse outfit. When she swapped the hideous garment onto the newcomer, nobody ever noticed.

And last night, she'd sent a message that did nothing to calm my nerves.

I'm back! Finally managed to escape the clutches of the Hollywood set. Why are the Yanks so fascinated with a British accent? I spoke to Emmett, and he is pissed with Vania. He reckons she recorded the video and sent it to you, and—I quote—ruined his future. So dramatic. And also bullshit because it was his dick that went a-wandering. But the upshot is, I think he was telling the truth. BTW, he has all these plans to win you back—a romantic weekend in Paris, a cosy holiday on Mustique, a yacht trip in the Bahamas. Can't believe the idiot forgot you don't do yachts anymore.

So...long story short, it wasn't Emmett.

I'll talk to Vania today and get her side of the story— wish me luck!

Plus I'm going to look at a yearling this afternoon—a filly this time, Hanoverian x Irish Sport Horse with impeccable bloodlines. Super exciting!

Laters,
P

I tried to convince myself that this was good news. Not about the filly, but that Emmett hadn't been playing amateur videographer. It meant the likelihood of me becoming an accidental porn star was lower. But *had* Vania been the culprit? Emmett's theory didn't quite make sense, because Vania wouldn't have wanted to become an internet sensation either. She'd just started her own interior design company, and we both knew the old saying about no publicity being bad publicity was a lie. The kind of clients she dealt with didn't embrace scandal.

Sending me the video on my wedding day was basically an open invitation for revenge. If I'd been that type, I could have released it to the world within minutes. Maybe she'd simply assumed I *wasn't* that type? No, that would have been a risky assumption to make, and as I'd found out, we really hadn't known each other well at all.

Which meant there was a third party involved.

A third party who'd at best activated the ejector seat and saved me from a loveless marriage, or at worst secretly recorded a lovers' tryst and who knew what else.

Had they been trying to help me or hurt me?

How could I find out?

I typed another message to Phil.

Emmett is delusional. Does he have no shame? I wouldn't take him back if he crawled on his knees over broken glass. Hasn't he learned by now that he can't buy me?
    And good luck—I'm quietly freaking out here.
    Do you really need another horse?
    G xoxo

So now I was waiting. If Phil was going to view the horse in the afternoon, then she'd be seeing Vania in the morning. Wouldn't she? Unless she planned to delay that until the evening... Dammit, I should have asked. Sometimes, having no cell phone felt liberating, but at other times, it was a pain in the butt. I should also have got Phil to remind me of her number, and then I could have asked Colt for permission to borrow the house phone. Although I wouldn't have put it past my mother's people to be monitoring Phil's calls, so perhaps it was just as well I hadn't tried to speak to her.

"Want us to bring you something to eat?" Brooke asked.

"I wouldn't say no. A sandwich would be lovely."

When she left with Kiki, the house felt so empty. I'd never minded my own company, but I found myself missing Colt. Wanting him. The longing had started in the early hours as soon as I'd crept back to my own bed. He thought it was too soon to tell Kiki about us, and I had to agree, given that I had no clue what the future held. But still, I ached for him.

What time would he be home? He'd left at eight when he got a call reporting slashed tyres on the other side of town, and he said he often worked overtime. *Slashed tyres.* I didn't mind admitting that the thought of some lunatic running around with a knife left me a little twitchy, especially since the other side of town was less than a fifteen-minute walk away. For the first time, I began to miss my bodyguards. They might have been intrusive, but now that I was alone, I realised they'd also been comforting in a fussy sort of way.

I staggered through to the kitchen to make myself a cup of coffee. If Colt kept this up, neither of us would need to use the gym-and-spa membership Nico had gifted us as a thank-you after the adventures on *Checkmate*. He said it was only fair since I'd saved him a towing fee, and although I could have been gracious and turned it down, I thought Colt might appreciate being able to use the fancy facilities whenever he pleased. There was also dinner and a bottle of champagne waiting for us at the Peninsula—again, Nico had insisted—and that part, I was looking forward to.

Of course, Phil's message appeared when I was out of the room. A watched pot never boils and all that. At least, I assumed a watched pot didn't boil—it wasn't as if I'd had much experience in that department.

Okay, here's the kicker... I'm not sure it was Vania either. She's as freaked as you are about the video being out there. Apparently, the asshole basically told her that what you and he had was more of a business arrangement, and therefore it was fine for him to screw her on the side. I guess she could've sent the video in a last-ditch attempt to stop him from marrying you, because she really did seem to care about him, but I don't think so. She said she liked the no-strings aspect of their relationship. Relationship! I was feeling almost sorry for her until she said that, but now I'm back to wanting to punch her in the face. And I'm tempted to drive over Emmett with a lorry. Then back up and drive over him again.

There's no such thing as too many horses ;)

P

Phil held an HGV licence for driving the horses around, so if Emmett was smart, he wouldn't go near England for a decade or two. Which meant he'd probably land at Heathrow next week. But if Vania hadn't made the movie, and Emmett hadn't either, then who the hell had?

If you end up in jail, I'll gladly give you bail money.

Did you ask Vania who she thought did it? If it wasn't her?

How many horses do you have now?

G xxx

A miracle happened and Phil managed to reply in under five minutes. Usually, she typed and ran.

Vania thinks Emmett recorded the video so he could jerk off to it later. Is she bitter? Yes, she's bitter. She's so bitter you could squeeze her into a G&T.

Nine and a half horses, but I have twenty-three stables, so...

P

That still left questions.

If Emmett didn't record it, then how did it get sent to me? There's no way he'd have Airdropped it himself. Does that mean someone else set up a camera? A peeping Tom? What the hell else did they film???

And how can you have half a horse?

G x

What else did they film? That's the question nobody can answer. Plus, where was the video filmed? Did you recognise the room? It seems Emmett and Vania were at it for some time, so they weren't able to narrow down the location.

As for half a horse, do you remember Scally? The skinny little thing that was meant to be with me for two

weeks max? Well, I only count her as a half because she's
so small.
P

Yes, I remembered Scally. She'd been more of a walking
skeleton than a pony when one of Phil's neighbours spotted
her abandoned outside their house one morning. Phil had
offered to foster her until a permanent home could be
found. Two days later, the pony had a name and Phil was
sending me photos with heart emojis, and I knew Scally
wouldn't be going anywhere.

But that was Phil's problem, not mine. Mine was much
less pleasant.

Who looks at decor when their fiancé's front and centre
screwing another woman?
G x

Did the video upload to iCloud?
P

No, I turned that off after Catherine's iCloud got hacked,
remember?
G x

Well, shit.
P

Shit was right. All we could do was wait to see what
surfaced, but the lack of control over the situation left me
with a knot in my stomach that tugged every time I moved.
There was a creep lurking in the shadows, possibly

somebody I'd considered a friend. Somebody I'd trusted. And that called *everything* into question because if I couldn't have faith in myself to make good decisions, then what hope was there?

If Brooke noticed my crisis of confidence, she didn't say anything when she returned with lunch, but Colt sure did when he got home. One look at my face, and he beckoned me towards the kitchen while Kiki watched cartoons.

"Shit, I need to oil that door." He closed it behind us with a *skreek*. "What's up?"

"Why would something be up?"

He smoothed his thumbs across my forehead and then kissed me, nothing heavy, just enough to show he cared.

"You have worry lines."

That moment, perhaps it was the most important moment in our entire relationship. Bigger than the sex, bigger than our first kiss. Because I realised Colt got me. He got me enough to notice those little clues I tried so hard to hide, and not only that, he cared that I was hurting. Which of course made me weepy, but he was prepared for that too with a clean handkerchief in his pocket.

"I'm s-s-sorry."

"Nothing to apologise for, princess. Want to talk about it?"

"Not really." But I did talk. I told Colt the full story of Emmett and Vania, and the results of today's conversation with Phil. "And now I just feel so powerless. Who would do something like that? Record people's most intimate, private moments without their consent?"

"You'd be surprised what some people get off on."

"I hate surprises."

"Noted. But putting my cop hat on, the culprit clearly

sent you the video to stop you from marrying Emmett. It's the motive that's troubling. Before that day, had anyone expressed reservations about the wedding?"

"Apart from my mother? No. And even she came around to the idea after she met his parents."

"Did you have any issues with friends or acquaintances? Any disagreements?"

"Again, my mother. We don't always see eye to eye. But away from home, I'm careful to steer clear of conflict. At least, I always thought I was."

"So maybe somebody had a problem with Emmett? If they wanted to hurt him, then driving a wedge between the two of you would've been an effective method."

"With hindsight, I'm not sure he cared enough about me to be hurt."

"Oh, he's hurting." Colt fisted my hair behind my head and kissed me properly this time. Deeply. Shamelessly. That tongue of his was wicked in all the best ways. "Trust me, he's hurting."

"I hope so," I murmured.

"There is one other possibility."

"Which is?"

"That someone wanted to help you."

I'd already considered that, but... "By hurting me? By shocking me? By ruining my wedding?"

"Would you rather have found out about the affair afterward?"

"I guess not."

Married and divorced at twenty-five—I could just see the headlines in the gossip rags now. The legal wrangling would have gone on for months, two families at war with me caught in the middle. Stuck in no-man's land. That's if I was allowed to get a divorce at all—Mor would have fought it in favour of those oh-so-important optics.

"We have someone like that around here. I guess you might call them a vigilante. A person who does bad things for good reasons. But if you want to find out who *your* mystery person is, I do have one idea. You said you still have the broken phone?"

"Phil has it."

"I know a guy, a geek over in Coquille. Met him when he was consulting for the sheriff's office. He's good with electronics—computers, cameras, phones, that kind of thing —plus he knows how to keep quiet about sensitive issues. He might be able to recover the video from the chip or the drive or whatever it's stored on. The metadata should tell us where it was filmed."

The meta-what? I had no idea, but the video wasn't the only thing on my phone. My secrets were hiding there too. My name, photos of me at official functions, my calendar... And if Colt's friend and, by extension, Colt found that information, he'd realise just how much I'd been holding back. If I took him up on his offer, I'd need to tell him everything before the results came through. *Everything.*

"How long does the process usually take?"

"If I got him to do it in his spare time for beer money? Couple of weeks? A month? He'd have to fit it in around other jobs."

A couple of weeks. Could I lay myself bare in that time? "Can I think about it? A part of me just wants to let the whole affair fade into the distance."

"Sure you can. But I have another question for you. A big one."

"Okay."

Colt took my hand. Why had my mouth suddenly gone dry?

"How do you feel about watching Kiki while I'm at work tomorrow? She could go to the Craft Cabin with Brooke, but she gets bored after half a day, and it's a lot to ask when Brooke has a job to do as well. But if it's too much trouble…"

Look after Kiki? Of course I would, but Colt was right— it *was* a big question. And it only served to highlight the trust he was putting in me versus the trust I wasn't putting in him. I owed him more. I owed him the truth.

For so long, I'd taken the safe option and tried to make everyone else happy, but now that I'd had a chance to step away from all I knew, I realised that by toeing the family line, I'd only been making myself miserable. I had to change. I couldn't go back to the status quo. And the first step on that journey would come by being open with Colt.

I had two weeks to find that courage.

"It's no trouble whatsoever. Spending the day with her will be a joy. And I think Brooke left some craft materials behind, so we'll have plenty to do."

"I'll leave you enough cash to take her out for lunch. And if she starts to get stir-crazy in the house, then the beach is only ten minutes away. Just don't let her go in the sea. She'll try to convince you she's allowed, but she isn't a strong enough swimmer yet."

"I promise to keep her away from the water. And Colt?"

"Yeah?"

"Could you ask your friend if he's able to look at my phone? I can ask Phil to mail it here."

Along with my purse. Good thing Colt hadn't asked to see my driver's licence when we first met because getting arrested for driving without it would certainly have added an interesting twist to our relationship.

"Sure, I can ask him."

"I'd really feel much better if I could get to the bottom of the mystery."

"*We'll* get to the bottom of the mystery, princess. You're not on your own anymore."

16

GABRIELLE

"So, how was the hot date last night?"

When Brooke dropped by during her lunch break yesterday, I'd assumed Colt had sent her to check up on me. And I couldn't have blamed him—I'd probably have done the same thing if a new... I didn't know what to call myself... Had I reached girlfriend status? We'd only been on one proper date, but we were living together. It was confusing. Anyhow, if I'd invited a new person into my child's life, I'd have wanted to be sure everything was okay too.

But now it was Wednesday, and Brooke was back again. With donuts.

"I brought these over for Kiki. She knows that every second Wednesday, I buy some kind of cakes or donuts or pastries in bulk, and there'll be hell to pay if I forget to bring hers over. Where is Kiki, anyway?"

"Taking a nap. She tired herself out in the garden this morning." Ever built a makeshift crazy-golf course with a small child? It was exhausting. "Why do you order cakes in bulk?"

"I run a support group for women affected by abuse. Sexual assault, domestic violence, stalking—they're all linked. Sometimes we need a pick-me-up."

"The group is here in Baldwin's Shore? I'm—" Shit, I almost admitted that I was the patron of a domestic violence organisation in England. "Never mind. That's a wonderful thing to do." Then I realised that when Brooke had referred to the women affected by abuse, she'd included herself. "Gosh, I'm so sorry. I didn't realise you'd been through... through such things."

"You weren't to know. It was big news at the time, but the gossip has subsided now."

I reached out, squeezed her hand in a gesture of sympathy that had become ingrained over the years.

"I'm so incredibly sorry that somebody hurt you, Brooke. Words always feel so inadequate at times like this, but if there's ever anything I can do to help..."

"Actually, talking helped me a lot. I used to bottle up the trauma inside, and it was like storing poison in my body. Once I started sharing, the burden got lighter." Now it was Brooke's turn to squeeze *my* hand. "If ever you want to join us, you'd be more than welcome."

"But I haven't been abused." My bodyguards kept everyone with ill intentions away. "Nobody's hurt me."

Brooke's cheeks turned a shade pinker. "Sorry, I shouldn't have said anything. I just see this haunted look in your eyes sometimes, and it reminds me of... I shouldn't have made assumptions."

Did I look haunted? Somebody—I never found out who —had left a pamphlet about PTSD on the coffee table at Emmett's place once. I'd always thought PTSD was something that happened to soldiers at war, but as I flicked through the pages, I'd ticked off the symptoms in my head. I had nightmares and flashbacks. I'd avoided boats for years in case they triggered the same panic that had overcome me after the accident. I struggled to focus. Relaxing was impossible for me, and I tried to block out my feelings because it had become easier to feel nothing at all. And if we were talking about stalking, the paparazzi had been hounding me from a distance for years. Telephoto lenses were invented by Satan himself.

At the time, I'd brushed off the idea that I might have PTSD, but what if Brooke was right?

Perhaps I *had* been storing up trauma?

This time in Baldwin's Shore was teaching me about who I was and who I wasn't. Last week, I'd finally taken myself away from the source of the pain, and I didn't just mean Emmett. And I was learning so much. About my own psyche, about what was important, about the future I wanted. It felt as if all the parts that made me had been broken down and reassembled in a more comfortable way, but now I had to get used to the feel of them.

I loved my home in Valetia. I loved my family. I loved the people I was sworn to serve. But that didn't mean I had to give them *everything*.

"I do have some issues from my past that I'm trying to work through. And you're right that sharing helps. I've been talking to Colt a little, but it's hard."

"Colt's a good listener."

"I'm finding that out. And maybe...maybe someday I'll come to your group, but I don't think now is the right time."

"I completely understand. At least you get the donuts this week, right? They're jelly ones."

"Right." I was grateful to Brooke for switching to a lighter subject. "And speaking of jelly, Nico swung by to talk to us while we were eating dinner at the Peninsula last night." Kiki had come too, and she'd behaved beautifully. "It was a jellyfish that got sucked into the yacht's water intake. Maybe even two or three of them judging by the mess."

"Oh, yuck."

"I believe that's what the marine engineer said when he started dismantling the hoses."

"We have a bunch of different jellyfish in the ocean around here, but thankfully they don't wash up on shore too often. I got stung by one when I was a kid, and Aaron tried to convince me that peeing on it would help, but luckily I didn't listen to him because that turned out to be a complete myth."

"We have them at home too, but mostly the *Aurelia aurita*, which is completely harmless. Although when I was small, my brother threw one at me, and I *did* pee on myself."

"Brothers are a pain in the ass, huh? Are you close to yours?"

"Not as close as we once were." Jens had grown into his designated role, while mine still felt too big. Whenever I assumed my duties, I felt like a kid running around in too-long trousers, just waiting to trip over. And I did trip frequently. "But you and Aaron are?"

"We have our ups and downs, but yes, we've always been close. So have Luca and his sister, although Romi's definitely more of a wild child than me."

"Does she live in Baldwin's Shore too?"

"Romi doesn't live anywhere. She's a nomad, but quite an affluent one. She's always had this look—beautiful but with an edge—and when she was backpacking in France, she got scouted by a guy from a modelling agency, so now she lives in hotels and spends her days in front of the cameras."

Wow. Somebody actually *chose* that life? Just thinking

about it made me shudder. But wait a second... Romi... Romi Mendez... *Romina* Mendez? That was Luca's sister? I'd met her once, and thank goodness she wasn't here because there was a good chance she'd have recognised my face.

Yet another reason I needed to tell Colt the truth.

"Rather her than me."

"Better her than both of us. For me, home and happiness are where the heart is..." Brooke giggled. "And the hot guy, and that's Baldwin's Shore."

Where was my heart? Part of it would always be in Valetia, but I got no peace there. England was dear to me too, but in Baldwin's Shore, I'd found an unexpected tranquillity. I could be happy here.

And I'd definitely found a hot guy.

Footsteps stomped overhead, first walking and then running down the stairs. Amazing how such a small child could sound so loud. If I didn't know better, I'd think Colt was keeping a baby elephant hidden away.

"Are there cakes?" Kiki demanded. "I want a cake."

"There are donuts, and it's 'I'd like a donut, *please*,'" Brooke corrected.

"Please can I have a donut? Please?"

"One donut. And don't forget to wash your hands first."

"And then can we play hide-and-seek?"

"That's up to Brie."

I didn't want to play hide-and-seek again. Not because I always lost—which I did—but because when we'd played yesterday, Kiki had squeezed herself into all sorts of tiny spots, and it didn't feel right poking around in Colt's home to find her. Checking behind garments in his closet felt somehow...intimate, which was perhaps a bit dumb seeing as we'd been sleeping together, but it made me uncomfortable nonetheless.

"Why don't we go for a walk instead? Get some fresh air?"

"To the beach?"

"If that's where you'd like to go."

Brooke ruffled Kiki's hair. "Kiki will never turn down a trip to the ocean."

A girl after my own heart.

———

"How was your day?" Colt asked.

I opened my mouth to reply, but Kiki got in first.

"We went to the beach! And Brooke brought donuts from her talking-about-mean-people club, and I ate two."

"Two?"

"Brooke said I could have one, and Brie said I could have another one." *För helvete.* Tattled on by a seven-year-old. "And I found a shell on the beach. A pink one. Let me show you, let me show you!" A pause. "Where is it?"

"In your room?"

She ran up the stairs singing, "One donut, two donut, three donut, four. Five donut, six donut, seven donut, mooooooore," and I groaned.

"I only let her have an extra donut to stop her from eating seaweed," I said to Colt, then quickly realised I'd made things sound even worse. "I'll do my utmost not to let it happen again, I promise."

He raised one gorgeous eyebrow. "Seaweed?"

"She said it was icky, so I told her it could actually be quite a delicacy, and I explained to her about vitamins and sushi, and the next thing I knew, she was putting it in her mouth. I'm so sorry."

"Don't worry about it. One time, I didn't cook dinner fast

enough for her liking, and when I turned around, she was on the floor eating kitty kibble."

"Euch."

"Yeah, well, she told me it tasted just like my chicken biscuits, and that was the point when I decided to take an online cooking class."

"No more burned Eggos, huh?"

Colt smiled faintly, then wrapped his arms around my waist and pulled me in for a kiss. A proper kiss with tongues and heat and hands squeezing my ass. How different this new life was. With Emmett, I used to get a peck on the cheek as he went to pour himself a glass of wine, and I'd thought that was totally normal.

I was gasping for air when we broke apart, and Colt's breathing was deliciously heavy too.

"Is this what I have to look forward to from now on?" he asked. "Both of the women in my life ganging up on me?"

"I hope so," I said without thinking.

"You hope so?"

"Uh, what I meant is that I hope I can stay as one of the women in your life."

"You and me both, princess."

Kiki thundered down the stairs, and we stepped back from each other reluctantly, our gazes the last thing to part. I thought... I thought that maybe I loved this man. Which meant I had to tell him everything, and soon. His friend had my phone now—Phil had sent it by express courier—and the clock was ticking.

17

GABRIELLE

*M*orning sex was a new thing for me. Five a.m. sex, to be precise, because we needed to leave enough time for me to sneak back to my room before Kiki woke up. And Colt was a cuddler. He wasn't averse to shoving me against the wall and fucking me until I bit my own tongue to keep from crying out—I'd found that out in the shower yesterday morning—but in these early hours, he liked to make love with a lazy intensity that left my legs weak and my heart swollen with need.

And talk.

He liked to talk as well.

"Did you mean what you said yesterday?" he asked, his breath feathering over my ear as his arms cocooned me. "About wanting to be in my life?"

There were few certainties in my world right now, but I knew with absolute confidence that I wanted to spend more time with Colton Haines.

"Yes, I meant it."

"Good. Because..." His arms tightened. "Fuck, I know this is soon, but I've fallen for you, princess. And I can't bear the thought of you returning home at the end of the month and never coming back again."

"I can't bear to stay away either. And I won't. Somehow, I'll come back. But...but I may need a little time. My mother will be difficult, I know she will, and the logistics..." My bodyguards would need a place to live. I'd have to buy a home, one with high walls to keep the photographers at bay. I'd still be expected to make appearances on behalf of my family, which would take careful coordination, and was there even an airport around here? "If you still want me after all that, then I'll come back."

"Of course I'll still want you. After I lost Hannah, I thought I'd never find another woman who'd fit so perfectly into my life. Into Kiki's life. I want you to be ours."

"I'm already yours. But there's something I need to—"

A wail cut off my big confession. A high-pitched, panicked wail. *Kiki.*

Colt was out of bed and tugging on a pair of sweatpants before I could blink.

"What is it? What's wrong?" he called, and I heard the panic in his voice too.

"Brie's gone! She's not in her room and she's not downstairs and I can't find her."

Voi vittu. It wasn't yet six o'clock. Why was Kiki even awake?

The door handle rattled, and Colt didn't make it halfway across the room before the door crashed against the wall. Shit, shit, shit! Why was there no damn lock?

Kiki's gaze swung between us, and that cute-as-a-button mouth dropped open.

"You're cuddling with Brie?" Her words were aimed at Colt, her tone accusatory. "You're cuddling with Brie and not with me?" A second later, she launched herself at the bed and landed right in the middle. "*I* want cuddles too. Can we watch cartoons?"

Kiki scrambled around, looking for the TV remote, and I clung on to the sheet for dear life. Lesson number one: if there was a child in the house, get dressed immediately after sex.

Colt's expression had morphed from horror to shock, but now the corners of his lips twitched. Was that asshole laughing? This wasn't freaking funny. Well, okay, maybe it was a tiny bit funny, but I was still trapped in bed with only a thin sheet preserving my modesty.

Finally, Colt found his tongue. "Why are you up so early?"

"Because Brie said we could do yard work today, and I want to grow things."

"Herbs," I choked out. "Brooke said the feed store sold pots and seeds and that sort of thing, so I thought we could start a herb garden."

When Phil sent the courier with my phone, she'd also sent my purse as requested. So now I had my passport and my wallet, and although I couldn't use my credit card—not only was it issued in my full name, but my mother's people would track it immediately—I had some cash. US dollars, euros, British pounds, and Valetian kroner, although I'd have to be careful with the latter because the notes had my father's face on them and our features were too similar for comfort.

"If you grow the herbs, you have to eat them."

"I ate seaweed yesterday. It was weird."

"Probably tastes better if you cook it first. C'mon, kiddo, let's watch cartoons downstairs."

"Don't call me kiddo."

But she took Colt's hand, and a moment later, I heard

the TV switch on, followed by the sound of the kitchen door and then the tap. If Colt was making coffee, I might just be in love.

I blew out a long breath. That had been a lucky escape. Or had it?

Kiki might have taken my relationship with Colt in her stride, but I still hadn't told him about *my* family, about the burden of expectations that could rip us apart. About the changes that would be forced upon him if we were going to be together.

Tick-tock, tick-tock, tick-tock.

Why hadn't I borrowed Siri's car again? The feed store was less than a mile away, but when you were lugging a bag full of pots and compost and garden tools, that sure felt like a long walk. Kiki was carrying the cakes, because of course she'd convinced me to stop at the coffee house on the way back. Okay, maybe I'd wanted to stop at the coffee house too, but I'd certainly earned a sweet treat. My arms had stretched an inch by the time we reached the house.

But we had basil, parsley, chive, thyme, mint, and sage seeds, and if the packages were to be believed, they might even start sprouting before I left for Valetia. With any luck, I'd return before they were ready to harvest.

Extricating myself from my life wouldn't be the work of five minutes. When I wasn't studying or attending my own doomed wedding under the pretence that it was a friend's, my mother expected me to be available. To pull my weight.

But that weight was crushing me.

I couldn't carry it any longer, especially now that I'd finished my degree and three months of hell each year was about to turn into twelve. I'd agree to some official duties, but not all of them. And I'd still support the charities I was a patron of to the best of my abilities. But the never-ending carousel of parties and balls and black-tie receptions... They'd have to go. My sister would be an adult soon, so let her attend. Elin lived for attention. Thrived on it.

There'd be a negotiation, and I didn't doubt it would be painful, but I couldn't back down. Not this time. Though I didn't want to hurt my family. I did love them, my brother especially, but my mother had turned into Queenzilla since my father's accident. I understood why—she needed to feel as if she was in control—but that didn't make her demands any easier to live with.

My hard line in the sand? I wanted to spend enough time in Baldwin's Shore to give a relationship with Colt a fighting chance. The bodyguards would have to back off. And if I managed to make my life seem boring enough, perhaps the paparazzi would lose interest?

As soon as we got into the house, Kiki dived straight into the nearest bag.

"I want to plant the mints first. Will they taste like Life Savers?"

"Not exactly." I nudged the bag out of reach. "And before you do anything, you need to change into old clothes. You can't garden in that dress."

"Why not?"

Because it was a pale pink satin ball gown, and it looked handmade. I suspected Darla's handiwork.

"It might get dirty. Let's go and find some shorts, okay?"

Mud would come off skin easier than it would come off satin. Upstairs, I found her a pair of denim cut-offs that looked as if they'd seen better days, plus a T-shirt that was slightly on the small side but which would do for messing around in the yard. Where were her hairbands? Usually, they turned up all over the house, but could I find one when I needed one? Could I heck. I was checking under the bed when I heard the *skreek*.

And I knew exactly what that noise was.

Somebody was downstairs.

Somebody was downstairs, and they'd just opened the kitchen door.

My pulse went from steady to oh-hell, oh-hell, oh-hell in half a second.

"Kiki?" I whispered, hoping it was her who'd snuck off to find a snack, but knowing in my heart it wasn't.

"Now can we plant the mints?"

It wasn't Colt either. He always called out when he got home. *Always*. And Brooke knocked. Who else might walk in unannounced? I couldn't think of anyone, and that meant one thing.

Bad news.

Voi vittu.

I couldn't breathe, couldn't move. The only phone in the house was in the hallway, and if whoever was inside had moved from the kitchen to the living room, they'd be able to see me if I tried to reach it. For the second time in my life, I missed my bodyguards. Was this the danger they'd always warned me of? I'd heard the whispers, the mutterings about how I was a target. A kidnapper had tried to snatch me from the hospital right after I was born, tried and failed thanks to my mother realising what was going on and screaming bloody murder, and she'd always been fearful it might happen again. After twenty-five years, I'd written it off as paranoia, but now? Now I wasn't so sure.

Alone, I could have climbed out the window, but Kiki couldn't, not without risking injury.

Was that a footstep on the stairs?

I couldn't leave Kiki behind. If I escaped, she'd be at the mercy of whoever was in the house, and I didn't know how long it would take me to find help. Or if I'd even make it that far. What if more people were waiting outside?

I wanted to believe there was an innocent explanation for the noises, but my gut told me trouble had come to Baldwin's Shore. Beads of sweat popped out on the back of my neck, and I forced a smile for Kiki.

"Let's play a different game first. Hide-and-seek, except today you have to hide in your room."

"But—"

"In your room. I'll go outside and count to twenty."

"Twenty? But we always do fifty."

"New rules. Be quick. And you absolutely mustn't come out until I find you. Promise me."

"I—"

"Promise me."

She must have heard the tension in my voice because she stopped arguing and nodded, her face solemn.

"I promise."

"And I promise I'll come back."

Another *creak* sounded as I hurried to the door, and I recognised it as coming from the step at the not-quite-top of the stairs. Last night, I'd giggled when I trod on it, hoping that the sound didn't disturb Kiki as Colt and I crept up to his bedroom. Today, it sent a ripple of terror through me.

I tugged the door open, heart pounding against my ribcage, hoping for the best but expecting the worst.

And all my expectations came true.

18

COLT

"That was our turn," Luca said.

"Huh?"

"Are you tired, spaced out, or just daydreaming about Brie again?"

Guilty as charged. And fuck it, I'd driven right past the end of Joe McIntyre's driveway. Traffic was light on the highway south of Baldwin's Shore, so I did a U-turn and pointed the patrol car back the way we'd come.

"I told Brie this morning that I want a future with her."

Luca sucked in a breath.

"What?" I asked.

"You don't think you're moving kinda fast? What happened to dating first?"

"Just because you took a decade to tell Brooke how you felt doesn't mean the rest of us have to dither."

"How well do you know Brie? I don't want to sound negative, and she seems like a nice woman, but you don't think she's cagey?" Luca snorted. "Although Brooke used the word 'mysterious.'"

"Yeah, she has issues, her family mainly, but she's started

to open up. I'm not going to push her, but I don't want to let her go either."

"What sort of family issues?"

"Apart from the cheating fiancé? Her mother's pushy and tries to run her life, and her father's in a coma from an accident Brie blames herself for. Plus there's a brother and a sister, but I don't know much about them."

"A coma? Shit."

"Yeah, for three years. She hates talking about it, and she seems closer to her friend Phil than any of them."

"Her best friend is a guy?"

"I made that mistake too. Phil's a girl. Philomena. As I said, Brie's talking, but she's also hurting, so I'll let her take her time."

"Did you try checking her social media?"

"She doesn't use social media." I sighed. "But I tried googling her, and the only Brie Westerburg that comes up is a porn star."

Embarrassingly, I wasn't even sure how to spell her name. But I'd tried every possible combination of Bree and Brie and Vesterberg and Vesterburg in order to cover all bases. Then I'd remembered that some European folks pronounced W as V and searched those options too—Westerberg and Westerburg.

Luca glanced sideways at me as I slowed to turn into Joe McIntyre's driveway. "You don't think...? I mean, she has a great rack."

"Shut the fuck up, man." Although I'd had the same thought. And from the back, porn-Brie had looked similar, so I'd watched the whole damn video of her sucking some chiselled guy off, feeling sicker and sicker, only to realise when she turned around that she was a completely different person. And my Brie's rack was definitely natural.

Spectacular, perfect, and real. "That's my future wife you're talking about."

"Future wife? Are you serious?"

"How old was I when I told you I was going to marry Hannah?"

Luca fell silent for a moment, remembering that day at the diner and probably his laughter too. "Fifteen?"

"And how long had I known her?"

"Like, a week?"

"Precisely. Because I knew she was right for me. And I did marry her. We'd still be married today if... Fuck."

My throat tightened, and I swallowed hard. I wasn't replacing Hannah—she was irreplaceable—and I was at a new point in my life, but it still hurt to remember what I'd lost.

"Sorry, buddy. Shit, I'm sorry. And I get it—you fall fast, and you fall hard. Everybody's different. Have you thought about how you'll break the news to Kiki?"

"Kiki's been doing her own thinking." And she'd nearly given me a coronary when she marched into the bedroom this morning. "She knows I'm close with Brie. When I was making her breakfast this morning, she asked me if Brie was gonna be her new mommy."

"Was she upset?"

"No, the opposite. I asked her if she *wanted* Brie to be her new mommy, and she said yes, and could she be a flower girl at the wedding?"

Luca burst out laughing. "Like father, like daughter. You're both smitten with the same damn woman."

"Yeah, but I'm not going to rush into getting married again. Hell, I'm not sure Brie would even want to after the number her ex did on her. But I sure like the idea of going home at the end of the day and knowing she's there."

"Do you think her family will be difficult?"

"They can't be any more difficult than mine. But you're right—I doubt they'll make things easy, and I'm certain she comes from money."

"She does? I guess there's the fancy accent, but she doesn't act pretentious."

"She said her father had boats, plural."

"Seb Candless has several boats, and he holds his pants up with string because he can't afford a belt."

"Seb's a fisherman."

He'd been fishing the waters off Baldwin's Shore his whole life, and so had his father before him, but there wasn't much of a market for his fish now. Too many cheap imports. Seb had tried diversifying into boat tours, but folks with money didn't want to ride in an old fishing vessel, so he just carried on scraping by. Such a waste. Nobody knew the sea around here the way Seb did.

"Just saying. Did Brie ever mention what her parents do for a living?"

"From what I can gather, her family runs some kind of PR business. Is that Joe waiting outside for us?"

Luca squinted through the windshield. The patrol car needed a wash, but I had other priorities at the moment.

"Sure looks that way."

"I'll let you do the talking. It'll be good practice."

"Good practice? How many missing goats do you usually investigate?"

Joe had called yesterday, complaining that he'd had two goats disappear in the last month. George and Gertie. Vanished without a trace, so he claimed.

"Missing goats are few and far between, thankfully."

"Reckon the goats are with the cats?"

"Who the hell knows?" I parked our vehicle beside Joe's

truck and jammed my hat on. Just another day in the life of a Coos County deputy. Brooke's drama earlier in the year aside, not much ever happened around here.

———————

"Guess I solved my first case," Luca said as we climbed back into the patrol car two hours later. "Do I get a trophy for that? A medal?"

"The departmental budget doesn't run to that, but I might buy you a beer later."

"Only one? I found three goats."

Yeah, three. Joe hadn't even realised the third was missing, probably because he'd been drinking since breakfast, which was also the reason he hadn't noticed that he'd left the pen's gate wide open. Luca had tracked their little hoof prints through the forest until we found the trio foraging for whatever goats ate in a clearing, then we'd managed to get ropes around their necks and lead them back home.

Wouldn't surprise me if Joe called with the exact same problem next week, though. He'd struggled to stay sober since his wife died last year. At least now that there were two of us on the job, Luca or I would be able to check in on him more often. Sometimes, being a deputy in a small town was as much about listening to people's problems as it was about making arrests.

We wound our way down Joe's driveway, bouncing over the potholes, and turned back onto the road. Since it was a Thursday, that meant lunch at the coffee house. Call it an informal town-hall meeting—residents knew I'd be there, and I welcomed them raising any questions or concerns they might have. Plus it was time to introduce the new guy.

There was a tiny substation attached to the library—basically a room—but nobody visited me there. You could call the coffee house an unofficial office.

A loud horn sounded, and I raised a hand in greeting as Jimmy Burns rumbled past in his logging truck. Once upon a time, he used to transport finished goods for the paper mill, but after the place closed down, he'd gotten a job at a local timber company.

Things changed, sometimes for the worse, sometimes for the better.

And some things stayed the same.

My phone rang, and I groaned when I saw the name flash up on the car's dash. Elmira Fairbanks. A pain in my ass, a thorn in my side, and the only person I wanted to speak to less than the Baldwin clan.

"Is that your personal phone?" Luca asked.

"Yeah."

"So don't answer it." He'd crossed paths with Elmira too. To say her attitude was abrasive was an insult to sandpaper.

"If I don't, she'll show up on my doorstep this evening."

Which would upset Kiki and interrupt my time with Brie. So, I gritted my teeth and answered.

"How are you, ma'am?"

"How am I? Furious, that's how I am. This town's full of damn animals."

Technically that wasn't true, not if the number of missing cats was anything to go by.

"Watch out for this asshole," Luca muttered as a red SUV crossed the white line into our lane.

I jerked the wheel, kicking up stones as two wheels hit the nature strip, and glared at the JFK lookalike in the driver's seat as he sped past. On any other day, I'd have pulled him over and issued a warning for the shitty driving and for the illegally tinted rear windows too, but this morning, I had bigger problems to deal with. And I meant that in a literal sense—Elmira was built like a tank.

"What's upsetting you today, ma'am?"

"This...this *maniac* nearly killed me."

"Do you want to report a crime? Because you need to call central dispatch for that."

"Well, you're the deputy, so I'm calling you."

This was one disadvantage of working in a small town. Everyone had my number. Most folks were respectful enough to go through the proper channels, but Elmira Fairbanks wouldn't know respect if it bit her on her ample ass.

"What happened?"

"One of your neighbours nearly ran me off the road."

Hoo boy. "Which neighbour?"

"How should I know? He was looking away from me, and it all happened so dang quick."

"Then how do you know it was one of my neighbours?"

"Because he turned out of your street."

"What model of car was he driving?"

"A big red SUV. Knocked my side mirror clean off, and did he stop? Did he heck."

Only two of my neighbours drove red SUVs—the Snyders, who weren't due back from their vacation until Saturday, and the Mitchells. Mr. Mitchell was in his seventies, and he'd had cataract surgery last year, but he'd always been a careful driver.

"Can you remember anything about the driver? You said it was a male?"

"Either that or a woman with short brown hair. And the passenger looked like Bill Clinton."

What was it with ex-presidents driving like loons today?

"It was the asshole who just went past us," Luca whispered, quiet enough that Elmira didn't hear. "His side mirror was damaged."

Ah, shit.

I forced myself to take a calming breath and slowed the patrol car. It was our civic duty to turn around and catch the guy, although I might be tempted to give him a pat on the back for the so-called attempt on Elmira's life rather than a ticket.

"Okay, ma'am, I'll look into it. But you still need to call dispatch and file a formal report."

"Fine. *Fine*."

She hung up, and I turned on the lights. No siren just yet because I didn't want to give our prey too much warning.

"First case, first car chase..." Luca grinned and checked his seat belt. "You're really spoiling me today."

JFK and Bill Clinton. The folks in dispatch were gonna laugh their damn heads off when I called this in.

Except dispatch beat me to it.

"Twelve-seventy. Distressed child called nine-one-one, says she wants her daddy."

The dispatcher read out an address, and my whole world stopped as I realised whose address it was.

Mine.

19

COLT

"Twelve-five."

I asked the dispatcher to repeat the message, just in case I'd misheard, but I hadn't. Radio protocol flew out the window.

"That's my daughter. Is she still on the line?"

"She hung up. It might've been a prank?"

From Kiki? Never. She didn't always do what she was asked, and she could be headstrong, but she knew right from wrong and she'd never pull a stunt like that. I stopped the car at the side of the road, my chest so tight it was a struggle to breathe. My fingers shook as I dialled my home number. Where the hell was Brie?

"Daddy?"

Thank fuck. I sagged in relief at the sound of Kiki's voice.

"What happened, kiddo?" I tried to keep my voice calm. Normal.

"Brie... Brie..." Kiki gulped in air, struggling to get the words out over tears.

"Can I speak to Brie?"

"She's g-g-gone."

"Gone where?"

"They took her."

The chills came back.

"Who took her? Where?"

"Men! They came into the house and they took her. She told me to hide, but she's gone, they're all gone, and now I'm h-h-here on my own."

Luca already had his own phone pressed to his ear, calling Brooke. She was closer than us—five minutes away at the Craft Cabin versus our half hour. At least one of us was thinking straight.

"Did you see the men?"

"N-n-no, but I heard them."

Who the hell had come into our home? It couldn't have been Brie's ex, could it? She hadn't exactly broadcast her whereabouts, that much I was certain of. I'd assumed she just wanted some thinking time, but what if there had been a more sinister reason for that caginess Luca mentioned earlier?

"You're sure they took Brie? Maybe they were friends of hers and they went somewhere to talk?"

"No! They h-h-hit her. Friends don't hit you."

"When did they hit her? You *did* see them?"

Silence.

"Kiki, you're not in trouble, I promise."

"Brooke's on her way," Luca whispered.

"Brie said to hide, but I looked out the window when I heard the car start."

"What car?"

"A car like Sophie's. And when Brie didn't want to get inside, the man with the grey hair hit her and pushed her."

A car like Sophie Snyder's... A big red SUV. All the

jagged pieces began fitting together... Elmira's call, the SUV veering toward us. Two ex-presidents...

Luca's deep breath said he'd put the puzzle together as well. "You want my opinion? Go after Brie. Brooke'll be at your place in a couple of minutes, and I can call Aaron too. He's working from the office today."

Whatever I did, I had about thirty seconds to make up my mind. The presidents had a head start already, and a few miles on, the road started branching into a rabbit warren of trails and small towns. If they turned off the main highway, we'd never find them.

"Kiki, I need you to stay on the phone, okay? Brooke's coming to sit with you, and I'll be back soon."

"You p-p-promise?"

"I promise."

Was I doing the right thing? Kiki was my flesh and blood, but the need to serve and protect coursed through my veins as well. Not only had Brie wormed her way into my heart, but she was also in trouble and it was my job to help. I'd sworn that oath.

And I intended to uphold it.

Luca was dialling Aaron when I accelerated after the red SUV, and he was telling him to get his ass over to my place and take a gun. Holy shit, what had we ended up in the middle of?

"How far ahead do you reckon he is?" I asked.

"Speed he was going? Four miles? Five? Maybe we'll get lucky and he'll be held up behind Jimmy's truck."

Jimmy's truck... I tried doing math in my head, gave up because I'd never been that good with numbers, and relied on my gut instead. Jimmy must be a mile or two ahead of the SUV, and ahead of both of them, the road narrowed as it went through a ravine. Locals called it the Devil's Cutting because of the way the trees closed overhead, heavy branches turning it into a high-sided tunnel, dark even in daylight. One time, a flood had damaged the road there, and the closure caused havoc for weeks with delays and detours.

Delays...

The bad thing about living in a small town was that everyone had my number. The good thing? I had theirs.

"Call Jimmy Burns," I instructed.

"You talking to me? I don't have his number."

"I'm talking to the damn car."

The electronic voice came back. "Did you mean Jimmy Hearne?"

"No, you piece of shit." *Breathe.* "Call Jimmy Burns."

Finally, technology came through, and so did Jimmy. "Yello. That you, Colt?"

"Did you get to the ravine yet? The Devil's Cutting?"

"Just coming up to it right now. Why you askin'?"

"Has a red SUV blown past you?"

"Not that I recall, and I'm sure I'd've noticed a thing like that."

"Block it."

"Huh?"

"The Cutting. Block it. I don't have time to explain, but I need you to park your truck sideways across the ravine."

"Is this po-lice business?"

"Yes, exactly. Can you do that?"

"Sure, no problem."

"Do not let that SUV past."

I heard the hiss of brakes through the phone, a *creak*, then the rev of the truck's engine as Jimmy manoeuvred the vehicle into place.

"Okay, son, the road's blocked. You wouldn't fit a bicycle through front or back, let alone an automobile. What now?"

"Just sit tight. We're on our way."

"Eh, here they come. A red SUV, you say?"

"That's right."

"It's stopping."

"We're five minutes away. Don't engage."

Should I risk turning on the siren? Not yet. If Brie was in the back of that vehicle, which I very much suspected she was, then I didn't want to panic her abductors and risk putting her in danger. *More danger.* She was already in a whole world of trouble, and I still didn't understand the perpetrators' motives.

"The passenger be gettin' out. Say, he looks just like Bill Clinton."

"So I've heard."

Fake-Clinton shouted, his voice faint through the car's speaker. "Move that truck. You're blocking the road."

His accent was American, which fit with the possibility that Brie's ex was mixed up in this. Emmett? That was his name, right?

"Can't," Jimmy yelled back. "The starter's broke."

"I said, move the damn truck."

"Eh, he's got a gun," Jimmy said, speaking to me. "Thought them Democrats didn't like guns."

"He's not really Bill Clinton. He's a criminal."

"Ain't no damn difference."

"Actually there—"

"That ain't a gun, you stupid-ass motherfucker." Jimmy was back to yelling. "This is a gun." I heard a *pop* that might have been a .22, a guy shouting, "What the hell?" and then a *boom* that was unmistakably a shotgun. "Guess he's coming back your way now. He runs better than he shoots."

Fuck.

"Reckon we need to get the big guns out of the trunk?" Luca asked.

"Tell me I'm having a nightmare. Tell me I'll wake up soon."

"I shoulda stayed in the army. To think I quit for an easier life. I figured that in this town, I'd have to shoot less people, not more."

"When did you last shoot somebody?"

"Year and a half ago. You?"

I gritted my teeth. "Never."

Luca blew out a breath. "Okay."

The closest I'd come to shooting a man was when an outsider moved into one of the Baldwin family's vacation rentals. They had several dozen properties, and this was the worst of the bunch, a three-bedroom ranch that had seen better days. Most of the time, it sat empty, but they leased it to a guy from Wyoming for a month, and he brought his girlfriend. Except it turned out that she wasn't so much a girlfriend, more the fifteen-year-old he'd been grooming online, and her family, the FBI, and the Jackson Police Department were all looking for the pair of them. The guy had been aggressive, waving a gun around, but I'd managed to talk him down in the end. He'd gone to jail, and the girl had gone home to her folks.

A happy ending.

In my eyes, negotiation was always preferable to a bullet, but I couldn't deny I was pleased to have Luca by my side today, seeing as Fake-Clinton appeared to have an itchy trigger finger. A .22 might be a small gun, but it could still do a heck of a lot of damage.

I called in the details to dispatch, let them know that shots had been fired and assistance might be needed, but backup was at least a half hour away, so we were on our own

for the time being. At least Brooke had called back to say
Kiki was upset but unharmed, and Aaron would wait with
them both at the house. There was a vase smashed
downstairs, but no blood, which I had to take as positive
news.

Breathe. Keep breathing.

When the road narrowed and the forest closed in on
either side, I skewed the car across both lanes at an angle.
Not quite as good as the Devil's Cutting, but it would have to
do. That gave us a minute to put on body armour and get
the shoulder weapons out of the trunk. I'd brought a
shotgun, and Luca had added his preferred AR-15 to the
arsenal since he'd done the specialised training to carry one.

How long did we have left? Thirty seconds? Twenty?

"Take cover in the trees," Luca said. "Not behind the car.
We're not in a movie here, and the trees give better
protection."

I deferred to him. Firstly, because he had more
experience than me in these situations, and secondly,
because I was struggling to think of anything but Brie. Kiki
was safe, but when the ex-presidents rounded the bend and
saw my car lit up like a Christmas tree, they'd realise they
were trapped and then they'd have two options: surrender
or fight. Since they'd fired on Jimmy without hesitation, I
feared they'd opt for the latter.

And they had a hostage.

20

COLT

*T*he SUV rounded the bend, and I braced for impact. Either a literal impact, if the driver of the SUV tried to smash his way past the patrol vehicle, or the pain of seeing Brie hurt. Opposite me, Luca shifted, ready to aim at the tyres if the SUV didn't stop.

Which it didn't.

But rather than trying to get past us, it braked a hundred yards away, skidded around, and sped back the way it had come.

Well, shit.

"They've gotta know they're trapped," Luca shouted as he ran to the passenger side. "I'll call Jimmy and warn him they're coming back."

Every move we made, the situation got worse.

"Tell him to get out of the truck and hide on the other side. The suspects know he's armed, and this time they'll be prepared. Bet they've got more weapons too."

"Agreed. If they're crazy enough to kidnap a woman in broad daylight, then they've probably brought more than a single .22 to the party."

But where was the party going to be held?

When we exited the next series of bends, the highway straightened out, and there was no sign of the SUV. Sure, they'd had a head start, but we'd gone after them damn fast, and unless the engine was running on nitrous, the vehicle should still have been visible in the distance.

"Where'd they go?" Luca asked.

"I don't know."

"Maybe they crashed into the trees?"

I hadn't seen any wreckage, but then again, I hadn't been looking for it. I'd once attended an accident where a jeep skidded off the road during a rainstorm and got lodged in the branches of a sturdy oak, and fifty people must've driven past without noticing. The doors were wedged shut, the driver's phone got smashed in the impact, and he'd been forced to climb out of the sunroof and flag down a passing trucker for help.

My nerves stretched to their last frayed inch as I performed a hurried three-point turn and headed back through the bends, Luca checking one side of the road while I watched the other, but there was no SUV. Luca got back on the phone to Jimmy, and he reported that they hadn't shown up at the ravine either.

They'd vanished.

"Where's the fucking backup?" I muttered.

"At a guess? Leaving Coos Bay right about now. We'd better check the rest of the route, see if they've stopped somewhere else."

We'd reached the straight stretch again when we saw it. Or rather, Luca saw it. Faint tyre tracks on ground still damp from last night's rain, heading onto an overgrown track barely visible through the trees.

Luca groaned as we rolled slowly past. "Shit, they've gone into the forest."

"How far in, that's the question. They're probably waiting for us to drive on by so they can skedaddle back toward Baldwin's Shore."

Only we'd put a dent in their plans when we didn't go haring off to the Devil's Cutting.

"One of us needs to check."

And Luca had already decided it would be him. Before I could suggest flipping a coin, he'd cracked his door open and slipped out, sidearm in his hand. I turned the car around to face north and waited just out of sight, ready to back him up by whatever means necessary.

Three minutes felt like three years. Every rustle of the trees set warning bells clanging in my head, and the back of my shirt was damp with sweat. I radioed in, told the unflappable Janice in dispatch what was happening, and got the news that two more deputies were on their way from over near Bandon and they should be with us in a half hour, maybe more since they'd have to clear the traffic backed up by Jimmy's impromptu roadblock.

Finally, Luca climbed back into the car.

"We must've spooked 'em. The track carries on up the hill, and there's no SUV in sight."

"You're sure it's them?"

"From the tyres, it looks like the right size of vehicle, and I don't know where the hell else they could've gone."

Which meant we had to follow. I nosed the car under the overhanging leaves and gave my eyes a second to adjust to the gloom.

"Watch out for an ambush," Luca said. "If I were in their position, I'd send the car on ahead as a decoy and wait in the trees to pick off my pursuers."

Gee, that was a comforting thought. "You think we should wait for backup?"

"That would be the sensible thing to do. We have search dogs, right?"

"Yeah, but they'll take hours to get here."

And by then, the ex-presidents would be miles away, even in this terrain. And so would Brie. How resourceful were her abductors? If they managed to make it to one of the small townships dotted around the area, they could steal a vehicle and disappear into the damn sunset while we tripped around the forest on a wild goose chase.

"So you want to carry on?" Luca asked.

"When have we ever been sensible?"

Luca kept his handgun at the ready while I inched forward along the rutted track. Too wide for animals, but it could've been an old logging road or maybe a driveway for a derelict cabin. A number of them lay rotting in the woods, relics from an age where people prided themselves on being self-sufficient. We used to hunt them out as teenagers, use them as dens and make-out spots, although I didn't recall an abandoned homestead at this particular location.

The track carried on for the best part of a mile, the way barely passable in places. The undergrowth was gradually reclaiming the land, and in another year or two, you'd never know there had been a road through here at all.

"Wait a second..." Luca said.

"What is it?"

"See the broken glass? That's fresh. Looks like a sidelight."

"They came through in a hurry."

"Any idea where this track comes out?"

"Nope. But Thunderbird Creek is on the other side of

the hill, so unless the track turns to the north or south, it'll have to come to an end somewhere."

The creek wasn't wide, but it was deep in places, and with the amount of rain we'd had in the past several days, it would be flowing fast. Our quarry might be able to wade across if they picked the right spot, but they'd be taking a risk.

And speaking of water, did you ever hear the fable of the boiling frog? How if a frog gets put into tepid water that's brought slowly to the boil, it doesn't realise the danger creeping up on it? In hindsight, that's what the drive up the old track felt like.

Around the next bend, I slammed on the brakes as I saw the SUV up ahead, its way blocked by a fallen tree. Guess this was the end of the road as far as wheels were concerned. Three of the SUV's doors were open, two front and one rear, so it seemed our prey hadn't given up yet.

"Sit tight or carry on?" Luca asked.

"Carry on. I'll call it in first."

Except I couldn't because the radio only crackled and blipped, and my phone had no signal. My life had officially gone to hell. Was Walmart hiring? I seriously needed a change in career.

The oaks and maples and alders down by the road had given way to conifers as we got higher up the slope, pine trees mainly, and the carpet of needles meant we had few footprints to follow. But every so often, we'd spot a boot print in a patch of mud or the outline of a tennis shoe small enough to belong to Brie. Fifteen minutes later, we found ourselves in what had once been a clearing, and the prints vanished entirely.

"Any ideas?" Luca asked as we skirted around the edge.

Rusted machinery covered in greenery gave credence to the theory that this had once been a logging site.

"Nope. We can hardly shout out their names and invite them to surrender."

In the end, it was Brie who showed us the way. At the top of the clearing, I spotted a broken necklace on the ground, and I quickly recognised it as one Kiki had made with Brooke. Fat pink beads and smaller yellow ones. Kiki must have given it to Brie, and whether she'd dropped it by accident or on purpose, it acted as a trail marker.

We were getting closer, and my mouth was so dry I could hardly swallow.

"Over here," I croaked. "There's a game trail."

The narrow path went over the ridge and carried on down the far side of the hill, and before five minutes had passed, we heard voices ahead. The trees were thinner here, the land more grass than forest, which meant sound carried better on the wind but also made sneaking up on our targets harder.

Luca was ahead of me, and I realised how much he'd changed in his time away. He was in hunting mode, moving silently, sure of himself. A graduate of stalking school while I was still in pre-K.

What would our next move be? Follow our quarry until they were overcome by fatigue? Their nerves had to be shot to pieces by now. Or should we try to catch them by surprise? If Luca turned, I'd signal him to hold back so we could discuss it. Formulate a plan.

Oh, who was I kidding? Mr. Murphy of Murphy's Law fame was along for the ride today, and he didn't need no stinking plan.

A scream cut through the air.

High-pitched.

Feminine.

Brie.

Luca ran, and I followed.

We burst out of the trees into what might have been termed a large clearing or a small meadow, and I saw two men ahead of us with the woman I loved. JFK had a hand clamped over her mouth and a gun to her head—a .45 by the look of it—and Clinton was waving his .22 around like a lunatic. Unfortunately, when he stopped moving, the barrel was pointing in my direction.

"Put your guns down," I ordered, sounding far calmer than I felt. "We don't want anybody to get hurt."

Up close, I realised both men were wearing masks, the type you got for Halloween, but good quality ones. From a theatre or a movie set? And although I couldn't see Clinton's face, his eyes were wild. Either he'd lost his damn mind or he'd dabbled with illegal substances, neither of which was a palatable option.

And Brie, her eyes were wide with fear. She'd been gagged with a bandana at some point, but she'd worked it out of her mouth, and now it hung around her neck. Her hands were taped in front of her, and she had blood running from both of her knees and the side of her mouth.

I'd never wanted to kill a man before, never felt that thirst for blood, but today, something changed. I could easily shoot these men. Hell, maybe I'd even enjoy it.

Clinton cemented my first impression—that he was nuts —by laughing his head off.

"Well, boys, looks like we got ourselves a good old Mexican stand-off."

A twig cracked behind me, and Luca cursed under his breath. I'd have done that too if all the air hadn't been stuck in my lungs.

"No, no, no." Ronald Reagan circled us slowly, his .45 aimed at my chest. "In a Mexican stand-off, there's no clear advantage. Here, we have three on two, plus we have a hostage."

This guy, he was the dangerous one. His eyes were cool and calculating as he sized up Luca, and in the same way that I'd assessed him as the primary threat, he settled on Luca as his main adversary and switched his target. I wasn't sure whether to be relieved or insulted.

"Here's what we're gonna do," Reagan told us, his hand rock-steady as he kept the pistol pointed at Luca. Centre mass. He knew what he was doing. Only amateurs and show-offs went for the headshot. "You're going to meander back over the hill and drive back to your office, or the donut store, or wherever you usually hang out, and we're going to take the princess here and be on our merry way."

Princess? A chill ran through me. Did they know about my relationship with Brie? Did they know that's what I called her?

Had they been watching us?

That thought sent prickles up my spine because *I hadn't noticed*. But if they *had* been following, then they'd miscalculated, because no way would I allow them to walk away with my girl.

"Can't let you do that."

"Oh, relax. We're not going to harm a hair on her pretty head as long as her family coughs up the ransom. And they will. Ten million dollars is pocket change for them. Blondie here probably keeps that much in her checking account."

Was he serious? I'd always figured Brie for wealthy, but ten million bucks? That was *insane*. I glanced across at her, and our eyes met. She was terrified, and Reagan was right—his team had the advantage. Three against two.

"We have backup on the way."

"And how long will it take them to find you? I don't have a phone signal, so you don't either. By the time they trip over your bodies, you'll be cold."

"You won't all get away," Luca growled.

"It's a risk," Reagan admitted. "You two should just relax. Go back to your office, wait a few hours, and we'll drop the princess off at a gas station once the ransom's in our pocket."

Clinton laughed again, and this time, Reagan joined in.

And then he lost his head.

21

GABRIELLE

Colt was here.

Colt was here, and I should have been happy. He'd found me. He'd followed the clues and he'd found me, but now he had a gun pointed at his head, and it was all my fault. My fault because I'd dared to dream of living a life I chose rather than the one assigned to me at birth.

I didn't know who had taken me, but I knew why. Money. I'd made myself an easy target, and now they wanted ten million US dollars in Bitcoin paid into a designated account. Reagan had been talking about it in the car. Not to the two idiots with him, but to somebody on the phone.

The ransom demand had already been sent. Which meant my mother was probably being sedated right about now.

If the slimeball who looked like President Kennedy hadn't had his hand over my mouth, I'd have told Colt and Luca to do as Ronald Reagan said and go back to the car. My family would pay the ransom—Reagan was right about that. Ten million bucks was lowballing. Insulting, almost. Who were these men? I didn't recognise any of their voices, although I'd worked out from the various conversations in the car that Clinton was Reagan's dumbass brother.

Maybe they'd let me go, and maybe they wouldn't. Right now, I didn't much care. When Colt discovered all my half-truths and realised it was my selfishness that had put his daughter in danger, he wouldn't want to know me anymore. And I feared I'd lost my best friend too. I'd only told one person my address in Baldwin's Shore—Phil—and three days later, the goon squad had arrived to kidnap me. Had she betrayed me in the worst possible way?

The bastard with the gun against my temple tightened his grip, and I fought against gagging. Swallowed bile. He stank of stale nicotine, and he needed to find a better deodorant.

When Reagan mentioned bodies, I felt the tears coming, burning behind my eyes. I didn't need to go home, but Colt did. He had Kiki to take care of. I opened my mouth slightly and got ready to make a move. To take myself out of the equation. If I bit JFK, would he be mad enough to shoot me? Perhaps.

When I was a teenager, my papa used to take me to the shooting range. He said it was important to know how to defend myself. And I didn't mind the shooting, really. At least I didn't end up splattered across the floor like when I took the aikido lessons. Mostly, we used to fire at paper targets, but sometimes the instructor—who was also one of Papa's bodyguards—would line up other things. Empty tin cans, playing cards, my old school textbooks. And, on one memorable occasion, a watermelon. That thing *exploded*.

Just like Reagan's head.

One second, it was there, and the next...gone. *Bang.*

All that was left was a bloody stump.

Holy. Fuck.

I wanted to vomit, but first, I bit JFK's hand as hard as I could. He howled in pain, and I heard two gunshots, Clinton's *pop* and something louder, but the darkness I'd been waiting for didn't come. Instead, I hit the ground with Luca on top of me. A second later, he was on his feet, leaving me gasping for breath as he kicked JFK's gun away and punched him in the face.

"You have the right to remain silent. Anything you say can and will be used against you in a court of law." Another punch. "You have the right to an attorney. If you cannot afford an attorney, one will be provided for you. Do you understand the rights I have just read to you?" I winced at the *crunch* of JFK's nose breaking. "No? Too fucking bad."

I rolled to my knees, wheezing. JFK's pistol had landed next to me, so I released the magazine and threw both parts as far as I could into the bushes. *Colt.* Where was Colt? He was on the ground, but as I tried to crawl towards him, Luca grabbed my leg.

"Stay there. It's not safe."

"But Colt—"

"He's okay."

He wasn't okay. He was bleeding, I saw that now. A crimson rosette was blossoming on his shoulder, dark against his light-brown shirt as he somehow dragged Clinton towards us. Luca ran out to help him, hunched over in a crouch.

"You're hurt!" I tried to help too, but Luca shoved me backwards.

"I said stay there."

This time, I did as I was told. Partly because I'd caused enough trouble already today without disobeying more orders, but mostly because I was terrified. Luca was still on edge too, scanning the hill on the other side of the creek from the safety of the trees even as he pressed down on Clinton's chest. Blood was bubbling from a ragged hole over the dumbass's heart and out of his mouth as well.

"Did you shoot him?" Luca asked Colt.

Colt nodded, his mouth tight. "Who the fuck shot Reagan?"

"I don't know, but I caught a glint of light on the hill opposite."

"Muzzle flash?"

"More like a scope." Luca studied Clinton. "This guy's not gonna make it. I've seen enough men die to know that much. Even if we got him to a hospital in the next five minutes, they wouldn't be able to fix this."

Colt pinched his eyes closed and rocked back on his heels. I had no clue what to say or do that wouldn't make things worse.

"Are you okay?" I whispered.

"No, Brie. I'm not okay." *For fanden.* "Are you injured?"

"Not really."

"Your knees are bleeding."

"I just tripped a few times, that's all." And my twisted ankle was throbbing like crazy with every step, but that didn't matter. "You...you got shot?"

Colt glanced at his shoulder. "Yeah, but it doesn't hurt much."

A siren sounded in the distance, and both men glanced in the direction of the road.

"Reckon that's our backup?" Luca asked as he produced a knife from somewhere and cut the tape off my wrists.

"Damn well better be. But what the hell are they walking into? Who killed Reagan?"

"No idea, but they did a better job than John Hinckley Jr.

Whoever's out there, that was one hell of a headshot. They've gotta be eight hundred yards away and there's a breeze."

"Who goes for the head at that distance?"

"Either someone who missed his target and got lucky, or a fucking master."

Colt had already gone white, but now he paled another shade. "You think they were aiming for me? For you?"

"Possibly. And if they weren't, that wasn't just a kill shot, it was a message: they're better than us."

"So, how the hell do we get off this hill?"

"Very, very carefully." Luca didn't look any happier than Colt. "Brie, were there only three men with you today? Did you see a fourth person at any point?"

"No, but Reagan was talking to an accomplice on the phone."

"How recently?"

"In the car. Back on the road."

"Did he mention anything about cops? Cover? Positioning?"

"Not that I heard. Somebody shot at Clinton, and when he got back in the car, we turned around, and the three of them were mostly arguing. Then we skidded around again, and JFK was freaking out, and Reagan just kept telling him to find somewhere, anywhere to hide."

"If that's the case, then I doubt their accomplice is over on Thunderbird Ridge."

Nobody voiced the big question—who *was* over there? —but Colt tried to answer it.

"Maybe it was a hunter? Cougar quotas got met for the year, but black bear is still open."

There were bears around here? Just when I thought my day couldn't possibly get any worse...

"How many black bears have you seen in these hills?" Luca asked.

"Okay, so maybe someone thought they'd bag a deer out of season."

"They went out to illegally bag a deer, but then they decided to shoot a human instead? Go big or go home?"

"Could've been a wild shot."

"You don't really believe that, do you?"

Colt sighed, then winced. Now that the adrenaline was wearing off, the pain from his wound would ratchet up. I knew that from experience. Several years ago, I'd slipped on deck during a boat race and cracked my arm on the gunwale, finished first by the skin of my teeth, and then gone to the hospital to get the fracture fixed. Needless to say, Mor hadn't been amused.

"Colt, you should get your shoulder looked at." There was no exit wound, which meant the bullet was still inside, and I wasn't sure whether that was a good thing or a bad thing. There was blood, a lot of blood, but some of it was Reagan's and some of it was Clinton's. "We can't stay here."

"One of us needs to keep this asshole company in case he wakes up." Colt dodged my gaze as he answered, and I knew what that meant. The keel had just been torn out of my world.

"I'll go for help," Luca said.

He'd cuffed JFK and taken the man's mask off, but I didn't recognise him. A plain, nondescript white man with mousy brown hair, a man I'd have walked past in the street without a second glance. Every so often, he groaned, so he wasn't out cold, but he certainly wasn't compos mentis. Clinton had been unmasked too. Earlier, his eyes had been wild, wild and cruel, but now they were glassy. Even though he'd stopped breathing, his face was anything but peaceful.

He wasn't familiar either, and there wasn't enough left of Reagan for me to form an opinion. Who were they?

"No, I'll go. You stay with Brie."

Yes, Colt was definitely avoiding me.

"I could go," I offered.

"No!" they both yelled at me.

Okay, okay.

Before anyone could argue further, Colt disappeared into the undergrowth, keeping to whatever cover he could find. I caught the odd glimpse of his shirt, and then he was gone. Luca leaned back against a tree and groaned.

"Fourth day on the fuckin' job."

"I'm so sorry about all this."

"Ten million bucks, huh?"

"It's only money." And if I'd learned one thing in my life, it was that money couldn't buy happiness.

He gave a low whistle. "And you didn't tell Colt that you're loaded?"

"I didn't want it to matter."

"Maybe it doesn't matter to you, but it sure matters to someone."

"Clearly, with hindsight, I made a mistake." I sank onto the damp earth opposite Luca as the sun came out from behind a cloud. Light glistened on congealing blood, and the coppery tang worked its way into my throat and made me gag. "I just... When I came here, it was the first time in my life that people treated me as a person and not a cash machine or a status symbol or some precious object to be handled with kid gloves." My eyes began watering, and I blinked back the tears. "When Colt took me out for dinner, it was because he wanted to spend time with me, not because he could use my name to book a table at the restaurant. And going out for pizza and ice cream with friends may seem like a small thing to you because you probably do it all the time, but for me, it was a big freaking deal. Sitting beside a pool without people snapping pictures and whispering behind their hands was a big freaking deal. Being trusted to take the sweetest little girl to the beach was a big freaking deal. And spending time with a man who liked me for my personality and not my bank account? That was a *huge* freaking deal. So no, I didn't tell him. I screwed up, and I didn't tell him, and now I've lost that...that magic."

All the things I cared about... They were gone.

22

COLT

"You were very lucky, Mr. Haines."

Lucky? The nurse and I had very different ideas about luck. I'd been shot, for fuck's sake.

"Are you kidding me?"

The words came out as a croak, and the nurse held a cup of water with a straw bent so I could sip.

"The bullet missed your vital organs. An inch to the right and it would've nicked an artery, an inch to the left and it would've hit your lung. As things stand, the surgeon says that you should make a good recovery with rest and physio."

Her words filtered into my brain. Artery... Lung... My head was still fuzzy from the anaesthetic. But when she put it like that... The bullet wound hadn't felt so bad at first. Sure, it stung, but I'd been too concerned about the sniper on the hill opposite to focus on the damage. Plus there were the two corpses, Brie's injuries, my colleagues about to walk into a potential ambush, and the fact that I'd just fucking shot someone myself.

Killed a man.

Turned out there'd been nothing enjoyable about that at

all. I'd had no choice—it was him or me—but bile still rose in my throat every time I replayed the scene.

On the trip down the hill, my nerves had once again stretched to the breaking point, waiting for a shot I'd expected at any moment. *Brie's safe with Luca. Brie's safe with Luca. Brie's safe with Luca.* I'd repeated the words over and over in my head like a mantra. The temptation to stay with her had been almost overwhelming, but Luca was her best shot at survival. Not only was he uninjured, but he'd also had experience with warfare, and that was what we were involved in. A war. With a sniper on the next ridge, we'd been forced into a battle for survival.

By the time I stumbled across reinforcements, I'd been feeling a little giddy, although I hadn't admitted that. No, I'd tried to go back up the hill with the others until somebody physically shoved me into an ambulance. The EMTs had given me drugs for the pain, and I didn't remember a whole lot until I woke up groggy...ten minutes ago? Twenty? Longer?

"How's Brie?" I asked the nurse.

"Brie?"

"She was kidnapped. Did she come here? Is she okay?"

"Oh, you mean Miss Gabrielle? They patched her up and took her over to the sheriff's office."

"I need to speak with her."

"Mr. Haines, you don't need to be speakin' with anyone today."

"You don't understand. We have—"

"Yes, I understand perfectly." She jabbed a needle into the IV bag beside me, tutting. "Rest is what you need."

"Is Luca here? Deputy Mendez?"

"He's with John Doe. That man's face is real messed up."

"John Doe?"

"Fella won't tell us his name. But he's wearing handcuffs, so I'm not sure I care to know it anyways."

JFK. Had to be. Luca's fists had turned his nose into hamburger.

"Can you get him? Deputy Mendez?"

"Rest, Mr. Haines."

"I just need to speak with him for a few minutes."

"I'll tell him you're awake, but you need to promise not to move around."

"Sure, I promise."

I tried to cross my fingers, but they wouldn't cooperate. Still, the sentiment was there. As soon as the nurse left the room, I sat up, trying to ignore the dull ache that spread from my shoulder into the rest of my body. How was I meant to get the IV line out of my hand? Or should I just wheel the bag and stand around with me?

Fuck, even getting to the door would be an exercise in endurance, but I needed to find Brie. Needed to check she was all right, and Kiki too. Then I had to try and make sense out of everything that had happened today because right now, I was struggling. Vague memories filtered back. Ten million dollars... Was Brie really worth ten million dollars? Some rich heiress? I'd taken her out to a damn pizza restaurant.

A phone rang. Somewhere close. Was that *my* phone? I patted my pockets, then realised I didn't have pockets anymore because I was wearing a paper gown, and shit, my ass was hanging out the back of it. Good thing I hadn't made it into the hallway because I'd have had to arrest myself for indecent exposure.

There was a bag on the chair next to me, and I spotted my badge shining through the clear plastic. Plus my cuffs and the remains of my bloodstained clothing. Where were my guns? I had to hope they were someplace safe. The phone stopped ringing, but then started again two seconds later, and I rummaged with my good hand until I found it.

"Colt, can you talk?"

"Brooke? You okay? How's Kiki?"

"Kiki's fine. Shaken, but I've been distracting her with candy and crafts. Is Brie there? Luca called earlier to say she was at the hospital with you both, but now his phone's going straight to voicemail."

"Heard they took her to the sheriff's office." Voices buzzed in the background, and even in my groggy state, alarm bells rang. "What's wrong? Who's there?"

Brooke's voice dropped to a whisper. "Half an army just showed up at your door, plus there's a scary English woman who says her name is Lady Philomena Huntingdon, and they're all looking for Brie. And when I say Brie, I mean Princess Gabrielle of Valetia. Did you know? Did you know about this?"

"Huh?"

"Brie is royalty."

"Are you messing with me? Where the hell is Valetia?"

"No, I'm not freaking messing with you! It's an island off the coast of Denmark—I looked it up. Small and very, very rich. They call it Monaco of the North."

Could it be true?

No.

No, no, no.

Yes.

Aw, shit. All the little pieces clicked into place.

Weeks ago, I'd nicknamed Brie "princess" because she seemed kind of regal and I thought it was a cute joke. But now I realised the joke was on me. Brie acted regal because she *was* regal. She must've thought I was the dumbest idiot that ever lived. Had she been laughing with Phil behind my back?

"I... I don't know what to say to that."

Another voice spoke in the background. A guy, and he sounded annoyed. "Where is the princess?"

"I've gotta go, Colt. I'll call later."

Shit, I needed to find Luca. My brain ordered me to the door, but my body didn't get the message, and I slumped back onto the bed. That syringe... What had the nurse put into the IV? Darkness clouded the edges of my vision, and I stared at the ceiling. The squiggles on the tiles reminded me of veins, or worms, or the network of streams around Thunderbird Creek, but then they blurred into a patchwork of grey squares and then into...nothing.

23

GABRIELLE

Scheiße, the circus had come to town. And the ringmaster? The one person I didn't want to speak to. No, not my mother—okay, there were two people I didn't want to speak to right now—but Phil.

Who told my bodyguards I was at the sheriff's office? I'd hoped to slip away, to get back to Baldwin's Shore and hide out until I could explain matters to Colt, then beg for his forgiveness. But now that plan had been scuppered.

"Your Highness," Aksel said from the doorway, as if that answered my unasked questions. He'd headed up my protection team since the accident, when Mor had replaced the entire crew of the chase boat that shadowed Papa and me whenever we went sailing. I'd tried to tell her that what happened wasn't their fault, but she'd overridden me, and Aksel was the result. I didn't much like him, and I couldn't imagine he was too fond of me either since I'd given him the slip in Gold Beach. He'd probably be getting his marching orders soon.

At least, I lived in hope.

"This is a private room."

My voice was hoarse from smoke and crying, my throat scratchy and raw. The deputies had set off the smoke grenades while they cleared the scene in the forest, just in case the sniper was still lurking, and when I finally got into the back of an ambulance, the true horror of the day's events had hit and I'd sobbed all the way to the hospital.

"We have orders to take you home."

"And where is 'home'? If you mean back to the palace, then I don't want to go."

"It's for your own safety. You just got abducted."

"And I also just got rescued."

Phil barged past Aksel, arms outstretched. She'd cut her auburn hair shorter in the two weeks since I'd last seen her —it was shoulder-length now—but despite the West Coast summer, she was still as pale as a ghost.

"Bloody hell, woman! I nearly had a heart attack when I heard about the ransom note. Your mother's losing her mind."

"What's new?"

Phil pulled up short when I didn't reach out for her. "You okay?"

There was no point in beating about the bush, was there? "No, I'm not okay. They came to the house, Phil. They snatched me out of the *house*. And I only gave one person the address."

The smile slowly slipped off her face as she realised what I was saying.

"No. No, I swear. I told nobody. Well, not until after the ransom demand arrived and these arseholes strong-armed it out of me. And I didn't even tell them which street until the helicopters were about to land."

"She didn't," Siri said, sliding past Aksel, iPad in hand.

She was surgically attached to the thing. "Phil only told us the town."

I wanted to believe Phil, I really did, but I struggled to believe in coincidences.

"Maybe you didn't realise. Did you write the address down?"

"Yes, but I memorised it and tore it up before I booked the courier."

"What courier?" Aksel's tone was harsh. "What did you send her?"

"None of your beeswax. And I didn't address the package to Princess bloody Gabrielle. Only a fool would've done that."

That was true. She'd sent it to Ms. West, and it would've been a big leap for anyone to connect that name to me. But if she was telling the truth, then how had the presidents found Colt's house?

I didn't want to believe Phil had betrayed me, but more than that, I couldn't understand what her motive would have been for doing so. She didn't need ten million dollars, and even if she did, I'd have gladly given it to her if she'd asked. And how would she have arranged the kidnap squad? She was connected in the horse world, not the criminal underworld. Which made me feel a little better, but not much.

"If it wasn't you, then who was it?"

Aksel looked around disdainfully. "Probably an inhabitant of that shanty town you were staying in."

It must have been, but not Colt or Brooke or Luca. Who else did that leave? Not Nico either—he wasn't short of cash. Paulo? Darla? Addy? Ernie? One of Ernie's customers? A shopper at the grocery store? A holidaymaker at the resort?

One of those people—people I'd chatted with and smiled at
—had outed me.

I'd wanted to make Baldwin's Shore my home, but how
could I do that if I didn't trust anyone?

"It's not a shanty town," I told Aksel.

But nor was it the paradise I'd once imagined.

Aksel just shrugged, indifferent. "We need to leave. The
jet is waiting at the airport in Medford."

"Where's Colt? I need to speak with him."

"And who is Colt?"

I wasn't about to explain our relationship, or more likely
former relationship—and the thought that it might be over
brought a lump to my already sore throat—to Aksel. He
wasn't the touchy-feely type. If he had a girlfriend, she
probably came with a remote control.

"Colt Haines. He's one of the deputies who rescued me."

Another deputy, one I didn't recognise, eyed us warily
from the doorway. "Uh, folks? I need to ask Miss Gabrielle
some questions."

"You will address her as Princess Gabrielle or Her Royal
Highness," Aksel informed him snootily. How in the devil's
name did he end up on my protection team? He'd clearly
missed his calling as a butler. Those guys always came with
a stick up their ass, and Aksel had a whole tree stuffed
up his.

"Sorry, ma'am. I mean Your Highness. Royal
Highness."

"Gabrielle is fine."

"Her Royal Highness is under no obligation to answer
your questions."

"But I *will* answer them."

Aksel huffed. "If you insist on that, then you should have
a lawyer present."

Siri began tapping away at her iPad. "I'll get right onto it."

Phil rolled her eyes.

"Stop! Everyone, just stop. Of course I'll answer any questions you or your colleagues might have, Deputy... I'm sorry, I don't know your name?"

"Brett, Your Royal Highness ma'am. Deputy Brett Pinkerton."

"Do you know where Deputy Haines is?"

"Uh, he was at the hospital earlier, but they might've let him go home now."

"He's okay?"

"The doc took the bullet out. I heard he'll be right as rain in a few months."

Thank goodness.

"If you can find a room suitable for an interview, then I'll join you. And I don't need a lawyer."

"Yes, Your Royal Princess, ma'am."

He backed away, bumped into the wall with his ass, changed course, and made it out of the room. It had to be Aksel making him nervous, right? I wasn't a scary person.

"Aksel, make yourself useful and find out where Colt is while I answer Deputy Pinkerton's questions."

"I have to stay by your side."

"I'm in a police station, Aksel. Nobody's going to kidnap me from a police station, and you can leave a couple of men from your goon squad behind." If I had to deal with both Aksel and rehashing the day's events, I'd scream, and Deputy Pinkerton would probably spend the whole interview stuttering out random royal titles. "They can stand outside the door."

"*I* will stand outside the door. Soren can locate Deputy Haines."

"Fine."

"Want me to stay?" Phil asked.

I nodded, and then I hugged her tight. I never should have suspected her, but stress did funny things to a person.

"Siri, would you mind finding us some coffee, please?"

"Right away," she said, the same way as she always did. Siri had been with me for five years, always quiet but the model of efficiency.

She scurried off, and I let out a long breath. Out of the frying pan and back into hell.

24

GABRIELLE

*D*eputy Pinkerton set up a video camera while I steeled myself for the interrogation. We weren't in one of those dingy little interview rooms you saw on the TV, more of a conference room with windows looking out onto the parking lot. Special privileges? I suppose I had to be grateful for that.

It shouldn't have been hard, simply telling Pinkerton what I'd seen, but every time I thought about what happened up on the hill, I pictured Reagan's head exploding. Again and again and again. At the time, it had seemed quite surreal, and perhaps there'd been an element of shock involved, but now I felt nauseated. Siri had found me a cappuccino with two sugars, just the way I liked it, but I couldn't drink a drop because my hands wouldn't stop shaking.

Sheriff Newman himself sat in on the interview, although he let his deputy do most of the talking. I got the impression that detective work wasn't really Newman's forte, but he liked the prestige that came with the badge.

"So you say you left the Haines home willingly with these men?" he asked, brow furrowed. Judging by the deep lines scoring his forehead, puzzled was his default operating mode.

"No, I'm saying two men had guns pointed at my head, so I didn't make a fuss. There was a seven-year-old girl in the house, Sheriff. What would you have done?"

Kiki was okay; they'd told me that much. Brooke was with her, and another deputy was standing guard outside the house until they rounded up the remainder of the gang. Plus the sniper, who was still at large.

"Right, yes, I understand."

"Good. Kiki's safety was my priority. I couldn't turn back the clock to undo the fact that I'd caused those men to be in her home in the first place, so the least I could do was make them leave without further incident."

"How did you get into the position of minding Kiki Haines? Doesn't seem like the kind of thing a princess would normally do, though I'll admit I'm not all that familiar with royal protocol."

"Colt helped me out when my car broke down a couple of weeks ago, and we became friends."

"Did you go to Ernie's auto shop? He usually fixes vehicles faster than that."

"I stayed on for a vacation."

"Well, we certainly have some beautiful scenery around these parts."

"Yes, I know. I saw most of it when three psychos took me on a tour this afternoon, so do you think we could possibly finish discussing that? I'd really love to leave sometime today."

Pinkerton shuffled the papers in front of him. "Sorry,

Princess ma'am. Could you talk us through what happened after the men took you out to their vehicle?"

I told them about Clinton's erratic behaviour, the way Reagan had slapped me around, seemingly for his own amusement, and how JFK had seemed more nervous than anything else. The phone calls, the men's panic when they found the truck blocking the road, and the hike up the hill where I kept falling over because I couldn't use my hands to balance properly.

"You're certain none of the men with you shot Reagan?"

"They were as shocked by it as I was."

"Did you see movement on the hill opposite? A person? Anything at all?"

"No, but I wasn't looking in that direction before the shot, and afterwards, I was on the ground while Colt and Luca handcuffed JFK and tried to save Clinton."

Pinkerton checked his papers again. Mostly he seemed to be using them as a prop, but he actually paused to read a sentence or two this time.

"Yes, the handcuffs... Brinkley claims that as he was being taken into custody, Deputy Mendez punched him several times."

Gosh, I didn't want Luca to get into trouble for something I'd dreamed of doing myself.

"Really? It looked to me as if he just tripped over while he was resisting arrest."

"You're certain about that?"

I looked Pinkerton dead in the eye. "Are you calling me a liar?"

He gulped and broke my gaze. "No, ma'am. Your Royal Highness, ma'am."

"Did you say Brinkley?" Phil asked.

"That's right—Duane Brinkley."

"I've heard that name recently. Or seen it."

Come to think of it, so had I.

"We identified him through AFIS—uh, fingerprints. He's a two-bit criminal out of LA. Abduction seems like quite a step up for him, and we're still looking into that. You think you might know the man?"

"I didn't recognise him," I told Pinkerton.

But that name... I was good with faces, but Phil was better with names. We always joked that if we could combine the two attributes, it would make all the events we had to attend a doddle.

"It would've been somewhere in LA..." Phil said, then snapped her fingers. "Got it! When I was helping Siri to move her stuff into her boyfriend's apartment, I knocked a pile of mail off the table. The envelopes were addressed to somebody Brinkley."

"Her boyfriend's name is Dayton, not Duane, and that definitely wasn't him on the hill today. I met him once or twice. But... But..."

But there were similarities. They both had brown hair and a light build, and they were roughly the same height. And maybe there was something about the face shape...

"Siri's the girl who brought the coffee?" Pinkerton asked.

"Yes."

No. No, no, no. Siri wouldn't have got involved in this. Would she? She was such a sweet girl, always so kind-hearted. Every time we walked past a panhandler, she insisted on stopping to give them cash, and last year, she'd raised money for an animal shelter by running the Los Angeles Marathon. The thought of her being involved in a plot to kidnap me was preposterous. Wasn't it? I hadn't exactly been the best judge of character lately.

"I definitely didn't tell Siri where you were," Phil said.

"Did she know about the package?"

"Well, shit."

"She *did* know?"

"I asked her how to book a courier, and she found me the number."

"What package?" Pinkerton asked.

I told him. I told him, knowing the whole time that Siri was waiting for me outside the door, and every word from my mouth felt like a betrayal. Siri wasn't just my assistant, she was my friend. At least, I'd always thought so.

"Rest assured we'll look into this right away," Sheriff Newman promised. "I think maybe it's best if you stay here for the moment, ma'am. We'll arrange to have lunch brought in." He glanced at his watch. "Dinner."

Food? How could I even think about eating? They wouldn't let me see Siri, wouldn't let me ask for her side of the story, but when Phil poked her head out the door, Siri wasn't in the hallway anymore. Where had they taken her? Should I try to get her a lawyer? How would I go about doing that? Knowing these things was Siri's job, not mine. What about Brooke's brother? Would he help? Perhaps, if I could work out how to get ahold of him. Over a week in town, and I didn't even know Brooke's freaking surname.

"Danish?" Phil asked, holding out a platter of pastries from the table.

"How can you possibly expect me to eat?"

A half hour passed, and I was tired from pacing the tiny room. I'd asked for Luca, but he hadn't shown up, Aksel wouldn't let me out the door, and nobody was telling me a thing. Phil had her phone, but who was I supposed to call? My mother? If it had been daytime rather than evening, I could have searched for the number of Ernie's Auto Repair or the Craft Cabin and asked for help, but they'd both be closed at the moment.

"This is a nightmare," I whispered. "We didn't do anything wrong, so why are we the prisoners?"

"Because Aksel's an arsehole and your mother's a control freak."

"Do you think those windows open?"

"Are you joking?"

"I'm not staying in this room for the rest of the night."

"You're crazy."

"Says the woman who zooms around the countryside on a half-ton animal with a mind of its own."

"Hey, horses are smart."

"Exactly my point. That makes them scary."

Phil shook her head, but she still headed over to the nearest window and tried the catch. The window opened an inch, and we stared at each other.

"Do you have money?" I asked.

"About a thousand bucks."

"That should be enough to get a cab to Baldwin's Shore, right?"

"Is that a serious question?"

"Don't look at me like that—I usually take limos, not cabs."

"I bet you don't know how much those cost either."

No, because Siri handled that stuff. "Shut up. Are you climbing out first or second?"

"Second. If we're going through with this cockamamie plan, then the least you can do is catch me."

"We're on the ground floor. Stop being so melodramatic."

Phil paused for a moment. Smiled. Why the hell was she smiling?

"What?"

"The whole Vania-escape-kidnapping thing might have been awful, but do you know something? This is the first time since the accident that I've seen the old Gaby. Your spirit's come back. With Emmett, you were like this shell of a person."

Really? Was Phil right?

The whirlwind of the past fortnight had jumbled my thoughts, but at the same time, the fog that had been hanging over me for the last three years had lifted. I felt a spark of life again. A spark that could die out or fuel me or consume me, depending on what happened next.

Yes, Phil *was* right.

I had one leg over the windowsill when the door opened.

For fanden.

Did anything else want to go wrong today?

"Where are you going?" Aksel demanded. "Get back inside."

"Would you believe I needed to use the bathroom?"

"There's a bathroom on the jet. You can use that one."

"Wait, wait, wait. The jet?"

"We're leaving right now."

"What? Why? I don't want to leave."

"It's been confirmed that Siri's boyfriend masterminded your abduction, and we don't know where he is or who else is involved. It's not safe here."

The spark dimmed, and I sagged back against the windowsill. "It's your job to make it safe."

"Need I remind you that there's a sniper out there? We can't control every variable, and the queen is insisting that you return to Valetia."

Of course she was.

"Where's Siri? What's happening to Siri? Was *she* involved?"

"Siri will be staying here to assist the police with their enquiries."

"You can't just throw her to the wolves like that. You don't even know if she's done anything wrong."

"She was living with the man."

Perhaps that was true, but I'd been living with Emmett without having any idea he was screwing Vania behind my back.

"She needs a lawyer."

"The queen's secretary will arrange for representation." Aksel gave an imperceptible signal, and two of his men moved forward. "Please, we must leave."

"I don't have my passport."

"We collected your purse from that hovel you were staying in."

I considered making a run for it, but how far would I have got? There were more of them than me, and I had no money and no phone.

"I'm not leaving without speaking to Colt."

Aksel's nose wrinkled. It did that a lot. "Deputy Haines is currently recovering from surgery. Soren located him, but he expressed no desire to see you."

Colt didn't want to see me? After the way he'd avoided me on the hill, I'd feared he wouldn't, not when I'd put his daughter in so much danger, but still, I'd hoped...

Phil held out a hand. "If there's a sniper around, sitting on the windowsill isn't a great idea, babes. Maybe everyone needs some time to think things through?"

What was the point? What was the point of anything anymore? I'd loved, and I'd lost. If Colt didn't want to see me, then I couldn't go back to Baldwin's Shore. I didn't want to cause any awkwardness. Not for him and Kiki, or for Brooke and Luca. It was over. They'd all been so good to me, but it was over.

I let Phil help me back inside, and then I followed Aksel to the waiting car.

25

COLT

"*D*addy!"

Kiki hurled herself at me, but Brooke caught her in mid-air before she could slam into my chest. I had to be grateful—my shoulder hurt like a bitch.

"Welcome home, Colt."

It was times like this that I appreciated my friends. During the two days I'd spent in the hospital, Brooke and Luca had stayed in my house with Kiki. Deck and Aaron had added extra locks to the doors and windows, Addy had come over to help clean up, Darla had sent craft materials and a cuddly toy, Paulo had given Kiki a painting lesson, and Nico had provided meals. But none of that filled the gaping hole Brie had left in my life.

She'd just gone. Flown back to Valetia without so much as a goodbye.

Ripped out my damn heart and taken it with her.

In its place, she'd left grief and sorrow and, yes, a touch of bitterness. Maybe what we'd shared hadn't meant much to her, but it sure as hell meant something to me. She'd come into my life, kept secrets, secrets that exposed my little girl to danger, and then vamoosed as quickly as she'd arrived.

That really fucking hurt.

The only person from Valetia left behind was Siri Froberg, and she wasn't talking other than to say she knew nothing about anything. Her high-priced lawyer—some suit from Portland—was running rings around the sheriff's department, and since I'd been placed on administrative leave until the shooting was investigated, there wasn't a damn thing I could do about it. Sheriff Newman had been apologetic when he came to speak to me, but he still had to follow procedure. He'd given me an update on the search for the sniper too. Whoever shot Reagan, they'd gotten away clean. By the time the helicopter got into the air, the only thing left in the area that was bigger than a deer was a young couple who were left red-faced when the crew swooped in for a closer look.

Without us knowing the sniper's exact position, the tracking dog had run in circles, probably chasing after wildlife or day trippers rather than our suspect. One deputy spotted bear scat on the trail. There'd been no further shots, which we had to take as a positive, but the fact that a stone-cold killer was on the loose in the area left me twitchy. I'd be keeping the drapes closed for the foreseeable future. And although Luca wouldn't admit as much out loud, I knew he was spooked too.

I gave Brooke a one-armed hug. "Thanks for taking care of everything."

"What are friends for?"

"Still, I appreciate it."

"I can't believe Brie upped and left like that. I thought she was a friend too."

Addy muscled her way past Luca and Aaron to kiss me on the cheek. "She's a freaking princess. *I* can't believe she was staying in Baldwin's Shore in the first place. If her car broke down, why didn't she call for her helicopter?"

"She'd just walked out of her wedding. I guess she needed some space."

I'd tried to give her that space, and then I'd ended up as her rebound. If I'd known back then what I knew now, would I have done things differently? Hell yes. I'd probably have offered her a bed for the night, but I sure as hell wouldn't have given her my heart as well. The former would have meant a neat anecdote to tell my future grandchildren, while the latter promised another year of grief. Not only mine but Kiki's too.

Brooke had brought her to visit me in the hospital, and I'd had to break the news that Brie wasn't coming back. There'd been tears. There'd been disbelief. And then Kiki had blamed herself, which broke my heart all over again.

"Brie promised to come back. She *promised*."

"Sometimes people say things they don't mean."

"Did she go home because I broke *my* promise?"

"What promise?"

"She told me to hide, and I promised I wouldn't come out until she came back. But I went to the phone to call you, and now she's gone. Is it my fault?"

"No, kiddo, it's not your fault." And Kiki's quick thinking had probably saved Brie's life. "It's a grown-up thing."

"Can't you call her? Tell her I'm sorry?"

She hadn't even left a number. "Wish I could, but I can't."

So now my little girl was miserable, and there wasn't a whole lot I could do to change the situation. More fool me for getting involved with a woman again.

"Dinner's on the table," Addy said, handing me a beer. "We set it up buffet-style. Nico sent finger food on account of your arm being in a sling. Isn't he just the sweetest? Anyhow, I guess I can understand Brie needing space. Have you looked her up on the internet?" No, I'd been trying to avoid that. "Man, the European tabloids are *brutal*. Did you know they call her Princess Piggy?"

"What?" I almost spit beer all over Addy.

"It's true. And her dad had a boating accident. Did you know about that?"

"She told me."

"Brie, well, I guess she went into mourning afterward even though he's still kind of alive, and she put on a few pounds. The paparazzi took photos of her on the beach in a bikini. I think it was a private beach, but they have those long lenses, haven't they? And they savaged her. I mean, who doesn't have cellulite? Okay, okay, Romi, we all know she's a goddess, but I'm talking about normal people."

Did Brie have cellulite? I hadn't noticed, and she certainly wasn't fat. If that was how people treated her, then no wonder she had hang-ups about wearing a bathing suit.

"That's insane."

"What's insane is that the really trashy reporters said she tried to kill her dad."

"Tell me you're joking?"

"Wish I was. Apparently, the royal family released a statement saying the boat hit a whale, but whales are rare in that part of the sea, so some people think she made a mistake and then tried to cover it up. Do you think she made a mistake? Because she seemed like a pretty good sailor to me, although I don't know much about boats, so I could be wrong, but she did win an Olympic medal."

Aaron wrapped a hand over Addy's mouth. "Colt just got

home from the hospital. How about you let him eat dinner before we start dissecting Brie's visit?"

"Fine, whatever. Did you try those little spiral pastries? The ones with the cheese and ham? They're to die for."

"Less talk about dying too," Luca muttered.

I'd noticed all the drapes were closed when I arrived home, and for that, I was grateful. Would the paranoia ever ease? The feeling of being watched? Dayton Brinkley was still on the run, but nobody thought he was our sniper. He was a marketing executive with a gambling problem. Duane had finally started talking, and according to his statement, his brother had heard from Siri that Brie had taken off and come up with the idea of demanding a ransom to clear his debts. Clinton had been Duane's buddy, and they'd recruited Reagan onto the team due to his previous experience. And what experience was that? Well, he'd turned to breaking and entering after being dishonourably discharged from the army, and an ex-girlfriend alleged that he'd held her prisoner for three days, although the charges were later dropped. The details made for unpleasant reading, and although the loose sniper scared the shit out of me, I couldn't be too upset about Reagan's death.

I was just thankful that Brie hadn't been forced to spend another minute with the man.

Fuck, I missed her.

The pastries might have been good, but I barely tasted a mouthful, and when the others left, I felt more relieved than anything else. Relieved that I didn't have to act strong when I was cracking inside. I read Kiki a story, deflected more questions about Brie, and then crawled into bed. I knew from my experience with Hannah that time would dull the pain, but right now, everything was so damn raw.

My head said not to, but when I failed to fall asleep, I

couldn't stop myself from looking up Brie online. Or Princess Gabrielle Katrine Henrika Westerburg von Lindegren, if we were going to be formal, which it seemed she usually was. Hundreds of photos taken at official functions showed her smiling, but it was a fake smile, a beauty pageant smile, all teeth and no eyes. The tabloid photos were much, much worse. If she realised the cameras were there, her expression was tight and miserable, and when they caught her unawares, they chose to print the worst pictures possible, every one of them accompanied by a caption pointing out some imagined flaw. The only time she looked truly happy was when she was on a boat. Sailing with her father, she came across as businesslike, and alone, she looked free. The way she had on board *Checkmate* as we sailed for the Peninsula. The way she had playing with Kiki. The way she had in my bed.

My heart ached for her as well as for myself.

Even though she'd left me, I still wanted her to be happy.

I just wasn't sure she ever could be.

26

GABRIELLE

"*T*his sucks arse."

Jens looked up from his newspaper. "Philomena, please. America was a bad influence on you."

"Who died and made you king? Oh, that's right—nobody. So quit being all pompous."

A sigh escaped my lips. Phil and my brother had a volatile relationship. She'd always complained that he was stuffy and strait-laced, while he thought she was a loose cannon. Then two years ago, they'd spent one drunken night together, and they'd been at each other's throats ever since. I couldn't admit I knew about their shenanigans, so instead, I was forced to play mediator in the hope that they might one day learn to forgive and forget.

"Don't you have a horse to prance around on?"

"I'm here to support Gaby since you're not doing a very good job of it."

"Why does Gaby get all the attention?" Elin asked. She was home for the summer break and kept complaining she was bored. "I went to the opening of the new theatre with Mor last week, and only a handful of reporters showed up."

"Try leaving your dress tucked into your knickers next time," Phil suggested, and Jens glared at her.

"Philomena's joking."

Phil shrugged and helped herself to another asparagus tarteletter. "Worked for Gaby."

"Hey, I didn't do it on purpose."

I'd been only fourteen at the time, in a hurry to give out the trophies at Cowes Week with Papa. It was my first big foreign event, and afterwards, I'd spent the whole night crying in my hotel room as Papa tried to reassure me that everyone would forget by tomorrow. That was a lie. They didn't forget, ever.

Elin's nose crinkled. "I'm not sure I want people to see my underwear."

"Good. That's a good plan. No underwear."

"*No* underwear? As in don't wear any?"

"No!" all three of us shouted. *Give me strength.*

"Wear lots of underwear," I told her. "Granny panties, a girdle, thick tights."

"But the pretty kind," Phil added.

Jens put his head in his hands. "Can we stop talking about underwear now?"

"Sure." Elin smiled brightly. "Will somebody tell me what went on in America? Gaby, did you really get kidnapped by a serial killer?"

"You have to stop getting your 'news' from the internet."

"Well, nobody else will tell me what's happening."

"There was no serial killer." At least, not that anyone was aware of so far. "It was just a bunch of crazies who wanted money."

The ex-presidents. At least by the time I walked into the palace, the staff had thought to remove the pictures of my father and grandfather meeting the real Clinton,

Reagan, and JFK. I didn't need more reminders of that awful day.

"And they blew each other's heads off?"

Elin never gave up, did she?

"That's not quite true."

"Then how did they die? They died, right?"

"Two of them got shot."

"By who?"

Jens stepped in again. "Can we stop talking about shooting people as well?"

"You lot are so boring." Elin shoved her chair back and flounced to the door in the way that only a sulky fifteen-year-old could manage. "I'm going swimming."

What time was it? I checked my watch. Half past eight on a Monday morning, which meant Mor would be finishing up with her personal trainer right about now. When she was at home, her routine never deviated. She worked out every weekday in the gym with Marcella, then took a shower and came in for breakfast. If I ate quickly, I might be able to escape before she arrived.

"Thanks," I said to Jens.

"No problem. Elin's just concerned—we all are—but she doesn't need to hear the gory details. At least they've caught Dayton Brinkley now."

We'd heard the news late last night via Aksel's replacement. The police in Utah had picked him up at a gas station, trying to buy fuel for a stolen car with a stolen credit card. At least nobody else had been injured during the arrest.

"I'm still so worried about Siri. Why won't Mor let me speak with her?"

"Because she doesn't want you getting hurt any more than you have been already. You've got a soft heart, Gaby."

"Why do you say that as if it's a flaw?"

"Perhaps it is?"

"I'll never believe that."

A shrug.

"Just because you've closed yourself off to all human emotion doesn't mean the rest of us have to. Don't you want to feel the warmth of human connection? The joy of friendship? The thrill of falling in love?"

"Love is for fairy tales."

"That's not true."

"If you think your transactional relationship with Emmett was love, then you need to open your eyes."

Now *I* shoved my chair back and headed for the door, although I didn't flounce as well as Elin. "You're the one who's blind, Jens."

"I—"

Phil was hot on my heels. "She's not talking about Emmett, you idiot."

"Then who—"

I made it into the hallway and started walking, then running. At least inside the palace, I didn't have Aksel Mark Two following me everywhere, or else I'd have been tempted to grab one of the swords or maces mounted on the wall and start swinging.

"Wait up," Phil called.

"Speed up," I shot back.

I didn't stop until I reached the sanctuary of my private quarters, although privacy was relative in a place like this. The maids rearranging my stuff took one look at me and backed out the door, but they'd return. They always did. Phil closed the door behind us, and I sank onto my bed. I'd grown up in this apartment—two bedrooms, two bathrooms, a closet-slash-dressing-room, a sitting area, and a small study—but it had never quite felt like home. When I was small, I used to stand out on the balcony and stare across the sea, pretending I was free, but as with everything in my life, it was just an illusion. I'd always be bound to my birthright, and as I'd got older, the chains had become tighter, not looser.

"C'mon, talk to Doctor Phil. You know that shit freaks me out, but for you, I'll listen."

"I wouldn't put you through that."

"Then what can I do to help? Do you want wine? A punching bag? A dartboard with Emmett's face on it?"

"How about a time machine?"

"That's a big ask. Don't you remember how bad I was at physics? I only passed because you helped me with my coursework. And anyway, what point in time would you want to go back to? Pre-Emmett?"

"Honestly? I don't know. Pre-accident, I guess, but then I'd never have met Colt."

"He made a big impression, huh?"

"The biggest. I thought... People talk about soulmates, and I always thought that was a myth, but then I ended up in Baldwin's Shore, and...and..."

"I hate to say it, but the two of you couldn't have been that in tune if he won't speak to you now."

"Ouch."

"You know me—I'm not going to beat about the bush."

"Yes, I do know you, and don't you dare tell me to get back into the saddle, either literal or metaphorical."

I was half-surprised she hadn't suggested a bran mash and a month of box rest.

"Dammit. Okay, so...wine?"

"It's not even nine o'clock in the morning."

"There's no law against it."

"If my mother saw me open the bottle, she'd try to get one introduced."

"So no alcohol, no horse riding, no rebound of a rebound... I'm at a loss here."

"I think that maybe I'll just go and sit with Papa for a while."

"Is that a definite maybe?"

In the past, I'd have gone sailing, but I wasn't sure I was ready for that yet. My boats glistened in the sun, docked neatly in the harbour below the palace. Mor had wanted to get rid of them all, but Jens had fought her on that when I wasn't strong enough to do so. He'd arranged for them to be maintained too. Our relationship wasn't always the smoothest, but beneath the bickering he cared, no doubt about that.

"Yes, I'm going to the hospital."

"Want me to come with?"

"I'll be okay on my own if you want to visit Lemon."

"You're sure?"

"Positive."

I wasn't sure at all, but Phil had sat with Papa and me yesterday and the day before, and I didn't want to bore her. Plus she hadn't seen Lemon since she arrived.

Lemon, of course, was a horse.

The island of Valetia was tiny, only twenty-one miles long and twelve miles wide, and with space at a premium, much of the land was developed. But several generations ago when a princess from the Danish royal family had married into ours, we'd been gifted an estate across the Valetian Strait as part of the celebrations. We used the house—Vandenburg—as a country retreat, and Mor had set up a scheme to let underprivileged children from all over the world take vacations there. There were stables in the grounds, plus a riding arena and paddocks, and Phil had been staying with us when a local charity that usually rescued dogs had asked for help with a skinny little foal that had landed in their care. That was Phil occupied for the rest of the trip. She bottle-fed Lemon through the nights, and when he'd grown older, she helped to break him to saddle. They still had a bond, even though he was enormous now.

"I'll just go for an hour."

Which meant three hours. "Take your time."

I appreciated Phil coming home with me to provide moral support and also to deflect some of Mor's ire. As the person responsible for aiding and abetting my escape from Emmett, Phil had already been on the receiving end of a stern lecture on personal safety and the risks facing young ladies in today's world. Phil's apology to Mor had struck all the right notes, but when I'd apologised to Phil, she'd shrugged it off and promised she'd totally help me again next time.

Next time.

How could there be a next time?

Didn't she realise there was nothing of my heart left to break?

With Siri still detained in America, Jens's assistant arranged for a car, and I rode across the bridge to Denmark with Phil to give Lemon a pat on the nose and a carrot before Aksel's clone escorted me back to Valetia. The hospital occupied the site of the kingdom's original infirmary in Kessin—more commonly called the Old Town by locals—although it had been entirely rebuilt since those early days.

Valetia had been settled centuries ago by Slavic

marauders, and for decades, it changed hands between various tribes who fished its waters and settled amongst its craggy cliffs. In the nineteenth century, skilled weavers had brought prosperity and helped to establish the island's position on one of the old trading routes, a position my ancestors had exploited for the benefits of the Valetian people. And in more modern times, a favourable tax regime had allowed the country to flourish as a financial centre and millionaire's playground.

All of this meant that our main hospital was a state-of-the-art facility with a reputation for hush-hush cosmetic surgery as well as excellent clinical care. The thought of having my face stretched and stapled left me cold, but the medical team there had been wonderful with my father over the past three years, and for that, I had to be thankful.

A nurse greeted me with a smile. "Good morning, Your Royal Highness."

"Good morning, Lena." At least I'd managed to get her to stop curtseying now. We were still working on the "Your Highness" part. "How is he today?"

"The physiotherapist finished a few moments ago. You're here to sit with him?"

"For a while. I'll call if we need anything."

I wouldn't call. The only thing I needed was tissues. For the past few days, I'd managed to stay upbeat when I visited, and in front of Phil, I'd stuck to mundanities, but today... today, I couldn't hold back the tears. I had to talk, and my father had always been a great listener.

"Papa, it's been such a shitty month. I don't know if Jens has told you, but I didn't marry Emmett. Which I'm actually glad about. What I really wanted to do was slice off his balls with a lawnmower and feed them to hungry sewer rats, but I left instead. Are you proud of me? That should have made

Mor happy because you know how she hates scandal, but of course it didn't. But she did fire Aksel, or demote him, or something. Whatever, he's gone, but the new guy seems more like a robot than an actual person."

Could the robot hear me? He was stationed outside the door, probably listening with superhuman ears. I lowered my voice a smidgen.

"So I ran away. I ran away, and it was *wonderful*. I found friends, Papa. Real friends, and even though I had nothing, they were so nice to me. I fell in love. *Love*. It was crazy, and beautiful, and I got the tiniest taste of what real life was like. Of what freedom was like. Freedom is watching cartoons at ten a.m. while eating cold pizza. Freedom is walking on the beach without half an army following you. Freedom is comforting a little girl who's upset because other little girls said mean things and she didn't have a team of bodyguards to step in and stop them. Freedom is drinking too much and regretting it the next morning. I experienced the good and the bad instead of being trapped inside a protective bubble, and while I can't say I enjoyed every minute, I could breathe the whole time. Is that weird? I could *breathe*. And now I'm back here, and there's this weight pressing on my chest that I just can't shift."

Tears had plopped onto Papa's arm, and I wiped them away as the monitors beeped quietly in the background. His heart rate was a tiny bit faster than usual. Did that mean anything? If it got any higher, I'd have to call the nurse. Good thing I hadn't worn mascara today because I was a mess.

"I wish I could have stayed in Baldwin's Shore forever. Truly, I do. Here I am, living Cinderella's dream, and what I actually need is the genie and the lamp. Although knowing my luck, that story would turn out really, really bad. Once upon a time, there was an ungrateful princess..." I choke-laughed and squeezed Papa's hand. "Do you remember the time I asked Mor if I could resign from being royalty? After I accidentally wore that see-through dress?" Bright sunlight, white cotton, and dirty-minded photographers didn't mix well. "And she said there was no such provision in Valetia's constitution? Well, the constitution was obviously written by a man. Sorry, but it was."

I wiped my eyes and looked down at my father. Had his head turned? Or was it my imagination? He often moved his arms and legs—reflex responses, the doctors said—but not normally his head. I fluffed his pillows in case he was uncomfortable and gripped his hand again.

"That's not to say that all men are assholes. Colt was the sweetest man I've ever met, so caring and...and..." I sniffled once more and regretted not bringing a second box of tissues. "So brave. He and Luca came to rescue me after I got kidnapped, and he got shot, and then he realised I hadn't been entirely truthful with him, and now he doesn't want to see me, and *fuck*, I made such a mess of everything."

What I really needed was a hug, but I had to settle for resting my head on Papa's chest. At least I could feel his heartbeat, strong and steady. He was still in there; I knew he was.

"Don't...cry."

Great, now I was hearing things.

"I'm so sorry, Papa. I was never cut out to be a princess. In the US, I worked in an auto shop for a week, and believe it or not, it was more enjoyable."

The heart-rate monitor began beeping faster, and my pulse sped up too. Was he okay? I sat up, reaching for the call button, and found...my father watching me.

His eyes were open.

His eyes hadn't been open for three long years.

Oh. My. Goodness.

"Papa?"

"Brie," he managed, and it was clear that even the whisper had been an effort, but his eyes tracked me as I moved.

I leapt for the call button and held it down. Where was the medical team? What was I meant to do? To say?

"I love you, Papa."

"T-t-too."

"Don't make yourself tired, okay? Just rest. The doctors are on their way."

The door burst open, and a dozen people ran in, some wheeling equipment and every one of them wearing a panicked expression.

"What happened?" the doctor in front asked, breathless as if he'd just run the length of the hospital.

"He's awake. My papa's awake."

Well, that stunned them.

Then they leapt into action, checking vital signs and reflexes because clearly my word wasn't good enough. The lead doctor leaned in, looking equal parts overjoyed and surprised.

"Your Highness, can you hear me?"

Oh, call him Magnus, for crying out loud.

"If speaking is difficult, you can blink once for yes and twice for no instead."

One blink, and my grin stretched from ear to ear.

"We need to run some more tests. Are you comfortable?"

One blink.

"Good, good. This is excellent. A lot of people are going to be very happy to see you."

Understatement of the century. I had to call my family

and break the news, and then I had to prepare for the media onslaught because the whole country would want to know every detail. But first, I bent to kiss Papa on the cheek.

"I've missed you so much," I whispered. "Thank you for coming back to me. *Thank you.*"

27

GABRIELLE

*I*f a month ago, somebody had asked me what I longed for more than anything else in the world, I'd have said I wanted my father to wake up. And maybe the genie did exist after all, because that wish had been granted. Papa was back with us.

Okay, not back, exactly—he was still in the hospital and would be for quite some time—but we could hold a short conversation with a mixture of words and blinks. There were times when he got upset and agitated, but the doctors said that was a good sign, that it was all part of the recovery process, and his mind was becoming sharper hour by hour. He was unmistakably Papa.

I'd spent the past three days at his bedside with Mor, Phil, Jens, and Elin taking turns to join me. Elin was visibly frustrated by the lack of progress, and even though I'd tried to explain that the human brain wasn't a light switch—it didn't simply blink off and on—she didn't stay for too long. Mor, well, she was hard to read. We'd never been close, which seems a terrible thing to say about your own mother, but until the accident, we'd gotten along okay. That damned whale had driven a wedge between us, and although it might have loosened a little this week, it was still undeniably stuck.

Papa sensed the tension and told me to give her time.

Time.

I didn't have time.

Because every second that passed was a second longer since I'd seen Colt, and I had no idea what to do about it. How to fix things, or whether they were even fixable.

"Just call," Phil said.

I'd found the Craft Cabin's number on the internet, and I even got as far as dialling once, but when Darla picked up, I'd panicked and disconnected. What if Colt didn't want to speak to me? Was not knowing worse than getting an answer I didn't want to hear?

"I don't know what to say."

"Tell him how you feel and that you're sorry you forgot to mention the whole princess thing."

"I'm not sure that'll be enough. He got shot because of me."

And I still wasn't sure how badly. A small segment on a local news website said he was home now, but the hospital wouldn't give me any information, even though they'd been happy enough to accept my credit card when I called to settle Colt's outstanding medical expenses.

"Well, he didn't die, so that's a point in your favour."

"Dammit, this is a conversation I need to have in person."

Phil snorted. "Good luck with that."

I'd forgotten just how much I hated these family conferences. They were the equivalent of a royal board meeting, where we discussed the state of affairs in Valetia and agreed upon future tours and appearances. On the agenda this week was a tree planting at the high school in Nordbruk, the naming ceremony for the new lifeboat, and a visit to a day-care centre for differently abled adults. Plus the usual round of dinners, parties, and speeches, yadda yadda yadda. Mor's private secretary always presented a segment on media coverage, and without fail, I cringed through the whole thing. Today was no different, except I got to feel Mor's disapproval in person rather than via Zoom. Life with Emmett had offered *some* benefits.

"Gabrielle, what were you thinking?" Mor muttered for the hundredth time this week.

"I was thinking that I needed a few days alone."

"Time alone isn't compatible with your role in life."

"Then I quit."

"We've had this discussion before. Being a princess isn't a job; it's a responsibility."

"I'm twenty-five years old. I should be allowed to live my own life."

"You're a twenty-five-year-old working royal, and that comes with obligations. But I understand you've been under a lot of strain lately. Perhaps we could arrange a short vacation? Gerhard, could you take a look at the schedule?"

"A vacation?" Hallelujah. "Sounds perfect. I'd like to go back to Baldwin's Shore."

Now that I'd had time to think things through, I realised I couldn't give up on Colt, not until I'd at least spoken with him face to face.

"Baldwin's Shore?" Mor sucked in a breath. "No. No, that's out of the question."

"Why?"

"Need I remind you that there's a sniper skulking around that place? The police haven't caught him, nor do they appear to even have a suspect."

"The sniper didn't shoot *me*."

"You don't know for certain that he wasn't *aiming* for you."

"I'll take bodyguards. Aksel 2.0 or whatever he's called."

"Malthe. He's called Malthe. Gabrielle, please make an effort to learn people's names. And he can't protect you properly if the threat's coming from half a mile away."

"But I have friends there. I just walked away without thanking them, or apologising for the problems I caused, or...or..." Or telling Colt that I loved him.

"We can send a donation to their community fund. They must have one."

"That's not enough."

Jens spoke before Mor managed to say "no" again, and I could have hugged him right then.

"Sending money is so impersonal, don't you think? And you're always telling us that our public image is important. Why can't Gaby take an armoured limo? Generate some good PR for once?"

Okay, that last part stung, but I was still grateful he'd spoken up.

Mor softened a touch. She always had respected Jens's opinions more than mine.

"When the police have apprehended the sniper, we can look into it."

So basically never, then.

"But—"

"Gabrielle, there are times in life when you have to compromise, and this is one of them. Your safety is my primary concern. Now, who's going to attend the orchid exhibition at the botanical gardens?"

Elin stuck up her hand. "Me!"

"No...party?" Papa asked as I slipped into his room with two kinds of pizza.

His speech was gradually improving, but conversations were slow going. He'd started eating morsels of solid food now as well, but I had to help him with the fork, something that irked him to no end but which we both accepted was a necessity for the moment.

"I'm currently excused from parties. Mor says I've exceeded my quota of scandals for this month. She's breaking me in gently with a visit to a children's art exhibition next week because surely even I can't manage to screw that up."

Papa's mouth twitched in what might have been an encouraging smile. Or a laugh. "Yes...can."

"Gee, thanks."

The nurses had propped him up with pillows today, and he pointed to himself with one shaky hand.

"Still...excused."

"Don't count on it for long, buddy. As soon as you can smile and shake hands, she'll have you out there in your wheelchair."

Papa's bodyguards had cleared the hospital garden today, and the nurses had wheeled him outside for a short while—his first breath of fresh air in three long years. A breeze was blowing off the sea, and he'd closed his eyes and inhaled the salty air. A look of quiet determination came over his face, the same way it used to at the start of every boat race. The road to recovery would be long and undoubtedly twisty, but he'd damn well walk it. My papa didn't give up.

I began cutting the pizzas into pieces, one pepperoni pie and one loaded with vegetables. Got to get his five a day in.

"Klara...op...op..." He was trying to say "opera," but he got annoyed if I finished words for him, so I waited. "Opera?"

"Yes, opening night at the Copenhagen Opera House." Mor had been to visit Papa this morning, so she must have told him of her plans then. "Jens is entertaining a group of children at Vandenburg, and Elin has friends over."

Phil was at Vandenburg too—Mor had roped her into helping with pony rides—so I was fully prepared for her to be in a foul mood tomorrow. Why couldn't she and Jens just kiss and make up? Actually, forget the kissing part—that would only make things worse.

"You...feeling...better?"

I wanted to say yes, but I'd always been honest with Papa. "Not really. I miss Colt so, so much. Kiki too. And Brooke, and Luca, and Addy... All of them. When I asked to go back to Baldwin's Shore, Mor said not right now, so I'll have to try phoning, but I don't know where to start."

"Wait?"

"I'll be waiting forever."

"She...cares. Own...way."

"Yes, I understand there's a lunatic running around with a sniper rifle, and yes, I'm grateful she doesn't want me to die, but doesn't she realise that being stuck here is killing me too, just more slowly?"

"Not...ad...adventurous."

"You're telling me." Mor's idea of adventure was travelling to Copenhagen by helicopter instead of by car. "I don't suppose she'd like Colt either, seeing as he isn't wealthy and he doesn't have a title."

"Colt... Good...man?"

"The best. The absolute best. Not only did he take me in like a stray and then save my life, but he's also a wonderful father to his little girl."

"Daughter?"

"Yes, Kiki. She's seven. Her mother passed away when she was young, but Colt made sure she was never short of love. In two weeks, I learned so much. About the person I want to be, about the kind of man I want to share my life with, and that man is *definitely* not Emmett. Thank goodness I didn't marry him. I'm actually tempted to send Vania a thank-you card."

That got a chuckle. I smiled back at Papa, then helped him to spear a piece of pizza and lift it to his mouth, and he chewed slowly, thinking. Although his body was letting him down temporarily, he hadn't lost his mental acuity. Yesterday, he told me that he'd been able to follow conversations for a while, but responding had been a step too far. At least, until my tears combined with his fatherly instincts had given him that extra push.

"Follow...heart."

Was Papa actually encouraging me to go behind Mor's back? It sure seemed that way. When I was eighteen, we'd anchored up for a break during a morning's sailing, and over sandwiches and a thermos of coffee, he'd told me that he and Mor wouldn't be following tradition and trying to match me up with a suitor. That it was up to me to find my own way in life, which included choosing a husband if I felt so inclined. I knew that was Papa's decision rather than Mor's—she'd not-so-subtly arranged for my path to cross with any number of eligible bachelors over the years—but before the accident, she hadn't meddled too much. So Papa's words didn't totally surprise me, but his willingness to join me in the doghouse did.

"You think I should go to Colt?"

"If...that's...what...you... want."

"How? How can I? Mor's become overprotective to the point of ridiculousness. I can't even get off the damn island. And say I did manage to ditch my bodyguards and my driver and borrow a car, someone would raise the alarm the moment I crossed the bridge." There was a border-control checkpoint at each end. Steel barriers. "The guards would chase me, and can you imagine *those* headlines?"

"Who...said...anything...about...driving?"

What other options were there? To get to the US, I'd have to fly. Valetia didn't have its own airport, only a heliport, which meant I'd have to get to the international airport in Copenhagen, almost a hundred miles away by road.

"You think I should hijack a helicopter? Are you crazy?"

There. That was a definite eye-roll.

"You...know...what...to... do."

Oh.

Oh, right.

28

COLT

"What the heck is this?"

I sat up in bed on... Hell, I didn't know what day it was, nor was I certain whether it was morning or afternoon. The drapes were still closed, and time had all melded into one long, depressing sludge. Did Kiki want breakfast? I should make her breakfast. No. Wait. I'd already done that before I took her to the Snyders' place. Why were Brooke and Luca in my room? And Aaron? And was that Nico standing behind them with Meli? I squinted into the gloom. Yes. Yes, it was.

Shit.

Brooke put her hands on her hips. "This is an intervention."

"A what?"

Kiki darted past Brooke. "Daddy, you smell *really* bad."

"Have you even taken a shower this week?" Brooke asked.

"The docs said to keep the dressing on my shoulder dry."

Aaron took his sister's side. Traitor. "Well, buddy, you'd

better figure out something because otherwise Brooke says me and Luca have to give you a sponge bath, and trust me when I say that none of us wants to go down that road."

A subtle sniff told me the room did indeed smell funky, but what did it matter? I wasn't asking anyone to share it with me.

"Thanks for the concern, but I'm fine."

Meli tore the drapes open, and as I was blinking in the unexpected beam of sunlight, Brooke yanked the quilt off the bed. Thank fuck I was wearing boxers.

"You're not fine."

Nico wrinkled his nose in disgust. "Perhaps I should send a housekeeper over?"

"I don't need—"

"Believe me, you do."

"Just leave me alone."

Brooke tried again. Had they planned the tag-team act in advance? "You can't stay in bed forever."

"I don't intend to."

Only for another week or two. Maybe a month. Time healed, the past had taught me that, but time was going so damn slowly.

"You have a pile of unopened mail, your refrigerator has mould in it, and Kiki's bored."

Who cared about mail and mould? "Want to go to the beach, kiddo?"

"I want Brie to come with us."

"She's been saying that the whole week," Meli told me. "There's no chance...?"

None at all. Brie had up and disappeared. Vanished. Taken off without leaving a forwarding address. For the first few days, I'd clung to the hope that she'd call, but as the hours ticked by with no contact, I'd lost hope. Lost my heart.

Lost the will to do anything. Brie had moved on. I shouldn't have been surprised, now that I knew her big secret, but it still stung like hell. First Jacqueline, then Princess Gabrielle... My judgment was fucked.

Yesterday, I'd ordered a Fleshlight from the internet, and with a tumbler of whisky as my witness, I'd sworn off women for good.

"Brie's gone. Radio silence."

"Maybe she's just distracted," Brooke suggested. "Did you hear her father woke up from his coma?"

"Yeah."

I'd been checking the internet every night, some might even say obsessively so. Three days ago, King Magnus of Valetia had opened his eyes, and reporters had been camping outside the hospital ever since. They'd given me my first glimpse of Brie since the day of the shooting, silent and stony-faced as a team of bodyguards herded her inside to visit. I figured she'd look happier. A part of me was glad she didn't, but a bigger part felt shitty for even thinking that.

Her people had released a statement detailing an amicable split with Emmett, and members of the press were speculating that the break-up was the reason she was still upset. Plus there was interest in the abduction, although everyone was remaining tight-lipped about that.

"So maybe she'll get in touch when things settle down?"

"I doubt that. She doesn't care."

"She does," Luca said. "She called the hospital and paid your outstanding medical costs."

"Huh?"

"All the out-of-pocket expenses."

"How do you know that?"

"Because when Nico called to do the same, they told him the bill had already been settled."

"And they said it was Brie?"

Nico shrugged, hands in his pockets. "Technically, they weren't meant to tell me that, but I can be very charming when I want to be."

Meli giggled, even though she was married. Smooth, Nico. Real smooth. My head throbbed as I processed this latest piece of information.

"Thanks for trying to pay. You didn't need to do that."

Although I'd had no idea how I was going to pay the deductible myself.

"You got shot in the line of duty. It seemed the least I could do. I don't suppose there's any news on the one that got away? The sniper?"

Luca shook his head. "Not yet. No witnesses, no trace evidence, no clues whatsoever."

So they were still out there. "Can somebody pull those drapes closed?"

Luca did the honours, and Brooke turned on the overhead light instead. How much did bulletproof glass cost? The fact that there was a trigger-happy hunter meandering around in Baldwin's Shore made me more uncomfortable than I cared to admit.

"You should try getting in touch with Brie," Luca said. "Now that the dust's settled."

Was outright rejection better than assuming the worst? "Not sure that's a good idea."

"You know what I think?" Brooke asked. "I think her bodyguards hustled her out of town so fast she didn't have time to catch her breath. They were real assholes when they came to the house, especially the one who seemed to be in charge. Someone should tell them that politeness doesn't cost a cent."

"I don't think they get paid to be polite."

"Well, they should. Nonna always said you catch more flies with honey. And Luca's right—you should try calling Brie. She might be feeling guilty over you getting shot and that's why she hasn't called you."

"I can't call her. I don't have her number."

"So go and see her," Nico said, as if it were the most obvious thing in the world. Possibly in his world, it was.

"In case it's escaped your notice, Brie is a real-life princess. What do you expect me to do? Walk up to the palace and knock on the door?"

"Tsk-tsk-tsk. Always so negative. Brie is a working royal, and as such, she'll be attending events. All you have to do is find out where she'll be and show up. If she wants to speak to you, then she will."

"And how exactly do I find out where she'll be?"

Nico waved his phone at me. "It's on the royal family's website. One second... Yes, she'll be opening an art exhibition in Obodriti next week. That seems to be a town in Valetia."

"Which is on the other side of the world."

"In 1903, Wilbur and Orville Wright came up with a wonderful invention, which later evolved into what we in modern times call an 'airplane.'"

"Thanks for the history lesson."

"Don't mention it."

"We can look after Kiki," Meli offered. "You should follow your heart."

"What if it doesn't work out?"

"What if it does?" Brooke countered. "You have to try."

I let out a long sigh. As usual, she was right. Even if another rejection put a final nail through what was left of my heart, I had to try.

"How long will we be on the airplane?"

Five days later, I sat in the departure area at SeaTac with Kiki by my side. As with all good plans, ours had gone wrong right out of the gate when we realised the art exhibition wasn't some fancy affair with champagne and canapés and paintings of weird-coloured fruit, but rather a contest for kids with workshops from well-known artists and a prize-giving ceremony at the end. Not the kind of place a twenty-eight-year-old guy could hang out on his own without getting arrested.

Hence Kiki was coming too. Her first foreign vacation. I'd wanted to take her on a trip abroad last year, but the roof had sprung a leak and the repairs had to take priority, so we'd gone camping in Olympic National Park instead. Poor kid tripped over a tree root and learned the dangers of poison ivy first-hand, and now "camping" was a dirty word in our household.

"About thirteen hours, but we'll have a little break in Amsterdam in the middle."

"Hamsterdam? Will we see hamsters? Is that where they live?"

"No, but we might see tulips when we fly over."

The intervention had been very necessary. The whole house had smelled revolting, and once I'd cleaned up with the help of the others, I'd focused on the glimmer of hope I'd been offered. A chance to see Brie again. And if it all went wrong, Nico had offered a consolation prize. It turned out that the Peninsula wasn't the only resort he owned, and if things didn't work out with Brie, then Kiki and I had the option to take an all-expenses-paid vacation in England, France, or Croatia. The pain in my shoulder had subsided into a dull throb, and I had to be thankful for not only my friends but also the administrative leave that was allowing me to spend some quality time with my daughter.

Focus on the positive.

Hannah had said those words to me so many times, and I'd forgotten to listen to her wisdom.

"Tulips? Like flowers?" Kiki asked.

"Yes, and maybe windmills too. Keep your eyes peeled."

"When we find Brie, will we get to stay in a castle?"

"I don't know, kiddo."

"Does she have a crown?"

"Probably. You want an ice cream?"

"Yes!"

Kiki had spent the week making gifts for Brie, stringing beads with Brooke and painting with Meli and Sophie. Me? I was empty-handed. I had little to offer Brie apart from myself, but would it be enough?

Thirty-eight hours until the art exhibition. I was flying in a day early to allow for any delays, but that wouldn't give me time to adjust for jet lag or the amount of sleep I hadn't gotten over the past week. Was I being a fool for thinking Brie might want a nobody like me? Probably, but if I didn't make the trip, I'd spend the rest of my life regretting it.

One way or the other, I had to know.

29

GABRIELLE

"You've lost your freaking mind. Your mother's gonna flip, you know that, right?"

"I'm fully aware, and thanks for reminding me. How does my hair look?"

"Flick the sides forward a bit. Here, let me do it."

Phil adjusted my wig, and I did the same for hers, then I gave a twirl.

"Okay now?"

"As good as it's gonna get." She flung her arms around me dramatically. "I'm a dead woman walking."

"We're...all dead," Papa said from his bed.

Since negotiations with Mor had reached an impasse, I'd once again been forced to resort to drastic measures. And also eBay. The wigs had arrived yesterday, one auburn, one blonde, and although they weren't perfect when you got up close, they'd pass muster from a distance. I had to send thanks to Emmett because if it hadn't been for the aborted wedding, not only would I never have met Colt in the first place, but I also wouldn't have lost enough weight to fit into Phil's clothes. We'd switched outfits in Papa's en-suite bathroom, and if I sucked my stomach in, I could just about do up the trousers.

My voice was a little higher than hers, but since Malthe was new and I'd barely said two words to him, I was confident we could get away with the deception. Thanks to the time I'd spent at boarding school, my upper-class accent was on point.

"Wish me luck?"

"Break a leg," Phil said, and Papa groaned.

"Don't break...anything. Especially yourself."

He sounded stronger every day, and I leaned down to kiss him on the cheek as Phil took her position in the chair beside him. Fortunately, they'd always gotten along swimmingly. Phil's own father was a pompous ass who was now on his fourth wife—or was it the fifth?—and during school holidays, she'd spent more time in Valetia than at home. Papa had even taught her to sail, although she loved boats about as much as I loved horses. She flashed me one last grin and then turned away. Now if anyone glanced through the door, all they'd see was a blonde woman holding Papa's hand the way I always did.

I felt guilty about skipping the children's art exhibition tomorrow—especially as I'd enjoyed painting so much with Kiki—but Phil had promised to go in my place, provided of course she was still alive. And I'd make it up to the kids when I got back. Organise another workshop or invite a group to Vandenburg, something like that.

Now or never. I blew one last kiss, slung a bag containing a few essentials over my shoulder, tucked my head down, and pushed the door open.

"Ta-ta, chaps. Got to ride."

"Is Brie ready to leave?" Malthe asked as I headed along the corridor.

"She said something about watching a movie. You can probably take a coffee break."

"We're not allowed to do that."

I raised a hand and waved him out of my life. "Whatevs."

Slow and steady, Brie. Don't run. When I reached the front of the hospital and strolled right out the door, I could have cried with relief. I was free again. Free! But my problems were far from over. The harbour was a five-minute walk away, and there, the *Penguin* awaited.

My nemesis.

Her mast had broken in the accident, but after she'd been towed to shore, Jens had arranged for her to be repaired even though Mor had fought him all the way. She'd wanted the boat destroyed, and if not for her public image, she'd probably have headed down to the harbour with a sledgehammer herself.

These days, the *Penguin* was berthed between the *Hawk* and the *Kestrel*, a sixty-six-foot luxury yacht and an old wooden ketch we'd bought as a restoration project respectively, and she looked more like a hummingbird. Small and shiny. Delicate, with azure water rippling against her twin hulls.

The Royal Harbour nestled between two cliffs, and despite the name, anyone with enough money could join the waiting list to keep a boat there. Small, colourful cafés had sprung up along the promenade behind, and it featured in every guidebook as a tourist must-see. An Instagrammer's dream. I'd been watching the weather forecasts, waiting for the right conditions, and today the wind was blowing hard to the north, bringing a chill to an otherwise sunny day.

As I hurried down the steep stone steps towards the piers, I expected to see a crowd, but not this much of a crowd. Why were there so many people? They were six deep, lining the promenade while they took pictures and ate ice creams. I pushed my way past, focused on the single guard at the end of our private pier. He looked young, and I hoped that I was as unfamiliar to him as he was to me. An hour ago, I'd paved the way by calling the harbour office to let them know Phil would be passing by to collect a sweater I'd left on board the *Hawk* yesterday, but if the guard was feeling particularly conscientious this morning, my daring escape could be thwarted before it even began.

And then I saw him.

For fanden.

Why hadn't I paid more attention during those stupid family conferences? Jens was standing next to the new lifeboat with Elin at his side, ready to swing a bottle of champagne against the hull and give the naming speech. That was today? I could have sworn Mor said next week, but obviously I'd been wrong. Our gazes locked, and Jens did a double take. Shit! Should I run? Hide? Since he was intimately acquainted with Phil, there was no way I could fool him.

I edged towards the *Penguin*, heart pounding as I waited for Jens to signal to the bodyguards standing on either side of him. But the signal never came. Was he actually going to let me get away with this?

I thought the answer might possibly be yes, but then Elin looked in my direction, and I couldn't fool her either. Elin was an "act first, think later" kind of girl, and she opened her mouth on instinct, but before she could get a word out, Jens sidestepped and gave her a hard nudge. If there'd ever been any doubt that I loved my brother, it was all erased at that moment.

Later, he'd deny that he intended to push Elin right into the water, but whether he meant it or not, that was where she ended up. The splash was *glorious*. And of course, Jens had to play the hero and jump in after her. A collective gasp rose from the crowd, and then all hell let loose. I could have cartwheeled to the *Penguin* naked and nobody would have noticed, not even the pier guard, who'd grabbed a rope and run towards the lifeboat just in case.

The *Penguin* waited for me in all her malevolent beauty, sails begging to be unfurled. If I tried to reach Copenhagen by car, there were a multitude of potential obstacles— purloining a vehicle, getting past the checkpoint unnoticed, traffic jams, the Danish police, not to mention the bloody alternator failing. By sea, I had a clear run. In the *Penguin*, nothing short of a whale could stop me, and surely even I couldn't be that unlucky?

Five minutes later, we slid out of the harbour as Elin basked in the attention. She was shrieking, but it was a "woohoo, I'm famous" shriek rather than "help, I'm scared." And I felt like squealing myself once I reached the open sea. With joy. I couldn't deny that I was nervous too—who wouldn't be after capsizing so catastrophically?—but as the wind filled the sails and we began skimming over the water, I felt freer than I'd ever been. No companions, no chase boat, nobody at all between here and Copenhagen, and I was freaking flying. *Penguin*. I snort-laughed to myself as we headed north at something approaching top speed. This boat wasn't a penguin; it was the love child of a swan and a falcon.

"It's a tiara," I explained to the security agent at Copenhagen Airport. "There's nothing illegal about a tiara."

And before you judge, it was a gift for Kiki, okay? I never

wore the thing, and once she was done playing with it, she could sell it to pay for college. At least, she could if some jobsworth stopped prodding it.

He called a colleague over, and the new guy also studied the ends of the band. *For goodness' sake.* If I could kill someone using a tiara, then the chances were that I could also kill someone with my bare hands, so we were all wasting our time here. As I waited, I developed a new-found appreciation for private jets.

Until now, the trip had gone without incident. A friend of Phil's from the horsey world had met me at his family's beachfront villa and helped me to tie the *Penguin* up to the jetty there, and then he'd given me a ride to the airport. A good guy, Phil had said, too bad he was gay. Then I'd collected my boarding pass from the machine without any alarms or flashbulbs going off. To be honest, I hadn't been expecting any issues there. I'd used Phil's credit card for the booking, and who knew my surname anyway? To the world, I was Princess Gabrielle, not Gaby Westerburg von Lindegren, or sometimes Princess Piggy or Princess Potato or Princess Pudding if the gossip rags were involved.

Finally, the agent handed back the tiara and motioned for me to take off my shoes. Ugh, this was horrible. Did people really have to do this every time they flew?

"Put your belt in the box too."

Was he kidding? If I took the belt off, the top button of Phil's trousers would go with it. I sucked in a breath, held it, and nearly passed out by the time I got to the other side of the scanner.

An hour to go until my flight took off. I had to travel to Seattle, then take a taxi to Baldwin's Shore, which would also be a new experience for me. Phil assured me it wasn't that difficult. But this was the same Phil who'd promised karaoke was fun, and that had turned out to be a big fat lie.

A kiosk near the gate sold magazines and snacks, and I bought a bottle of water plus the half-dozen magazines that featured me on the cover. Those went straight into the trash, and I found a seat in a quiet corner to wait. And wait. Why was the damn plane delayed? I opened a news app to see if there was an update, only to find a video of a dripping Elin bowing to the media before swigging from Jens's bottle of champagne. Good grief. Mor was going to have kittens.

My phone buzzed in my hand, and I upgraded the kittens to baby Godzillas.

PHIL

SOS

My world stopped, *dead*. In Phil-speak, "SOS" stood for "Shit Oh Shit."

I'd been rumbled.

The first thing I did was turn off my phone. Should I try hiding in the bathroom? Would that help? Probably not, and knowing my luck, I'd miss the flight entirely. The only thing I could do was scrunch up small and hope. I wasn't religious, but I said a prayer to cover all bases and then crossed my fingers.

Would it be enough?

Would it?

It wasn't enough.

I was on the verge of a coronary when I spotted Malthe shouldering his way through the milling crowd, followed by the rest of the goon squad and a bunch of airport officials. My eyes prickled.

Why?

Why, why, why?

Malthe stopped three feet away from me, and when he beckoned, I couldn't make a fuss. Not unless I wanted even more column inches. I had no choice but to follow him through the terminal, trying to hold back tears.

So near, yet so damn far.

Would I get another chance? Probably not. The palace was about to become a very posh prison, and I wasn't even sure I'd be allowed the obligatory phone call. What about visitors? Would I get visitors? How about a new hashtag?

#FreePrincessG?

#FreePrincessBrie?

Even #FreePrincessPiggy would have been better than nothing.

A modern-day fucking fairy tale.

"*C*an I ride on the carousel again? Pleeeeeeeease?"

"Kiki, calm down and hold my arm."

It wasn't a fairground carousel, it was a baggage conveyor, and we'd nearly been hauled off by security. Luckily, the guy happened to have a daughter Kiki's age, and between that and my sling, I'd gotten the sympathy vote.

"Can we see the mermaid? Meli said there was a mermaid."

"Maybe later in the week, okay? We need to find our hotel and get some sleep today."

If Brie was at the art exhibition tomorrow, I needed to be awake to see her, although I wasn't certain she'd show up. When I'd checked the website after we landed, I noticed a "TBC" had appeared after the engagement, and that hadn't been there when we left Seattle. Was Brie pulling out? If she did, what the hell was I meant to do next?

"Can I have chips?"

"We can have dinner when we get to the hotel."

"Dinner? But it feels more like breakfast."

I'd tried explaining time zones twice already, but it was a

difficult concept for Kiki to grasp. I was about to make one more attempt when she wriggled free of my grasp.

"Briiiiiiiiiiiiiiie!"

Ever had a moment when you want to sink through the floor? Welcome to life as a parent.

"Kiki, shhh."

I took off after her, then stopped short. What the...?

A redhead was staring in my direction, and a second later, she started running too. One of the Secret Service wannabes behind made a grab for her, but they were left holding the red hair, and holy shit, it *was* Brie.

Kiki tripped over a guy's foot and splattered across the tiles, and there was blood, and then Brie was on her knees and we were all on the floor and I didn't know what the fuck was going on.

"Don't just stand there—find tissues," she snapped at the ninja behind her. The man had an arrogant set to his mouth, almost a sneer, and I recognised the Valetian royal crest on the breast of his jacket. "Find a doctor. Kiki, are you okay?"

I checked out the damage. Looked like a nosebleed, which wasn't entirely unheard of for Kiki. She got them from time to time when she was messing around in the yard, and it always looked as if there'd been a massacre.

"Lean forward and pinch your nose, remember?" I told her.

"It hurts."

"Yeah, I can see that."

Tissues magically appeared, and I cleaned up the mess as best I could. At least Kiki wasn't crying. She was trying to hug Brie instead, and fuck, could this have gone any worse?

"You okay?" I touched Brie on the arm, and she looked up at me with those big blue eyes.

"I-I don't know. That kind of depends on you. Why are you here, Colt?"

"You have this art gallery thing tomorrow? Or are you flying somewhere?"

Her wild giggle sounded more hysterical than happy. "Well, I was trying to get to Baldwin's Shore, but my plans were foiled."

"You were coming back to Oregon?"

"I wanted to apologise. For not telling you exactly who I was, for getting kidnapped, for you getting shot, for everything."

"Getting kidnapped was hardly your fault, princess." The endearment slipped from my lips, and it was my turn to choke out a laugh. "*Princess*. You must've thought I was dumb as a box of rocks."

"No, not at all. I thought it was sweet. Nobody's ever given me a nickname before. Not a nice one, anyway."

I wanted to take whoever had come up with "Princess Piggy" and feed them to the damn hogs.

"So, you really are a princess, huh?"

"Unfortunately."

The head ninja behind her cleared his throat, and she extended one delicate finger and flipped him the bird. If I wasn't hopelessly in love with Brie already, that would have sealed the deal.

"Being a princess isn't a good thing?"

"It's the pits. Honestly. When I heard you didn't want to see me anymore, it hit so hard, even though I knew I deserved it, and all I wanted to do was meet you face to face, to explain and say how sorry I was, but that got vetoed and I had to escape from the hospital in a freaking disguise and sail across the Sound to get here. And still they caught up with me."

That...that was insane, but at the same time, I was in awe of this woman. I didn't know what or where the Sound was, but if she'd gotten in a boat again despite her fears, then that was a big fucking deal.

But what was that bullshit at the beginning?

"Where did you get the idea that I didn't want to see you?"

"From Aksel."

"Who's Aksel?"

"Malthe's predecessor." She tipped her head at the ninja hovering over her. "He got fired."

"Good, because I didn't tell Aksel that. I never even met the guy."

"But...but he said... What were his words? He said that he'd sent Soren to find you, but you expressed no desire to see me."

"Yeah, well, that was probably because I was unconscious. By the time whatever the docs gave me wore off, you'd gone."

"I don't know where Aksel is right now, but when I find out, I'd very much like to kick him in the nuts."

Brie said it so primly, so sweetly, that it took a few seconds to register. I had to chuckle. That was my princess.

"I'll hold him down for you."

"So is there... Do you think we might have a chance? To be together, I mean. As I'm sure you can imagine, relationships are quite tricky for me, and I don't exactly have a great track record, but I'd give anything to try again. If you're willing, that is."

"Princess, I love you. I figured I'd tell you in some big romantic gesture, not on an airport floor, but I guess it didn't work out that way."

"I don't think we're meant for big romantic gestures. It's the little things that count. Like this."

She crawled forward and pressed her lips to mine, and it was only when the crowd cheered that I realised just how much of an audience we had. And most of them seemed to have camera phones. Sheesh.

"Daddy, that's yucky," Kiki mumbled through her tissue. "Stop sucking Brie's face."

"Sorry, kiddo."

"Don't call me that. If Brie's a princess and she's going to be my new mommy, does that mean I get to be a princess too?"

Nice, Kiki, way to scare off Brie completely.

But Brie only smiled. "I'm not certain of the rules in regard to that, but I did bring you a little gift."

Next thing I knew, Kiki was wearing a tiara. A fucking tiara, and it didn't look like paste.

"Is that thing real? I mean, the stones?"

"I should imagine so. It was a gift for my sixteenth birthday, but I've never worn it much, and I thought Kiki might get some enjoyment out of it."

"Enjoyment? She'll get mugged."

"That's what the bodyguards are for."

"Your Highness, we need to leave," the head ninja told her.

"Fine. We'll leave. All of us. Together. One of you can bring Colt's suitcase."

"I'm not sure Her Majesty will be happy about this."

"What's new? She's never happy. I presume you brought a vehicle, so how about you go and fetch it?"

The crowds parted as we headed for the exit, but I kept my good arm around Brie in case anyone tried to push forward. Kiki gripped Brie's shirt with one hand and held the tiara on with the other. We'd flown to Scandinavia, but what we'd landed in was a whole different world, and at this moment in time, I had no idea just how hostile the rest of the natives might be.

But I had Brie. And if I had Brie, then everything else we could work through together.

31

GABRIELLE

*A*s a teenager, I'd become all too familiar with the headmistress's study at school. It lay at the end of a wood-panelled hallway, and the brass plaque on the imposing door was always perfectly polished. Rumour said the headmistress's name was Cynthia, but I never heard her use it, and even her husband called her Dr. Crumpton. Papa had once confessed that she made him very nervous.

Dr. Crumpton had three hard chairs lined up in the hallway outside her study, and I used to break out in a cold sweat every time I sat in one, waiting for the inevitable bollocking. It wasn't that I deliberately set out to misbehave, but things just went wrong. Like the time somebody—and I never found out who—switched my bottle of ethanol for water, which I then squirted onto a piece of sodium, which accidentally set fire to the chemistry lab. Papa had paid for the damage, but I still had detention for a month.

Today, as I sat with Colt, Jens, and Elin in the room where Mor liked to hold our family conferences, I was transported back to my school days. The only thing missing was Phil. Nine times out of ten, she'd been sitting outside Dr. Crumpton's study with me, but today she'd disappeared.

"Uh-oh," Elin said. "I hear her."

The *click, click, click* of heels on tile got closer, and sweat beaded on the back of my neck. Colt squeezed my hand, and warmth spread through me from his support. This obviously wasn't the ideal way for him to meet my mother, but when I'd suggested he wait in my quarters, he'd just muttered, "For better, for worse," and wrapped an arm around my waist. At least Kiki had managed to escape. She was busy charming the butler in one of the drawing rooms.

Mor swept in and took her place on the other side of the table. Her secretary followed, a portly little man whose shirt buttons were working overtime. Unlike Siri, he preferred to print everything out, and this afternoon, he carried a thick wedge of papers under his arm.

Shit.

Mor studied Colt from her throne, sizing him up the way a boxer eyed an opponent. I only hoped the sling on his arm might invite mercy.

"Mor, this is Colt."

"Colt. My daughter seems to have gone quite gaga over you."

"The feeling's mutual, ma'am."

"The correct term is 'Your Majesty.' Has nobody schooled you in etiquette?"

Dying seemed like an attractive option right now. Why did parents always have to embarrass their children? Did they teach it in prenatal classes?

"Apologies, Your Majesty."

"Does it really matter?" I muttered.

"Gabrielle, please don't try me, not today. What were you thinking?"

"What was I thinking? I was thinking that I'm in love, and I wanted to see the man I'm in love with." Colt gripped my hand tighter, and I realised that in all the commotion earlier, I'd forgotten to tell him that part. I really was terrible at this relationship stuff. "What else was I meant to do? Send him an email?"

"You sailed thirty miles, alone, in that deathtrap of a boat. Have you lost your mind?"

According to Phil, yes, but that wasn't the point. "The *Penguin* isn't a deathtrap."

"It nearly killed your father."

"Technically, that was a whale," Jens said, and Mor turned her icy gaze on him.

"And you! How on earth did you manage to fall into the harbour at a boat-naming ceremony?"

"I was assisting Elin."

"And how did Elin end up in the water?"

Elin folded her arms, and her expression turned sulky. "I slipped."

What had Jens bribed her with to get her to say that? I had no idea, but it was worth every penny.

Mor pressed her lips into such a thin line that they almost disappeared. "Gerhard, what's the damage?"

Damage. She made it sound as if we'd destroyed the world. The only actual injury had been to Kiki's nose, and that had stopped bleeding after a minute or two. I'd arranged for a doctor to check her, just in case, but nothing was broken, thank goodness.

Gerhard shuffled his papers and prepared to deliver the bad news. "Clearly, we had some concerns with Elin this morning when it appeared she'd decided to follow in Gabrielle's footsteps—Elin, you mustn't let alcohol pass your lips until you're eighteen unless you're in Germany, and even then it's recommended that you stick to local products and only if the event calls for it. But thankfully, Elin's faux pas got overshadowed by Gabrielle's fracas at the airport."

Elin glowered, and I knew it was because she'd trended on social media for less than an hour before #RunawayPrincess shot up the list. I couldn't bear to look at the details myself, but Jens had told me.

"And really," Gerhard continued, "this was a surprise to all of us. Not that Gabrielle would do something so utterly reckless, but the way the public has reacted to her display of...well, I don't know what to call it—on the floor of Terminal Three. People seem utterly charmed. They're calling it a modern-day fairy tale, and of course the media wants to know who the child and the man with the injured arm are."

"As do we all." Mor turned to Colt. "So, who are you?"

"I'm the man who's in love with your daughter."

Holy shamoli. I melted. Freaking melted against Colt, and he wrapped his uninjured arm around my shoulders. Jens smiled, and even Elin didn't look quite so annoyed.

"That doesn't answer my question."

"My name is Colton Haines, Your Majesty. I'm a sheriff's deputy in Baldwin's Shore."

"I see. According to Philomena, you rescued Gabrielle after she had the misfortune to be abducted?"

"I was involved, yes."

"And how did you go from there to cavorting with my daughter on an airport floor?"

That was enough. "We were not cavorting! Kiki tripped over, and we were helping her."

"Kiki." Mor said the name as if it left a bad taste in her mouth. "Your child?" she asked Colt.

"Mine and my late wife's."

Mor froze for the tiniest second, and I knew she'd been expecting a divorce. "I'm very sorry for your loss."

"Appreciated."

"So, why are you here?"

"I came to see Brie."

"Yes, I gathered that. And what are your intentions towards my daughter?"

Colt turned, and when our gazes met, the heat in his told me my mother absolutely didn't want to hear his answer.

"We want to spend some time together," I told her.

The tension in her jaw said she wasn't keen on the idea, but she nodded once. "I'll have the staff arrange a guest room."

"There's no need. Colt can stay in my quarters."

"That's not in line with protocol."

Screw protocol. "Then I guess I'll be breaking yet another rule. And I also want part of our time together to be spent in Baldwin's Shore."

"Baldwin's Shore? Out of the question."

"Why? I lived in the US part-time for the last three years. You didn't have a problem with me staying when I was going to marry Emmett."

"That was different."

"Why?" I stood up and leaned over the table. "Because Emmett's rich? Because his parents move in the right circles?"

"Gabrielle, you have no idea what you're talking about."

"Then what? I'm sick of double standards. I'm sick of being a prisoner in my own home. I'm sick of being followed by a bunch of ghouls I can't stand, and I'm sick of having less freedom than a convicted bloody criminal."

"I've already had Malthe reassigned."

"That wasn't my point and you know it. We can't go on like this."

"You have—"

Mor had barely uttered two words before the door opened, and when I saw who was there, I sat down. In shock.

"Brie's right. We can't go on...like this."

Phil pushed Papa into the room and kicked the door closed behind them. He'd dressed for the occasion in slacks and a wool sweater that swamped his frail frame, but his eyes showed his old strength. How I'd missed that strength. Once Phil had settled him into his rightful place at the head of the table, she ignored the chair Jens had pulled out for her, gave him a filthy look, and went to sit on the other side of Elin. Uh-oh.

Mor goldfished for a moment and then found her voice.

"Magnus, you should be in the hospital."

"I've been in the hospital for three...damn years. I'm sick of being in the hospital."

"What if there's a problem? A complication?"

"There's a doctor outside and...an ambulance in the courtyard." He turned to face Colt and held one hand out, supported by his elbow on the arm of the wheelchair. "So, you're the man who's captured my daughter's heart. I'd come over to shake hands, but..."

Colt rose right away and offered a hand of his own. "Colt Haines. It's good to meet you, Your Majesty."

"Call me Magnus. Brie, how was the trip across the Sound? Did the *Penguin* behave herself?"

"The sea was a little rough, but the wind was with me and the *Penguin* flew."

"Penguins can't fly," Elin said, and Phil smacked her playfully on the head. "Ow."

"It's called a metaphor."

"I hear you took an unexpected swim, my girl? Bet that livened things up a bit."

"Don't encourage her," Mor scolded.

"Klara, I still remember the time you snuck out of a hotel on Mustique to go skinny-dipping at midnight."

Mor gasped, and her perfectly applied make-up did nothing to hide her blush. "That was a very long time ago."

"Almost another lifetime, it seems. I had an accident, and the only thing that died was your sense of adventure. What am I hearing about you trying to clip Brie's wings?"

"She wants to move to America with a man she barely knows."

"Which, I imagine, is nothing like you moving here from Finland to marry a man you barely knew?"

"Our parents knew each other."

"So invite the man's parents over for dinner and talk to them."

No. *No, no, no.* Mor was looking in Papa's direction, and I made a frantic cutting motion across my throat. Thankfully, he got the message.

"Or not." Phew. "Why not trust Brie to make her own decisions?"

"Because once again today, she demonstrated how little regard she has for her personal safety."

"Are you talking about the sailing part? Or the part where she gave her bodyguards the slip again?"

Mor threw up her hands. "All of it!"

"So what's your plan now? Order a giant roll of cotton wool and wrap her up in it?"

"If that's what it takes to keep my family safe."

"You don't think that might suffocate her?" Mor's face

crumpled, and Papa motioned to Gerhard. "Please, leave us."

He backed out of the room without another word. Papa was still king, after all.

"I just... I just don't want to lose anybody." Mor's voice cracked, and despite our difficulties, I couldn't help but feel sorry for her.

"If you love somebody, you set them free. Give Brie her wings, and she'll come back. Chop them off, and she'll forever be trying to fly away."

"But the danger..."

"Clearly, there will have to be compromises. Brie will need bodyguards, competent ones, but she should have a hand in their selection. And I share your worries about recent events. Siri's involvement and this sniper are of particular concern."

"Sir, uh, Magnus, we don't believe Ms. Froberg was involved in Brie's abduction."

She wasn't? I mean, I'd hoped that was the case, but how did Colt know?

"Could you explain?"

"Luca, uh, Deputy Mendez called me right before I left SeaTac to say that Dayton Brinkley has finally followed in his brother's footsteps and begun talking. He gifted the car that Brie borrowed to Ms. Froberg, and unbeknown to her, he'd arranged for an anti-theft tracker to be installed. When he found out Brie was taking some time to herself, he simply had the tracker activated and his brother followed her right to my door."

My goodness. I pictured the Audi, sitting where I'd parked it—badly—outside Colt's front window. A ticking time bomb. *I'd* been the one who told my kidnappers where I was.

"You think he's telling the truth?"

"I haven't spoken to either of the Brinkley brothers myself, but the explanation seems plausible."

Papa nodded. "And the sniper?"

"There's been no progress on that."

"Then we'll have to monitor the situation carefully. Colt, you were there—what's your honest opinion? Is the sniper a threat to my daughter?"

"Can't deny it shook me up, but the more I think about it, the more I'd have to say no. There was only one shot. Whoever pulled the trigger could have taken Brie out that day—could've taken all of us out—but they chose not to."

I still had nightmares about it. I'd seen Reagan's head explode a hundred times in my dreams. But Colt was right —the sniper had spared us. For whatever reason, he'd wanted us alive.

"Then it seems likely that we can achieve a threat level in Baldwin's Shore that we're all comfortable with."

"But—" Mor started.

"I'm not suggesting Brie boards a plane today."

"Does that mean I can go in the future?"

"Once we have arrangements in place. There's also the matter of royal duties. Whether we like it or not, I'm still a king and you're still a princess. And what do crowns mean?"

"Commitments." It was an old joke of ours. "I used to fly back once a month when I was with Emmett. It wasn't a problem."

"Is it a problem for you, Colt?"

"I understand Brie has a job to do, and I'll always support that."

"Good. So we're agreed on that point. Klara?"

"I'm not sure about this."

"Valetia is twenty-one miles long. How many

engagements can there be that require our attendance? You, Jens, and Brie can split the work. At some point, I'll be able to join you again, and Elin's getting old enough to take her share of the load."

"When can I start going to the parties?" Elin asked. "I've been waiting my whole life to go to the parties."

"When you're old enough to drink legally. Our constitution says that there must be a monarch in Valetia at all times, either myself or the queen, or one of our children acting as regent. That's our baseline. Other work and time off can be scheduled around that." Papa broke into a grin, a proper grin, and I hadn't seen that for a long time. "Klara, how do you feel about a vacation?"

"I—"

"Just say yes."

"Yes?"

"So, do we have agreement?"

I nodded because it was the best deal I could hope for. It meant I could have a life with Colt and Kiki as well as the new friends I'd made in Baldwin's Shore. And in truth, I did enjoy some of the engagements, especially when I got to work with children. Jens and Elin nodded. Then finally, finally, Mor acquiesced too.

Phil shrugged. "Don't mind me. I'm just here for the entertainment."

32

COLT

*C*ompromise.

An interesting word when it came from the mouth of a king.

A fucking *king*.

I was dating a princess, and it was official because everyone on social media said so. Brie seemed to be taking it in her stride while I pinched myself every morning I woke up beside her. Shit like this didn't happen to assholes like me.

Except it had.

A week after the airport incident, the memes were everywhere, but we found ourselves back in Baldwin's Shore.

Compromising.

Compromising meant Brie wasn't allowed to live in my house at the moment. The rear was too open, the walls too thin, the neighbours too close. Members of Brie's new security team—which was actually her old, pre-accident security team—were currently assessing every vacant property in town to work out which one would be suitable for her to buy, and while they did whatever it was that royal protection agents did, we were staying in the aptly named Royal Suite at the Peninsula. Plum velvet drapes skimmed a plush gold carpet, and in the seating area, three navy-blue couches clustered around a marble-topped coffee table that faced floor-to-ceiling windows with a view of Turtle Rock. We had a terrace. A hot tub. A private garden area. Unless the paparazzi borrowed a boat, they couldn't see in, and the bodyguards kept an eye on the ocean. Kiki had her own double bedroom with an en suite. The master bedroom had space for two more couches plus a walk-in closet. Even the master bathroom had an armchair next to the tub—my new favourite place to sit—and the kitchen looked as if it had never been used.

Brie had apologised for us having to stay there.

Apologised.

The suite was bigger than my damn house, and I'd balked at the cost initially, but then Brie told me how much her family was worth and once I'd picked my jaw up off the floor, I packed a suitcase.

"Don't worry; Nico's giving us mate's rates," Brie had told me.

Of course he was. They'd become quite pally now, despite the results of her security team's background check. Nico had a dark past. Or at least, his father did before he got assassinated. Lev Belinsky had been a shady Russian oligarch whose tentacles had stretched deep into the oil and gas industry until he was found dead in bed one night. A single stab wound to the heart, and the guards stationed inside his house hadn't noticed a thing until it was too late. Nor had twenty-year-old Nico, who'd been asleep in the next room.

Brie had choked up when she found out. She'd wanted

to give him a hug and tell him how sorry she was, but we had to respect his privacy.

If he hadn't told us, we weren't supposed to know.

There'd been concern that Nico might have followed in his father's footsteps in some areas at least, and certainly a number of Lev's competitors had shown up dead in the years after his untimely demise, but as far as Brie's people could ascertain, Nico had simply taken the man's money and run. First to London, then to Paris, and finally to the United States. His empire centred around the leisure industry, not fossil fuels or organised crime, and on the surface at least, he'd kept his nose clean in the twelve years since he left his mother country. After breaking up with a girlfriend in Los Angeles, he'd begun spending more time in Baldwin's Shore.

And Nico wasn't the only person in town with a skeleton in their closet. Turned out the car accident that had killed Sara Baldwin's parents wasn't quite as much of an accident as we'd been led to believe. As well as the usual dings, dents, and scratches caused by a vehicle tumbling down an embankment, her mother had a bullet wound to the head. Nine-year-old Sara had been found hours later, sobbing in the back seat, terrified but alive. Fuck knew where Brie's people had dug up the information, but the report came with a "TOP SECRET" stamp across the top. According to a footnote, Sara claimed she couldn't remember a thing.

I only hoped that was true.

So there we were. Camping out in a luxury oceanfront villa with twenty-four-hour room service, a killer view, and a butler. Midday, and I pinched myself again.

"Honey, I'm home." Brie bounced through the door with a Cheshire cat grin on her face. "Well, home-ish."

"'Honey, I've entered the hotel suite' doesn't have the

same ring, huh?" I hooked one arm around her waist as she pressed against me. She'd gone for the casual look today— jeans with a plaid shirt and cowboy boots. "Good lunch?"

When Brooke had asked Brie if she wanted to meet up for lunch at the coffee house someday, Brie had jumped at the chance. Now that I knew her better, now that I'd spent time around her family and seen their weird dynamic first-hand, I understood why she placed so much importance on life's simple pleasures.

And on friendship.

"Lunch was glorious. When we have an oven, I want to learn how to bake cakes. Brooke said she'd teach me, and so did Mary from the coffee house after the laugh we gave her today."

"Should I be looking for a new social media hashtag?"

"No, no, nothing that exciting. We were waiting to be seated when a blonde woman cut in front of us, so Brooke pointed out there was a line, and the woman said, 'Who do you think you are? Royalty?' So *I* said, 'Well, actually...' and *then* she recognised me and ran right out of the shop. Brooke said she was one of those awful Baldwin people. Don't you think it's a little pretentious, naming a town after yourself? Even my family didn't manage that."

"Did I tell you how much I love you?"

"Many times, but I'll never get sick of hearing it."

I leaned in to kiss her, and her lips parted on a moan. Making it here hadn't been easy, but in this place, at this point in time, Brie was the woman I was meant to be with. And my cock agreed with that assessment. I was half-hard already, and as Brie's tongue swept into my mouth, I turned to rock in an instant.

"Do we have time for this?" she murmured.

"Kiki isn't due back from school for an hour."

Meli was picking her up. It was an arrangement that had always worked well for us, and none of us saw a reason to change Kiki's routine for the new school term. She had enough to cope with already. Like life in the spotlight and a whole new family. Brie was helping Kiki to adjust, and so were her parents. Even Klara—we'd graduated from calling her "Your Majesty" now. I had no doubt she could be a bitch when the mood took her, but the other day, I'd walked into the palace's smaller dining room to find her eating fancy cakes with Kiki, going through each type of cutlery and teaching her how to use it. She was doing her best in her own way, and I had to be grateful for that.

I reached for Brie's shirt, cursing the sling for the hundredth time that day. The doctor was pleased with the way my shoulder was healing, but it had a ways to go yet, and the injury still hurt more than I cared to let on.

But I'd mastered one-handed buttons, and Brie let the shirt slide down her arms, revealing perfect breasts spilling over satin cups. Expensive lingerie was one of the few things Brie liked to splurge on—when she wasn't stealing my underwear anyway—and I had no complaints.

"Bedroom?" she asked, breathless.

"Yeah."

Too damn right.

33

GABRIELLE

*T*he backs of my knees hit the bed, but before I fell onto it, I needed to get Colt's shirt off. Easier said than done when he was wearing a sling, but I'd come to realise that there were few sights quite as delicious as a tanned six-pack, and passing up any opportunity to lick it would have been a crime.

"Could you just...lift your arm? Yes, perfect."

He *was* perfect.

Every last inch of him, and he had plenty of those. But quite apart from the magic cock, Colt had slotted into my life like a puzzle piece that had been missing for so long, the key to my soul. He accepted me for who I was, and all the baggage that came with being Princess Gabrielle.

I scooched up the bed, the sheets cool under my back, and Colt followed, covering me, allowing his weight to press me into the mattress. Two months ago, I'd felt trapped, cornered like a wild animal, and today I was still trapped, but in a very different way.

Colt made me feel beautiful. Wanted. Desired. When he looked at me with such heat in his gaze, those brown eyes blazing like coal in a fire, I wanted to be pinned under him forever.

"I love you," I blurted, as had become my habit at every possible moment.

"Love you too, princess." He caressed my breasts, gently massaging each in turn with talented fingers. "And I especially love these."

"You're such a *man*."

"Under the circumstances, is that a good thing or a bad thing?"

"Definitely a good thing."

He swapped his thumb for his tongue, and I swapped words for incoherent mumbles as he kissed his way down hot, damp skin. All the way down, and when his head sank between my thighs, my legs fell open and I gave in to his charms. If I'd learned one thing about Colton Haines, it was that he was a giver. He gave kindness, he gave happiness, and he sure as hell gave incredible orgasms. I arched off the bed as the flames tore through me, muffling my cries with a hand because although the villa was reasonably private, there were likely still guests within screaming distance.

"My goodness," I managed once I could speak again.

"My princess."

"Yours."

"*Mine.*"

I tangled my fingers in his hair and dragged his mouth up to mine. Tasted myself on his kisses. I'd always be his. I'd give him myself, I'd give him anything, although he often seemed reluctant and almost embarrassed to accept. Grinning like a lunatic, I wrapped my fingers around his cock and stroked my thumb over the head as his abs braced.

"And this is mine."

"Where would you like it, princess?"

"Where it belongs."

I guided him inside me, sending a silent thank-you to the physician at the palace who'd quietly prescribed me oral contraceptives without making a fuss. More children were in our future—we'd had the big talk—but for now, we just wanted to enjoy each other. I'd never tire of this, of the blissful feeling of fullness as our bodies joined. Of the way he rolled his hips to hit exactly the right spot.

Thrust after thrust, and that exquisite tension rippled through my core, wave after wave before Colt sent me spiralling over the edge again. His warmth filled me, and when he rolled us so I was on top, I buried my face against his chest, careful to avoid pressing on his sore shoulder. He'd been cleared of any wrongdoing in the shooting now—aided, I suspected, by his elevation to hero status when the media realised what he'd done—but he was still on sick leave. I couldn't complain about that.

"Is now a good time to tell you that I have news?" I asked, not wanting to spoil the moment but unable to keep it to myself any longer.

"Good news?"

"Yes. I mean, I hope so. Kasper may have found us a place to live."

"A house? Here?"

"Not exactly. It's more of a piece of land. There's an old paper factory on the outskirts of town, quite derelict, but the plot's a good size and Kasper likes the location."

"You want to build a house?"

"I know it might take a bit longer than we'd planned, but we could design it exactly the way we want it. Really make it ours."

"You realise if we go down that road, Kiki's gonna want a swimming pool? Probably a stable for a pony too."

Ah, yes. A pony. Phil had a lot to answer for.

"That all sounds perfectly doable."

Colt sighed a long, "Fuuuuuck."

My heart sank. "You hate the idea?"

"No, I just can't believe this is my life now. Talking about swimming pools and ponies as if that's normal. You're sure you can afford this?"

"Yes."

My family's wealth had brought me grief for my entire life, and it would be nice to use it for something I'd actually enjoy. A real home. And in time, I hoped to give back to Baldwin's Shore too, by funding local projects and maybe with volunteer work. I didn't want to hide away in an ivory tower; I wanted to be a part of the community.

"Then if you're happy, I'm happy." Colt paused, cradling my cheek in his hand. "I have news too, but I'm not sure you're gonna like it."

"Oh?"

"My tech buddy recovered part of the data from your phone."

Colt was right—I didn't like that news, not one little bit. But I was also glad he'd told me.

"The video?"

"The video, some pictures, contact data... You knew I'd work out who you were from that, didn't you?"

"I didn't plan on keeping it a secret forever. Just...just long enough to work out a way to tell you that wouldn't involve you kicking me to the kerb."

"That was never gonna happen. Took me less than a week to see the kind of person you are, and I liked what I saw."

If only I'd been able to see clearly back then too. But so

often, insecurities shouted their presence while confidence stayed silent in the background.

"You liked me at a time when I didn't much like myself."

"And that's why we make such a good team. Do you want to watch the video? If you'd prefer, I can destroy it."

"What would you do?"

"Me? I'd rather know what we're up against. As Roosevelt once said, 'In the long run, the most unpleasant truth is a safer companion than a pleasant falsehood.'"

"Then I suppose I should get dressed."

And also order a bottle of wine or perhaps something stronger. I had no desire to see Vania's perky boobs or Emmet's naked ass again, but at least this time around, it wouldn't hurt so much. How could it when their deception had led me to Colt?

I was about to roll out of bed when his phone rang, and from the way he tensed, it wasn't a call he wanted to answer. As a wannabe stepmom, I felt instant panic.

"Kiki?" I whispered. "Is something wrong?"

"It's my mom."

Oh. Wow.

"Are you going to answer?"

"No."

He got up and tugged on a pair of sweatpants, his movements jerky. The phone stopped ringing, and I waited with my heart in my throat in case she tried calling again. She didn't, but a minute later, I heard the telltale *ping* of a voicemail. I tensed for a moment. So did Colt, but then he pulled on a T-shirt and walked out into the sitting area.

What did his mother want?

Hadn't she hurt him enough already?

"Still sure about this?" Colt asked, his finger hovering over the "play" button on his laptop.

"Do it."

Kiki was asleep, and I'd fortified myself with red wine and chocolate. It was now or never.

On-screen, Vania straddled Emmett, her head thrown back, breasts jiggling as he urged her on. He never had been one for doing the work. Bile burned in my throat, but I forced myself to swallow it down and focus on the surroundings. The pale peach walls. The edge of the chandelier at the top of the shot. The view of the sea from the windows. Wait. The sea? Emmett's house didn't have a view of the sea, and neither did Vania's apartment.

"That absolute bastard!"

Colt squeezed my shoulder, offering comfort. "You recognise the place?"

"That's the beach house! The bloody beach house where we were meant to get married."

The tryst probably happened when I went for a walk with Siri and the goon squad to settle my nerves. Emmett and Vania must have waited all of thirty seconds before they started ripping each other's clothes off. Now that I thought hard about it, I recalled Emmett's face being slightly flushed when we got back, but I'd put it down to a case of mild sunburn.

"That's good."

"How is it good? It's *awful*. I was so freaking stupid not to see it."

Dammit, I needed more wine. I reached across the dining table, snagged the bottle, and poured the remainder down my throat. At a time like this, who cared about a glass?

"It's good because it narrows the suspect list. How many people were at the beach house with you?"

"Uh... Uh... Not many? On that day, just Siri, Emmett's assistant, my security team, and the wedding party. Oh, and Phil. The stylists didn't arrive until the following day."

"Phil wasn't in the wedding party?"

"Weddings freak Phil out. I'd never inflict bridesmaid duty on her."

"Hmm."

"What does 'hmm' mean?"

"It means I can see Phil having the balls to record Emmett and Vania."

"That I'd agree with, but it wasn't Phil. She'd just have told me without all the subterfuge."

"You're sure about that?"

"Positive."

She'd have sat me down with a stiff drink right after she chopped off Emmett's unmentionables and drop-kicked Vania into the ocean.

"What about the others?"

"Not any of the groomsmen. They're all suck-ups. The best man, too—he and Emmett were in the same fraternity, and it would go against their stupid bro code. And the bridal party... I can't see it, but I missed the fact that Vania was screwing my fiancé, so what do I know?"

"Let's take a look at the metadata."

"I don't know what that is."

"Additional information that comes with the video file." Colt opened a panel on the screen, and a bunch of numbers popped up. They meant nothing to me. "Okay, it has the GPS coordinates, but we've already identified the property. No serial number, which would have been useful, but it was filmed on an older iPhone. Image size, camera settings—those won't be much help. Date, we already know..."

"Wait, did you say an older iPhone? That's just not possible."

"It's right there on the screen."

"Nobody who was at the beach house uses that model. They all buy the latest one as soon as it comes out. For the last release, Emmett sent his assistant to queue outside the Apple store at midnight."

He'd presented me with a new iPhone as if it were some big romantic gesture, but I'd been more concerned with the fact that it was a cold night and his assistant's lips had looked kind of blue.

"Somebody with access to the house did. The landlord? Someone who worked for him? Who else knew you and Emmett were going to be there?"

Someone who worked for... I gasped as realisation hit. There *had* been one other person at the beach house that weekend, and I knew she had an older iPhone because when Emmett knocked her phone off the counter and broke the screen, I'd given her the spare I'd tossed into a drawer after the midnight queue fiasco.

"Rosa," I said. "It was Rosa."

"Who's Rosa?"

"Emmett's maid. He insisted she come with us to keep the place tidy." Which was a dick move because she had small children at home, but when I'd tried to persuade him to let her stay behind, he said her contract stated that she'd be required to travel on occasion. And she'd been right there when the video arrived. At the other end of the room, on hand in case I needed any help, a part of the background waiting to steal the limelight. Why had she done it? Out of spite? In all the conversations I'd had with Rosa, she'd never struck me as mean. "I need to speak with her."

"Is that a good idea?"

"I don't see who else it could have been, but I need to know for sure."

"Do you have her number?"

"No, but Siri probably does, and I need to speak with her too."

"Do you know what you're going to do about her yet?"

"Not yet. Mor doesn't trust her, but I think she just showed terrible judgment when it came to men. And goodness knows, that's a failing I can identify with, present company excepted."

"I think there's a compliment in there somewhere."

"Oh, my judgment has definitely improved. When I began listening to my instincts instead of overthinking and trying to please everyone else by finding a husband who fit in with a life I didn't want anyway, things got a lot better." I leaned in to press a soft kiss to Colt's lips. "A whole lot better."

"I'm mighty glad to hear that."

"Is it too early to head back to the bedroom?"

"With you, it's never too early, but I was hoping you might use some of those instincts to help me out first. You're not the only one who's been overthinking."

"What do you need help with?" He slid his phone onto the table, and when he unlocked the screen, I realised. "You haven't listened to the voicemail from your mother?"

"I don't know whether to listen to it, delete it, or ignore it forever."

"Shall I quote Roosevelt for you?"

He laughed, but his face was stony as he cued up the message.

"You want me to stay?" I asked.

"No more secrets, Brie."

No more secrets.

His mother's voice was sweet, melodic, and if I hadn't known better, I might even have been charmed. But I knew all too well that the brightest of lights cast the darkest of shadows.

"Colt, I heard on the news that you'd been injured, and my gosh, I hope you're okay. Your father and I thought that maybe we could pay a visit to Baldwin's Shore and meet up for lunch. It's been such a long while since we saw each other, too long, and it's time we buried the hatchet, don't you think? I see you've settled with a new girl too, and we'd love for her to join us. Just let us know when would be a good day for you, and we'll make the arrangements to fly up."

Wow.

The gall of the woman.

She just wanted to pretend the last ten years hadn't happened? I could think of a good place to bury the hatchet, and I didn't mean metaphorically.

Colt looked as shocked as I felt. "Wasn't expecting that. Why now? Why'd she call now? Caring about me getting shot, that's bullshit. She didn't call when Hannah died, and that hurt a hundred times worse."

"Call me a cynic, but I can take a good guess. Did you notice she mentioned me, but she didn't mention Kiki once?"

The hurt in Colt's eyes cut me like a rusty knife. His pain was my pain. How could a mother do that to her own son? I might not have met Mrs. Haines, but I understood enough about her that I didn't care to spend a single second in her company. I'd do it for Colt—if he wanted to have lunch, I'd sip tea and converse politely because I was a seasoned pro at that—but I wouldn't enjoy it. The whole time, I'd imagine yanking out her mean tongue with the sugar tongs and feeding it to the sharks she swam with.

"Fuck," he said.

"What are you going to do? Are you going to call her?"

Instead of answering, he reached for the phone, erased the voicemail, and held out a hand to me.

"Let's go to bed, princess."

Relief flooded through me. Relief that I didn't have to pretend to be nice to somebody I disliked so intensely, and relief that Colt was holding himself together. Not that I'd really expected him to fall apart. He was strong, much stronger than me. A rock.

My rock.

"That's a wonderful idea."

Except we didn't make it that far before the phone rang again.

And this time, it wasn't Colt's mother.

It was worse.

34

COLT

*M*y bare feet sank into the carpet as I paced the hotel suite, both regretting the beer I'd drunk earlier and wishing I could chase it with vodka.

"Luca didn't say what this was about?" Brie asked.

"Not exactly. Just that it was fucked up and had something to do with the Bad Samaritan."

"The what?"

"Last year, a psycho snatched Brooke. He drugged her, had her tied to the bed naked by the time we realised who he was and where they were. We were speeding across town to get to her, and Luca was ready to kill the guy, I swear he was, but when we got there, we found that someone else had beaten us to it."

"Who?"

"We never worked that out."

"He killed the guy who took Brooke?"

"The guy wished he was dead after the Samaritan finished with him, but no. He lived, and now he's in prison."

"That's sick."

Brie was right about that.

She was also right about my parents. We both knew why my mother had called, and it had nothing to do with my bullet wound and everything to do with the fact that I was dating a beautiful Scandinavian princess.

Well, tough fucking shit. I wasn't sharing her.

Ten long minutes passed before Luca knocked on the door with Brooke and Aaron in tow, and I put a finger to my lips.

"Kiki's asleep. Wanna talk outside?"

Luca shook his head, jaw clenched. "Inside."

Brooke's knuckles were white where they gripped his arm, and Aaron didn't look much more relaxed. I opened the door wider, and when they got inside, the first thing Luca did was pull all the drapes shut.

"What's the problem? You don't want to see the tsunami coming?"

"It's not a tsunami I'm worried about." He dropped an envelope onto the coffee table. "*This* is what I'm worried about."

"What is it?" Brie asked, but I knew. I knew the instant I saw my name printed on the envelope in neat black capital letters.

COLT AND LUCA

The Bad Samaritan was back.

"Where did you find this?"

"On Aaron's kitchen counter. Turn it over."

My guts threatened to heave their contents onto the polished wood as I flipped the envelope with a fingernail.

P.S. YOUR REAR CAMERA HAS A BLIND SPOT AND YOU SHOULD BOLT THE FRENCH DOORS WHEN YOU GO OUT.

"Brazen" didn't even begin to cover it.

"What French doors?" I asked Luca. Aaron lived on the first floor of the building, and as far as I recalled, he just had a regular front door and back door. But he was still having construction work done, so maybe I'd missed something?

"As far as we can ascertain, the ones onto the roof terrace," Luca said.

"He came in via the *roof*?"

"There's no damage anywhere, but I guess he could've picked the lock."

"How'd he get up there?"

"Crampons? A grappling hook? A jetpack? Hell, he might have fuckin' wings."

"What's going on?" Brie asked. "What does the note mean?"

"It means the Bad Samaritan broke into Aaron, Brooke, and Luca's mini Fort Knox of a home to leave us a note. Do you have any trips to Valetia planned? Because now might be a good time to take one."

"Why? We have guards. Despite what Mor might think, Kasper is well-trained and very experienced, and he's built an excellent team."

"With this guy, I'm not sure any of that matters." I blew out a long breath and fought back the fear. Hadn't Brie and Brooke been through enough recently? "You didn't open the envelope?"

"Thought since it was addressed to both of us, we should do it together."

"Shouldn't you call someone about this?" Brie asked.

"Call who? We *are* the law enforcement officers in this town."

"The FBI?"

"A break-in where nothing was taken doesn't fall under their remit."

"What about forensics people?"

"Based on past experience, there won't be any fingerprints. Who wants to do the honours?"

Luca nodded to me. "As my mentor in the field, it's all yours, buddy."

"Thanks. You might want to keep back."

I took the penknife he offered and slit the top of the envelope, half expecting an explosion or a puff of anthrax. The folded sheet of paper was something of an anticlimax, but the flash drive that fell out with it sent another jolt through me. What was on it? Did I even want to know? First things first—I drew out the paper and smoothed it flat.

"Is that a map?" Aaron asked.

"Sure looks like one."

I couldn't say it was crudely drawn—that would be doing the Bad Samaritan a disservice. It was neat but confusing. On the left side of the page, a dotted line began at a red diamond with the word "FAIRBANKS" printed inside it. As the line wound its way across the page, each turn was marked with a distance and a compass bearing before it finally ended at a blue rectangle with a picture of a cat in it. A few trees and flowers—fucking *flowers*—had been dotted about, and halfway across the page, there was a smiley face inside a yellow circle.

"I don't get it," Brooke said.

Glad she spoke up because she wasn't the only one.

Luca tapped a fingertip on "Fairbanks." "The red diamond is a military symbol. It means 'hostile,' and if that's meant to be the Fairbanks place, then I'd say Elmira definitely qualifies. The blue rectangle means 'friendly.'"

I tapped the smiley face. "And this?"

"No fuckin' idea."

"That's all there is?" Aaron asked. "Just a kid's map and a memory stick?"

"Yeah."

Brie turned the paper over. "Not quite."

> **MY SOUL IS BROKEN,**
> **AS DARK AS THE NIGHT,**
> **MY MIND IS TWISTED,**
> **BUT YOU'RE NOT IN MY SIGHTS.**

What the actual fuck? Was that meant to be a poem? It seemed almost...playful.

Brooke shuddered. "Gee, that's not creepy at all."

"Perhaps the flash drive will explain?" Brie suggested, and remarkably, she seemed less disturbed than the rest of us. Probably because she hadn't seen what the Bad Samaritan had done to their last victim.

Aaron huffed out a breath. "What if it has a virus? This could be a trap. No way am I putting that thing into my computer."

Both valid points. "I'm with Aaron."

"So why don't we try it in Kiki's laptop?" Brie asked. "All she has on it is games, and we can disconnect it from the internet."

The laptop had come from Brie's mother. She might not have been the easiest woman to get along with, but I couldn't fault her behaviour with Kiki, and she had the same generous streak as Brie when it came to handing out gifts.

"Kiki won't be happy if the laptop melts down."

"I can just buy her a new one." Of course Brie could. Why didn't I think of that? "And it might answer all of our questions."

Or, as it turned out, throw up some new ones. The flash drive contained a single file, a movie, and after watching Emmett and Vania's antics earlier in the afternoon, I hesitated to click on it. In the end, Brie reached across and did the honours for me.

A well-maintained yard appeared on-screen, edged by a high fence. Bright flowers exploded from flower beds in every colour of the rainbow, birds fluttered around a cluster of feeders, and the trees were pruned to within an inch of their lives. The lawn had razor-sharp edges and perfectly parallel stripes. Who had time to manicure their lawn that way? Brie's gardeners, obviously, but apart from that?

The answer? Gerald Fairbanks.

The camera stayed rock steady, so I had to assume it was mounted somewhere, and the picture was surprisingly clear. Whoever the Bad Samaritan might be, they had access to quality equipment. As we watched, Elmira Fairbanks walked into view carrying a wire cage, and that cage had a cat in it, a dainty thing wearing a neon-green collar. She shoved it into the trunk of the car parked in the driveway, Gerald scuttled out of the house and hefted a heavy-looking sack in alongside it, and then they both climbed into the front and drove off.

"What the fuck?" Aaron asked, and again, he spoke for both of us.

"That cat looked like the Snyders' Smokey," Brooke said. "He wears a green collar."

"What's he doing with Elmira Fairbanks?"

"Hell if I know, but it looks as if Deon's in the clear now."

"That's the only file on the drive?" Luca asked.

"Yup."

"Try checking the metadata," Brie said, and everybody stared at her. "Uh, I just learned about that stuff."

I looked, but of course it had been scrubbed. The Bad Samaritan wasn't going to make the same mistake as a maid, although he'd helpfully left us the date and the GPS coordinates. The footage had been filmed yesterday afternoon.

I picked up my phone and called Meli Snyder, and two minutes later, we'd learned that Smokey had vanished sometime in the last twenty-four hours and Sophie and her father had spent the evening combing the neighbourhood for him. They could probably stand down, but I didn't want to give anyone false hope that Smokey might be found, or worse, suggest he'd come to harm at the hands of Elmira Fairbanks, so I promised to put up some posters tomorrow and help spread the word.

"Did Elmira just steal that cat?" Brooke asked.

"Hard to tell. Does she own a cat?"

Shrugs all around. I played the video back several times and tried pausing it, but I couldn't get a good enough look at the caged feline to tell if it was definitely Smokey. But those puzzle pieces fit.

"This is insane," I muttered. "Is the Bad Samaritan really helping us to hunt down a cat thief?"

That was the piece that didn't fit. The Samaritan had taken a perverse joy in torturing a man, disappeared for months, and then broken into Aaron's place without leaving a trace apart from the note. On a scale of Austin Powers to James Bond, that put him around the level of Jason Bourne. And now we were expected to believe he'd morphed into Hercule Poirot?

"I've given up trying to make sense out of this shit," Luca said. "Guess I can cross becoming an investigator off my list of career ambitions."

"The way I see it, we have two options if we want to get to the bottom of this—either we talk to Elmira Fairbanks, or we take a trip out to that blue rectangle."

Luca made a face, which was understandable because neither of those options was an attractive proposition. On balance, a visit to the Fairbanks place was marginally less dangerous.

"Technically, I'm still on sick leave, but how about we both go talk to Elmira tomorrow morning?"

"I'd rather take my chances in the forest."

"Ten o'clock, and don't forget your body armour."

"What are we going do about the Bad Samaritan?"

"What *can* we do? All I can say is that if he wanted us dead, we'd be cooling off in the morgue. Right now, it feels more like he's toying with us."

"You think this is a game to him?" Aaron asked.

"More of a demonstration. *Look what I can do.*"

Brooke barely managed a whisper. "He was in our home, Colt."

Dammit, I hated hearing that quake in her voice, and Luca's mouth set in grim determination.

"Sweetheart, I'll sleep with a gun in my hand."

"I could arrange for more guards," Brie offered. "It might take a day or two, but..."

Damn, I loved this woman. Yes, we'd had a roller coaster of a start, but could it have worked any other way? If Gabrielle Westerburg von Lindegren had waltzed into town and announced she was a princess, I'd have kept my hands firmly off, insisted she call her family, and escorted her to the Peninsula to chow down on tea and cakes until her people arrived. I'd never have met the real Brie. But fuck, she'd agreed to work for car parts in the auto shop and done it with good grace too.

"What are you smiling about?" Aaron asked.

"Nothing."

But Brie linked my fingers with hers and squeezed. She knew.

"Colt's right," Luca said after a moment of reflection. "The Samaritan would get past any guards we put in his way. Hell, he'd probably see it as a challenge. Brooke, he's not after you. He *saved* you. And according to that note, he's not after me or Colt either."

"What about me?" Aaron asked. "The note was on my counter."

"He left a note there once before. Maybe it was habit? Or convenience? You were barely involved in the previous incident, and he's never mentioned you. I don't think you're a target either. And this..." Luca picked up the note. "Isn't a threat. The choice of placement was a warning—fuck with me and find out—but the message itself isn't menacing. I'd go so far as to say it's the opposite."

"So no extra guards?" Brie asked.

"Not for the moment. But as Colt said, we do need to talk to Elmira, so if your guys happen to have a spare riot shield..."

"Is she really that bad?"

"She makes a rabid wolf seem friendly."

"I believe we have some suits of armour back at the palace."

Brie wasn't kidding about that. "Just wish us luck."

35

COLT

"I don't know nothin' about any cats. Now, if you've finished interrupting my morning..."

Elmira Fairbanks tried to shut the door in our faces, but Luca put his foot in the gap. She wasn't a tall woman, but she was heavy, and what she lacked in height she made up for in attitude.

"You don't have a cat?" he asked.

"No, I do not."

"It's just that I heard you had a cat in your car a couple days ago, and we're trying to contact all the cat owners in the neighbourhood."

"Who's been gossiping about me?"

"I can't divulge that information at this time."

"Why?"

"Because this is an ongoing investigation."

"Investigation into what?"

"I'm sure you've heard that a number of cats have gone missing in town recently."

"Like I said, I don't know nothin' about that."

This woman was exhausting. "Mrs. Fairbanks, please just tell us why you had a cat in your car."

Her gaze lasered in on me, and I forced myself to stand my ground. When I was a kid, she'd scared the shit out of me.

"It was my sister-in-law's cat."

Elmira Fairbanks was an only child, and thank the heavens for that, which meant she must have been talking about Gerald's sister, Reba, who'd married Mike Sheeran. Mike used to be friends with my parents and, as I recalled, he was allergic to anything with fur. One time, he'd visited our house and broken out in hives when Mom's cat jumped into his lap.

"Reba's cat? You sure about that?"

"Are you accusing me of something?"

"Why was the cat in your car?"

"We took care of it while she went out of town."

"Are you a cat person, Elmira?" Luca asked, waving at the array of bird feeders on the lawn. "Figured they'd scare your feathered friends away."

"Can't say that I am, and that's 'Mrs. Fairbanks' to you."

At least she'd told one truth today. "Mrs. Fairbanks, my apologies. For someone who isn't a cat person, you sure do grow a lot of catnip."

"Catnip?"

The moment I walked along the path to Elmira's front door, I'd realised the problem. Before we confronted the dragon herself, we'd chatted with the neighbours who lived either side, and for years, Elmira had complained about cats congregating in her yard, shitting on the lawn, chasing her beloved birds, and scratching around in the flower beds. Then several months ago, she'd stopped complaining.

I swept a hand toward a flower bed at the front of the

house, brimming with purple flowers. "These plants—they're catnip. Cats just love the stuff. They'll come from miles around to roll in it."

"They...what?"

It was the first time I'd ever seen Elmira speechless, and I might have savoured the moment if it hadn't been for Tigger and Smokey and all the other pets who'd vanished.

"You didn't know?"

"I bought the pots at a yard sale years ago, and they didn't have labels. How do you know what they are, anyway? You don't strike me as much of a gardener judging by the state of your own yard."

"My mom kept a pot of the stuff on the porch. What did you do with the cats, Mrs. Fairbanks?"

"I... How dare you point the finger at me?"

"It'll be easier if you just tell us what happened."

"Get off my property, or I'm calling the sheriff!"

We had no choice but to leave. For now. I'd hoped Elmira might make things straightforward, but who was I kidding?

Sheriff Newman was mighty nervous of the woman too, so he'd tell us to back off until we had more evidence. Before we could count on his support, we'd have to gather proof that she was lying about her sister-in-law owning a cat, formal statements from the neighbours, and a timeline to show she was in town at the times the cats had vanished.

And we'd have to visit that blue rectangle in the forest.

Was it too late to change my mind about the armour?

My shoulder ached more than I cared to admit as we trekked along the path in the forest. Brie hadn't wanted me to come, and I understood her fears, but I couldn't let Luca go alone. So we'd compromised and Kasper was with us. Aaron too, although everyone had tried to convince him it was a bad idea.

"If you're going to do anything stupid, you should have legal representation on hand."

I wanted to say we wouldn't do anything stupid, but in light of recent events, there were no guarantees.

"You're a civilian."

"In this country, technically so is Kasper."

Valetia didn't have much of an army, just a handful of boats and a few hundred soldiers in the Royal Guard, but Kasper had been a commander in the Jaeger Corps, the Danish special forces. According to Brie, he'd won medals for bravery, although he always acted as if that was no big deal.

And at Aaron's words, Kasper had just shrugged. "Let him come. Four targets is better than three."

Ordinarily I liked the guy, but not so much today.

"Thanks for those words of comfort."

Now I was following Luca through the wilderness south of town with Aaron behind me and Kasper bringing up the rear. The rudimentary map wasn't drawn to scale, more of a glorified list of instructions than anything else, but if our interpretation was correct, we had a couple more miles to go. Whoever the Bad Samaritan was, he was meticulous, I'd give him that much. There was no ambiguity in the directions. He was athletic too—I was no slouch when it came to fitness, but this hill left me out of breath.

We took it slow and steady, alert for any danger, but even though I was half expecting trouble, my heart still leapt into my throat at Luca's whispered, "Oh, fuck."

"What?"

"You gotta see this."

"See what?"

The map. Luca was tapping the map, now laminated courtesy of Aaron. "We're right here."

On the smiley face. And then Luca turned to point west.

"Oh, fuck."

I added "versatile" to the list of the Bad Samaritan's attributes.

Our cross-country route had brought us roughly eight hundred yards as the crow flew from the location of our showdown with the ex-presidents just one short month ago. And from where we were standing, a gap in the undergrowth gave us a perfect view of the clearing where Reagan had lost his head.

"He's got to be kidding," Luca muttered.

"I don't think he's kidding."

"What's wrong?" Kasper asked, and I explained.

"So that's what he meant when he said you weren't in his sights. He was being literal. Literal, rational... I'm starting to like this person."

"You're crazy."

Kasper grinned. "Yes, my commanding officer used to say so."

Aaron had paled a shade. Having second thoughts about coming? "The freak's a magician. What did he do, follow Brie when she got abducted?"

Unlikely. The kidnappers had been all over the place, acting on a wing and a prayer rather than a well-thought-out plan, and besides, we'd have noticed another car on the road.

"I don't think so."

"Maybe he was out here making these instructions?" Kasper said. "They are very clear, yes?"

"With a handy sniper rifle?"

"A hunting rifle would make that shot, and everybody in America seems to own a gun. People take them to the supermarket, the gas station, the café..."

"Okay, okay, I get the point."

"To the pizza restaurant, the pet store, the hair salon... Why do they need their guns in a hair salon? To shoot the barber if they don't like the style?" Kasper shook his head. "Nobody does this in Denmark."

"Can we carry on now?"

Kasper gestured along the path. "Please."

Forty minutes later, we emerged into a small overgrown clearing. The mouldering remains of a log cabin loomed over us, dark and mossy, a good-sized home being gradually reclaimed by the forest. Tree boughs kissed the roof, scratching at the shingles as the breeze blew. Someone had cared for this place once, been proud of it. The remains of a rocker still sat on the porch, and ribboned drapes fluttered through holes in the broken windows.

"Spooky," Aaron said. "I didn't even know this place existed. Who wants to live all the way out here in the forest?"

"There's probably a back way in." Luca pointed to the far side of the clearing, at a gloomy tunnel through the trees. "That looks wide enough for a car."

"So why did we walk?"

The answer was simple.

"Because the Bad Samaritan wanted us to." That smiley face. *Another message.* "The bigger question is, why did he send us here? Did Elmira use this place as a feline graveyard or something?"

"If she did, who would ever notice? Actually, don't answer that. I don't want to think about it."

An angry yowl nearly gave me a heart attack, and a second later, a cat leapt through the nearest window and just missed landing on Luca. Holy shit—was that Smokey? It sure looked like him, plus the neon-green collar was a big hint.

Next, I heard hissing, and we all turned and looked at each other.

"Elmira wasn't bumping the cats off; she was dropping them off," Luca said as understanding dawned. "She didn't want them near her house, so she dumped them out here instead." A squirrel bolted past with a tabby in hot pursuit. "Bet they're having the time of their nine lives."

The cabin's front door sagged on its hinges, and when Kasper pushed it open with a long stick, the *creak* set my teeth on edge. But he couldn't see a booby trap. Probably the cats would have set them off if there had been any. And there were a *lot* of cats. I'd counted fifteen—or it might have been sixteen because they didn't much like keeping still— before I spotted a familiar face peering at me from the top of an old armoire.

"That's Tigger."

Kiki was gonna be so damn happy. Even though we couldn't live in our house at the moment, she still insisted we go back every day to top off the food bowl on the back porch and check for any signs of her buddy.

"You're sure?" Luca asked.

"Yeah, I'm sure. I need to take her home for Kiki."

"How? We should've borrowed Elmira's cage."

"I have paracord," Kasper said. "We can fashion some sort of harness, but we'll have to catch her first."

"Should've taken a handful of that catnip too."

There were empty paper sacks on the floor, torn open, and I flipped one over with my foot. Kitty Krunchies? Was that what Gerald had been carrying? He'd been feeding them too? It shouldn't have been funny, but hell, this was the most ridiculous outcome to a case I'd ever investigated.

"You laughing at me?" Luca asked as he made a grab for Tigger.

"Nah, I'm laughing at the situation. What are we meant to charge Elmira with? Is relocating cats a crime?"

Aaron, of course, knew the answer. "If you can't make a criminal complaint stick, there are certainly grounds for a civil case under tort law. Under the second restatement of torts paragraph two hundred and eighteen part (a), she's dispossessed another of a chattel."

Sheesh.

Luca made another leap for Tigger and missed, but his landing was followed by a splintering crash and he fell right through the rotten floor into the crawl space below. Fuck.

"We could try tagging personal injury onto that," Aaron said as I gingerly tiptoed to the edge of the hole.

"You okay?"

"Yeah. Stinks down here."

Kasper passed me a flashlight, and I shined the beam into the void. Cobwebs festooned the space, and spiders scuttled away into the darkness. Good thing Addy wasn't with us.

"Do we need a rope?"

"Nah, I can—" Luca started.

Holy fucking shit. "Don't move. Do. Not. Move."

He froze instantly. "What is it? A snake?"

No, not a snake. Or a venomous spider or a bear or a mountain lion. Not anything alive at all. Kasper appeared next to me with a second flashlight, a more powerful one, and now the skull two inches from Luca's left foot grinned back even brighter.

"*For fanden.*"

Slowly, slowly, Luca followed our gazes, and within seconds, his face had taken on a deathlike pallor. The skeleton stretched out beside him, hands in a pile beneath the ribcage as if they'd once been crossed over her stomach. And it *was* a "her" judging by the tattered remains of the dress she wore. After months and possibly years in darkness —how long did a body take to decompose?—the colours were still surprisingly bright.

"Luca, you okay?" Aaron asked.

"No."

One word, but he choked it out, a cross between a growl and a sob. Luca had seen death, I knew he had, so I guess I hadn't expected him to be so affected, but then again, I wasn't the one crouching in a crawl space with a corpse.

"The body's not fresh. It's probably been there for a while."

"Twenty years. She's been here for twenty years."

"How do you know that?"

He looked up at me, eyes glistening.

"Because the last time I saw this dress, my mom was wearing it."

A FEW WORDS FROM THE BAD SAMARITAN...

Want to hear more from the Bad Samaritan?
I've included a few of their thoughts in a bonus chapter,
FREE to members of my reader group.
You can join here:
www.elise-noble.com/c4ts

WHAT'S NEXT?

The next book in the Baldwin's Shore series is Aaron and Romi's story, *Buried Secrets*.

Model Romi Mendez has spent most of her life believing her mom abandoned her, but now the truth has been revealed, along with her mom's body. Now Romi has one goal: to make her father pay for his crimes. But as new leads come to light and masks get stripped away, the possibility of another funeral becomes all too real.

Three years ago, lawyer Aaron Bartlett forced Romi to confront her demons, and now she acts as if he's Satan himself. He can't hope for forgiveness, but maybe he can help to see justice served? When Romi teams up with sharp-tongued PI Blue Carver, Aaron's patience is tested, and so are his survival skills. Some people in Baldwin's Shore would rather their secrets stayed buried...

For more details:
www.elise-noble.com/buried-secrets

And if you're in the mood for more romantic suspense, why not try my Blackwood Security series, starting with *Pitch Black*? The folks from both series will be meeting up soon...

After the owner of a security company is murdered, his sharp-edged wife goes on the run. Forced to abandon everything she holds dear—her home, her friends, her job in special ops—assassin Diamond builds a new life for herself in England. As Ashlyn Hale, she meets Luke, a handsome local who makes her realise just how lonely she is.

Yet, even in the sleepy village of Lower Foxford, the dark side of life dogs Diamond's trail when the unthinkable strikes. Forced out of hiding, she races against time to save those she cares about.

For more details:

www.elise-noble.com/pitch-black

If you enjoyed *Secrets, Lies, and Family Ties*, please consider leaving a review.

For an author, every review is incredibly important. Not only do they make us feel warm and fuzzy inside, readers consider them when making their decision whether or not to buy a book. Even a line saying you enjoyed the book or what your favourite part was helps a lot.

WANT TO STALK ME?

For updates on my new releases, giveaways, and other random stuff, you can sign up for my newsletter on my website:
www.elise-noble.com

If you're on Facebook, you might also like to join Team Blackwood for exclusive giveaways, sneak previews, and book-related chat. Be the first to find out about new stories, and you might even see your name or one of your suggestions make it into print!

And if you'd like to read my books for FREE, you can also find details of how to join my advance review team.

Would you like to join Team Blackwood?

www.elise-noble.com/team-blackwood

facebook.com/EliseNobleAuthor

instagram.com/elise_noble

goodreads.com/elisenoble

bookbub.com/authors/elise-noble

tiktok.com/@EliseNobleWrites

END-OF-BOOK STUFF

Did every little girl want to be a princess when she grew up? Not me. No, this girl binge-read the entire Swallows and Amazons series and wanted to be a sailor. I even took sailing lessons and still have vivid memories of falling out the boat a lot, but as an adult, I realised I was more at home under the water than flitting around on top of it.

But hey, I figured it would be fun to write a book about a rebellious princess. With boats. Having grown up in the UK and seen the drama of first Diana and then Harry and Meghan play out, I don't think being a royal is quite the fairy tale Disney makes it out to be. I hope you enjoyed the story!

Colt and Brie will be back soon in Buried Secrets—I've just finished the second round of edits on that one, although I kept getting distracted by Steve the squirrel. He's now discovered the bird table that sits in front of my desk (with a window in between because it would be bloody cold otherwise). I bought him his own squirrel feeder, but he's decided he'd rather face off with the magpies and get chased by the dog.

I'm writing the Bad Samaritan's book at the moment, and having a lot of fun doing it. Plenty of drama, using whatever characters I want from whichever series I choose... Emmy's there in Baldwin's Shore, of course, plus Bradley— he can sniff out any craft store in a hundred-mile radius. Maybe Black will show up too :) And a few other people...

Thanks so much to all the members of Team Blackwood

—when I needed cat names, you guys delivered (and with photos)! Hopefully some of you spotted your moggies roaming around Baldwin's Shore!

Thanks also to my beta readers—Jeff, Renata, Musi, David, Stacia, Jessica, Nikita, Quenby, and Jody—and to Nikki for editing, Abi for yet another cover, and to my proof readers, John, Debi, and Lizbeth.

And thank *you* for reading!

Elise

ALSO BY ELISE NOBLE

Blackwood Security

For the Love of Animals (Nate & Carmen - Prequel)

Black is My Heart (Diamond & Snow - Prequel)

Pitch Black

Into the Black

Forever Black

Gold Rush

Gray is My Heart

Neon (novella)

Out of the Blue

Ultraviolet

Glitter (novella)

Red Alert

White Hot

Sphere (novella)

The Scarlet Affair

Spirit (novella)

Quicksilver

The Girl with the Emerald Ring

Red After Dark

When the Shadows Fall

Phantom (novella)

Pretties in Pink

Chimera

The Devil and the Deep Blue Sea

Blue Moon

Blackwood Elements

Oxygen

Lithium

Carbon

Rhodium

Platinum

Lead

Copper

Bronze

Nickel

Hydrogen

Out of Their Elements (novella)

Blackwood UK

Joker in the Pack

Cherry on Top

Roses are Dead

Shallow Graves

Indigo Rain

Pass the Parcel (TBA)

Blackwood Casefiles

Stolen Hearts

Burning Love (TBA)

Baldwin's Shore

Dirty Little Secrets

Secrets, Lies, and Family Ties

Buried Secrets

A Secret to Die For

Blackwood Security vs. Baldwin's Shore

Secret Weapon

Secrets from the Past

Blackstone House

Hard Lines

Blurred Lines (novella)

Hard Tide

Hard Limits

Hard Luck (2024)

Blind Luck (novella) (2025)

Hard Code (2025)

Hard Evidence (TBA)

The Electi

Cursed

Spooked

Possessed

Demented

Judged

The Planes

A Vampire in Vegas

A Devil in the Dark (2024)

The Trouble Series

Trouble in Paradise

Nothing but Trouble

24 Hours of Trouble

The Happy Ever After Series

A Very Happy Christmas

A Very Happy Valentine

A Very Happy Halloween

A Very Happy Easter (2025)

A Very Happy Thanksgiving (TBA)

Standalone

Life

Coco du Ciel

Twisted (short stories)

Books with clean versions available (no swearing and no on-the-page sex)

Pitch Black

Into the Black

Forever Black

Gold Rush

Gray is My Heart

Audiobooks

Black is My Heart (Diamond & Snow - Prequel)

Pitch Black

Made in the USA
Coppell, TX
06 November 2024

39765135R00182